# Robert White

Robert White is an Amazon best selling crime fiction author. His novels regularly appear in the top ten downloads in the Crime and Action and Adventure genres. Robert is an ex cop, who captures the brutality of northern British streets in his work. He combines believable characters, slick plots and vivid dialogue to immerse the reader in his fast paced story-lines. He was born in Leeds, England, the illegitimate son of a jazz musician and a factory girl. He hated school, leaving at age sixteen. After joining Lancashire Constabulary in 1980, he served for fifteen years, his specialism being Tactical Firearms. Robert then spent four years in the Middle East before returning to the UK in 2000. He now lives in Lancashire with his wife Nicola, and his two terrible terriers Flash and Tia.

# Novels by Robert White

**Rick Fuller Thrillers:**

THE FIX
THE FIRE
THE FALL
THE FOLLOWER
THE FELLOWSHIP

**Det Sgt Striker Thrillers:**

UNREST
SIX

**Stand alone novels:**

DIRTY
BREAKING BONES

# THE FELLOWSHIP

A Rick Fuller Thriller
Book FIVE
(The CIA Diaries Pt2)

By

## Robert White

www.robertwhiteauthor.co.uk

ISBN: 978-1791853396

For my wife Nicola

# Acknowledgements

I spent fifteen years of my life as a police officer, five as a member of a tactical firearms team. After leaving the Service I spent four years working in the Middle East and during that time I had the pleasure of meeting and working with several retired members of Her Majesty's Special Forces.

One evening, sitting in an Abu Dhabi bar, I was having a quiet beer with two such ex-servicemen I had grown to know quite well.

Casually, one broached the subject of a job offer. They needed a third man to complete a team who were to collect a guy from Afghanistan and deliver him across the border to Pakistan. The job was worth several thousand pounds each and would last three days.

I was extremely flattered to be asked.

I knew my two friends would be soldiers until they took their last breath. Even then, in their mid-forties, they missed the adrenalin rush only that level of danger could bring.

Personally, I didn't feel qualified enough to join them and turned down the offer, something incidentally, I have regretted ever since.

I would like to say a big thank-you to those two men, who, with their many late night tales of war and adventure, inspired me to write this work.

*"We know that without food we would die. Without fellowship, life is not worth living."*

(LAURIE COLWIN)

*November 1987, Sterling Lines, Hereford.*

# Rick Fuller's Story:

The immediate aftermath of the Libyan debacle had been hard on the whole squadron. As patrol leader, I'd had the job of informing Frankie Green's wife of his death. She, and his kids were devastated. Their lives torn apart. The worst thing about it was I couldn't even tell her where he was or if we'd ever find his body.

The lads had done the usual whip round. Beers had been sunk, tales had been told, but the mood was still bleak back in Sterling Lines. I, in particular, was finding it hard to come to terms with the loss.

Two days after we had returned to camp, our OC summoned me to his office.

"Not feeling yourself, Fuller, are you?" he'd asked.

"I'm okay, Sir," I'd offered, even though I knew he could see right through me.

He sat back in his chair and held a fountain pen between the fingers of both hands, as if he was about to snap it in half.

"Boy soldier, weren't you? Father served, killed in action, Aden wasn't it?"

"Yes Sir."

He took a deep breath and pursed his lips.

"Lads who have no experience of life outside the military, sometimes find dealing with family issues harder than those that have, how can I say, lived a little."

"You mean dealing with Frankie Green's family, Sir?"

"I mean seeing his wife and kids grieve, Fuller."

"I saw my mother grieve, Sir."

He blew air down his nose.

"I'm sure you did, but you were a child, Fuller. What I'm trying to say to you, is that grief occurs in all walks of life."

"Frankie was my responsibility, Sir."

"And you are a damned fine trooper, an excellent patrol leader and great servant to this country. Fuller."

"Thank you, sir."

"Look, son, I realise that you probably feel down right now, but all I can say to you, is that you have my utmost support, and that the next mission that comes along will go your way. How's that?"

"That makes me feel better, Sir. Always best to keep busy."

"Quite, Fuller. Well, good luck, off you trot."

And so, I did, feeling... well, not feeling much at all.

We'd lost Frankie Green attempting to kill Abdallah Al-Mufti, Muammar Gaddafi's right hand man. He'd been organising the sale of weapons and explosives to the Provo's, including the Semtex that had been used at Enniskillen.

Although we had caused major damage to Al-Mufti's operation we hadn't stopped the flow of weapons, and the intel coming back across the water was that the IRA's stockpiles were still growing.

Now, you might have thought that after the Remembrance Day disaster at Enniskillen, where eleven civilians were killed, the PIRA boys may have calmed down a bit.

Not a hope. The late eighties were one of the worst periods of the Troubles.

On 21st November, the Provo's placed three bombs in the Kildress Inn in Cookstown, County Tyrone.

On the 28th, two British soldiers were wounded when the PIRA launched three mortars at a temporary vehicle check point in County Armagh.

In early December, there were a series of attacks on both military and civilian targets where British soldiers were wounded, but it was when the UFF leader John McMichael was killed by a boobytrap bomb attached to his car, just three days before Christmas, that the Head Shed got the nod and we could finally pull our fingers out.

The OC made good on his word, and for Des Cogan, Butch Stanley, me and new boy, Si Garcia, the holidays were cancelled.

On the morning of December 25th, our patrol sat around a small square table. A large tin tea pot took centre stage surrounded by four blue mugs and a shed load of empty foil cups that had once held mince pies. We were waiting for our man from the ministry to brief us.

As the only married bloke in the patrol, Des was not a happy bunny. It wasn't how any of us had envisaged spending Christmas day, but for him with Anne at home, it was doubly hard. Then again, our OC was pottering around, so if he was giving up his festivities, we figured things must be serious enough to warrant pissing the wife off.

Just after 1600hrs, the boss wandered in with a tray of turkey sandwiches, four cans of bitter and another two boxes of Kipling's specials.

"Sorry chaps," he said. "Best I could do at such short notice."

"Thought we'd at least have had a cracker or two, Sir," said Butch tucking in, his huge drooping black moustache, instantly covered in stuffing.

"Thanks, Sir," I offered, cracking my can open. "What time is our man due?"

"He's here now, Fuller," he said. "He's just taking a call from London and he'll be with you."

The OC tapped the side of his nose. "Think this one is a little wet behind the ears, so be nice to him, okay?"

Wet or not, no sooner had we shovelled the last of our sandwiches down our necks, the face walked in. Unusually for a spook, he wasn't suited and booted. He wore an open necked shirt and jeans and looked ever so slightly dishevelled. Maybe all the senior guys were sipping brandy and smoking cigars in their London flats and this fella was all that was left. He looked to be in his twenties, fresh faced and lithe to the point of skinny.

He pulled papers from his briefcase and nodded towards our table.

"You lads had enough to eat?" asked our man.

There were nods as more foil cups were emptied of their contents.

He looked at our large tea pot. "Any left in there?"

"Help yersel," said Des, finding a clean mug.

"Cheers," he said. Pouring himself half a pint of over-brewed Typhoo.

"Right," he slurped. "First of all, sorry to cock up your holidays, but this is urgent and there isn't any time to fuck about."

He didn't pick up his notes, just rested his hand on them.

"Okay, we've known for some time that one of the roles of the IRA Southern Command, is to store and protect much of the organisation's arms, and that small stocks are regularly transported from the South to the Province. These are intended for the immediate use of ASU's (Active Service Units). There are, of course, smaller arms dumps in the border counties."

He looked at me.

"You will be well aware of those Fuller as you and your patrol ran a sur-veillance on one, late last year."

The guy knew his stuff alright. I'd headed a four-man patrol in Crossma-glen, the previous November. We'd had eyes on an IRA weapon stash, Des had been dug in for several days to give us the heads up. The intelligence was that several other players would be visiting the plot to remove the kit and take it to a forward operating base. The weather was atrocious, and we were all pissed off and wet through.

In the end, we were compromised by a bloody dog. We hadn't seen it. One of the players had brought it in the back of a van, under cover of dark-ness.

As often happens in the dark and bad weather, comms go down and tac-tics go to shit.

The firefight was horrendous.

Des was wounded on his approach.

I killed five people that evening. When we eventually cleared the scene, I saw that two of the Provo's I'd shot had been young women.

The spooks reward was the recovery of 40 firearms, including thirteen FN FAL rifles.

Mine had been another fucking medal that would sit in my drawer and not see the light of day.

I just nodded at the guy and let him get to his point.

He cricked his neck. "However, the bulk of the IRA's arms reserves are stored in dumps deeper within the Republic. They choose this strategy partly because it is easier to find a safe hiding place for the kit south of the border. Less cops, more fields etc..."

He took another slurp of tea.

"Our intel tells us that some of the most important dumps are in the Munster area. These are regularly replenished by arms from the continent, brought into local ports by trawlers and other small boats. Now, we have recently discovered that the IRA's quartermaster general is a man called McMullen, who lives just south of the border. However, his opposite num-ber is based in Limerick. He goes by the name of Connor Gallagher and it is his job to organise the transport of weapons, ammunition and explosives from the South to the ASU's in the North."

He shuffled through his papers and held up a grainy photograph.

"This is him, here. And the reason that you fine chaps are missing your turkey dinners, is that Connor and his pals are about to move three hundred and eighty gallons of nitrobenzene from a store just north of Tralee and drop the lot at McMullen's farm, which we believe is some ten miles south of Dundalk. Our informant says that the farm already holds a large stock of ammonium nitrate fertilizer. I don't need to spell out the problem with that, do I, chaps?"

Si Garcia, at twenty four, was the youngest in the patrol. Born not far away from Hereford, in Ross on Wye, he'd once played rugby for Gloucester. He was a sandy haired lad with a full set beard, broad shouldered and strong as an ox. He was quiet and unassuming with a dry wit when required, but it was always going to be hard for him, stepping into Frankie's shoes. That said, he'd kept his head down, done his work and we couldn't ask for more than that.

Si had been selected because, like Frankie, he had a wealth of experience when it came to blowing things up.

He knew exactly what the man from the ministry meant.

"Nitrobenzene was used to make the bombs for Bloody Friday," he said in his deep accented voice. "21st July 1972. At least twenty devices exploded in the space of eighty minutes. Nine dead, including two British soldiers and five civilians. With three hundred and eighty gallons of the stuff, mixed with AN. Fuck me, you could blow up half of Belfast."

The young face pointed at Si.

"Spot on old chap. That is exactly the problem. Our intelligence suggests that the Provo's are planning a spectacular. A massive bomb in Belfast, on New Year's Eve."

I raised my brows at that one. You see, Belfast in the eighties hardly invited partying. It was dour and grey, with boarded-up windows and bricked-up homes.

The Troubles had taken their toll. Belfast was never the Snipers' Alley that the press would have you believe, but the centre had become a ghost town. Where once there had been a glut of bars, clubs and cinemas, they were now few and far between. The youth of the city scarcely ventured out into the centre, forever cautious of what had happened in Birmingham and Guilford in the seventies.

The man from the Ministry read my thoughts.

"Things are changing over there, Fuller. Belfast is not all flared trousers and soul music you know? Dance music has arrived."

Des spat crumbs on the table as he spoke. "Ye mean that shite where every fucker just jumps up and down, stoned off their tits?"

The face gave Des a withering look. "Succinctly put, Cogan... These 'Raves' as they are being called are not held in traditional venues, but in disused warehouses and factories. They ship in massive PA and lighting rigs and people come from miles around to dance."

"And take drugs," I offered.

"Even so," countered the face. "The organisers are expecting two thousand people from all sides of the city, both Protestant and Catholic."

The guy finished his tea. "Now, we don't think the Provo's will risk slaughtering some of their own youngsters, but they aren't the targets."

"Then who is?" asked Des.

"The RUC," said the face flatly. "The cops are expecting trouble on the night and have cancelled all leave to deal with the influx of young people. Up to fifty police officers will be on duty around the venue."

Si Garcia had a puzzled look on his face.

"It still doesn't make sense," he offered scratching his thick beard. "The Paddies are moving too much gear for that kind of job. I mean, If I wanted to hit say, six or seven targets using a nitrobenzene and AN mix, I'd only need about a tenth of what they are moving."

The face held out his arms and shrugged.

"Chaps, half of my job is analysing intel, data, phone records and bugged conversations. The other half is surmising what they all mean."

"You mean guessing what they all mean," said Des, his eyes flashing with irritation.

The spook may not have had much experience, but he wasn't fazed. He looked straight into the Scot's face.

"Well then, Mr Cogan, on this particular occasion, it's our ... guess, that you chaps' had better stop this nitrobenzene ever making it across the border, or we're going to be picking up pieces of dead policemen off the streets of Belfast on New Year's Day."

He picked up the shot of Connor Gallagher. "And you can dispose of this gentleman at the same time if you please."

With that, the guy picked up his papers and was gone.

Throughout the briefing, our OC had been tucked away in the corner. Now it was his turn. He walked over, dropped a pack of documents on the table and spoke quietly.

"Maps of Tralee and the routes out of the area. Aerial photographs of the location of the chemicals and photographs of the two main players."

He sat on the edge of our desk. "Now, as the boys from Whitehall are unsure exactly when Gallagher will move the booty we need you over the water ASAP. So Fuller, that means you're dropping in HALO. No leisurely boat trips to sun drenched shores for you this time. Get your kit together and report to the RSM within the hour. And good luck chaps. Get this one wrong and I have a feeling it won't be a happy new year for anyone."

We all sat at the table in silence for a moment.

Si eventually broke it.

"How many HALO drops you lads done?"

It was a fair question. The Regiment was split into different 'troops.' Air Troop, where Butch and I had been taken from, were the freefall parachuting specialists. We were tasked with jumping behind enemy lines, either on our own missions or to pave the way for other squadron troops. We were the HALO experts. But, Des, had been seconded from Mountain Troop, his specialism was Arctic warfare, climbing mountains and sitting in snow holes until his dick dropped off. Si, our new boy, had been drafted from Mobility Troop, his forte being the desert, mechanics and anything that went bang. All of us had various levels of airborne training, but, since being recruited into one of the new specialist counter terrorism patrols, we had gotten used to having both feet on the ground.

"I've done three," said Des, finding his pipe. "And they were fucking hairy, I'll tell ye."

"Well, I've done two," offered Si. "And Des is fuckin' spot on. My oxygen failed on my first. I nearly shit myself."

"Don't be so fuckin' soft," said Butch.

Everyone ignored him.

The anacronym, HALO stands for High Altitude Low Opening. Each trooper jumps from 30,000 feet or higher, beyond the visual range of anyone on the ground. Then, you freefall most of the way down. Chutes are only deployed at the last minute to prevent the trooper being spotted. You have to wear special kit including oxygen to deploy HALO, and the big danger was, that if that kit didn't work for whatever reason, within thirty seconds, you were pretty much incapable of reasoning, let alone working out when you'd reached 2000 feet and it was time to pull the cord. Si was lucky to be alive to tell his tale.

It took us just shy of two hours to sort our weapons and jump kit, and as we approached the RSM's office, we looked more like fighter pilots than ground troops.

The RSM is considered to be 'primus inter pares' or 'first amongst equals,' and is primarily responsible for maintaining standards and discipline. He also acts as a parental figure to his subordinates, including junior officers, even though they technically outrank him. I always considered the RSM to be the most important rank in the squadron.

Ours went by the name of Bert Singleton and was about as tough a man as I'd ever met. He'd seen it all and bought the t-shirt, had a quick temper and took no bollocks from anyone.

I couldn't work out why we were reporting to Bert that evening, but one thing was for certain, I wasn't going to question him.

He was sat at his desk with a brew, and as usual, a fag burning in the corner of his mouth. As we lumbered into his office, he stood, stubbed out his cigarette and walked around to greet us.

"Just personal weapons and belt kit on this one boys, eh? No extras, no ID, Dog Tags, family holiday shots, you know the drill."

We all nodded. It was strictly forbidden to carry any family photographs on a mission behind enemy lines. Although we weren't at war with Ireland, should things go tits up and the Provo's get hold of any of our team, finding a family picture in your pocket only gave them an edge when it came to interrogation. That said, I'd never been asked to remove my Dog Tags before. As it happened, I didn't wear mine as they irritated me, but Des, Butch and Si did as they were asked and dutifully dropped theirs on Bert's desk.

"Right then," smiled the RSM. "You lads are off on a right jolly. Throw your kit in the back of the bus outside and I'll be with you in two shakes."

Moments later we were all crammed into a Transit eight seater, bouncing down the road in darkness.

We knew it was pointless asking the RSM where we were going, but the fact that it was he that was driving us, told me this was a very important journey.

Just a touch over two hours later, all became clear.

Our bus drove straight into Heathrow airport. We bypassed the main buildings and headed for the cargo zone. Even back in 1986, Heathrow moved millions of tons of cargo every month.

The place looked no different than any other large distribution centre. A cavernous structure with dozens of roller shuttered doors sat directly in front of us. Queues of HGV's waited impatiently for their turn to reverse onto their allotted dock and drop their cargo. As our bus rolled up to the first security checkpoint, we were met by a grey man in a grey suit.

He slapped a square sticker on our windscreen and dropped himself into the passenger seat.

Bert gave the guy a cursory nod and we were off again, speeding across the apron.

"I could do with one of them stickers, next time I go to Benidorm," chirped Si.

The grey suit didn't even turn around, he just pointed to a British Airways 737 in the far distance.

"That's yours," he said.

For years, there had been speculation that a top secret agreement between British Airways and the Regiment's Hierarchy was in place. In times of war, or great threat to the people of the UK, this arrangement would allow the Special Air Service the use of specially re-fitted BA planes, to deliver men and equipment into enemy territory. That speculation had just become a reality and, there was little doubt that if we were heading for Ireland in such secrecy, the job was of the utmost importance.

We collected our kit from the back of the Transit and stood at the bottom of the stairs leading to the body of the aircraft. The RSM stepped over to me and leaned in. It was as if he'd read my thoughts.

"Good luck, Fuller," he said, and took my hand. "If these fuckers aren't stopped on this one, there'll be a civil war in the North, mark my words."

I had nothing to say to that, just nodded and climbed the steps.

Once inside the aircraft, it quickly became apparent that our 737 was very special indeed. Every last bit of unnecessary kit had been stripped from the inside, and much to our consternation, that included every seat.

Even the Hercs had benches.

As we dropped our chutes and belt kits at our feet, we were joined by two very young looking pilots.

Both were fair haired and of similar height and build. The guy wearing the captain's epaulettes stepped forward. "Which of you chaps is Fuller?" he asked with a smile.

"That will be me," I said.

He offered a hand. "Splendid, splendid. Beard," he announced. "Captain Adam Beard, and this…" he nodded to his first officer. "Is my brother, Ryan."

We shook.

Ryan was holding a thick looking book and a chart of what was undoubtedly southern Ireland. He tapped the map with a finger.

"Our official flightpath is direct to Belfast, but shortly after leaving the Welsh coast, we'll declare a technical emergency and request an alternative landing. The Irish ATC will have to direct us away from Cork as it's blowing a hooly down there, so we'll head for Shannon. Just before we start our descent, we'll spin around and drop you chaps somewhere around the Limerick/Kerry border. The Paddies will kick up a fuss, but we'll tell them we got a bit lost and that my dear brother has decided to turn back for home." He gave me a cheeky wink. "All in a day's work."

Faking an urgent situation that takes a civilian aircraft into restricted airspace was nothing new. However, I wasn't sure if it had ever been attempted by the UK government before.

I knew many BA crew were ex-military, and Adam and Ryan did indeed wear the BA uniform, but from the look of the two brothers, I considered they were still serving. They had that edge about them.

"Ryan will sort the door opening and timing," said Adam. "You will have noticed that we don't have any cargo. That is because this is no ordinary flight, and this is no ordinary British Airways 737. As you are probably aware, the exit doors on the standard aircraft open outwards making a parachute drop impossible unless you blast your way out. Ours do not, enabling the seal to be broken after decompression by a single operator and at any height we require. We never carry cargo on these little jobs, as it allows me to slow the aircraft down to 120 knots before she stalls. Now, any questions?"

Adam's little speech instantly confirmed that he and Ryan Beard were not about to take me on my next package holiday to Spain.

"All very James Bond," said Des looking about the empty fuselage.

"Exactly," smiled the Captain. "Well, we're expecting a few lumps and bumps on the way, so you lads wedge yourselves in where you can. We're just going to run the rule over the aircraft and we'll be off in about ten minutes."

At that, Adam turned and busied himself on the flight deck.

Des was shaking his head. "My old man told me about this shite," he said, laying down his weapons. "Not with planes, like. He worked in the shipyards from being a wee bairn. He told me that during the Second World War, the men would camouflage warships to look like civilian vessels, to confuse the German U Boats, y'know, to stop 'em torpedoing them like eh?"

Butch Stanley didn't usually say too much, but he gave me a knowing look and gestured to the stripped out plane.

"They don't do this for nothin' though, do they? I mean, they don't go to all this trouble to disguise a drop, if this wasn't a big deal."

I looked at my patrol and considered I had some of the best fighting men in the world at my side.

"The big deal, Butch, is stopping these murderous bastards from killing dozens of RUC lads on New Year's Eve."

Des felt in his pocket for his pipe and gestured towards the flight deck. "Don't suppose them boys will mind if I have a burn."

"I will," I said.

\* \* \*

A typical HALO jump requires a pre-breathing period of about half an hour prior to the drop. This is where the jumper breathes 100% oxygen in order to flush nitrogen from their bloodstream and prevent decompression sickness, the same problem a diver suffers from with rapid ascents.

As I got my breather together, I felt the usual fluttering in my gut. I'd done eleven HALO drops and you never forget a single one. My concern was for the inexperienced lads in the patrol. I would have liked at least one dry run with belt kit and weapons.

Each member of the team had sorted their own webbing, and other than spare ammunition and a knife, it's pretty much up to the individual what he carries in there. How much weight, how much bulk. That said, dropping from such altitude, carrying anything other than your chute, is an issue. It destabilises the jumper and spinning or tumbling at thirty thousand feet is a recipe for disaster. Just fifteen seconds in, you reach terminal velocity.

That is 120mph, belly down arms out.

As Adam and Ryan started the engines and completed their pre-flight checks, I kept my concerns to myself and did what I often do in the circumstances.

I fell asleep.

The hand of Ryan Beard shocked me awake. His BA officer's uniform had been replaced with a full flight suit. After all, the second he opened the 737's door, he would be hit with air temperatures of between minus 25 and 35 degrees Celsius. Despite his oxygen mask, his voice was clear and calm.

"Okay, Fuller? Rise and shine old chap."

I stretched myself and checked my watch. We had been in the air less than thirty minutes. The 737 took a sharp left turn, straightened itself and I heard the engines step up a gear.

"We've decompressed," said the First Officer. "That was us changing tack for Shannon… we've caused quite a commotion I'll tell you. Adam will slow us to just above the stall and put the aircraft in a holding pattern above the drop zone. Get your shit together boys… ETA seventeen minutes… oh, and it's a tad breezy out there, blowing north-south, forty knots."

We all stood in a small circle and checked over each other's kit. Individually we each carried a folding stock Mp5k and a Browning Hi Power SLP. Si had the biggest payload as he had been given the task of bringing along some explosives. Everything had to be secured and as well balanced as possible.

This was going to be no ordinary jump. When the rear door was opened by the First Officer, we would be travelling just above the speed at which our particular 737 would stall. That means the minimum speed the Captain can fly at and still maintain altitude. There are lots of variables he has to think about, including his payload and the weather conditions, but either way, we would be jumping out of an aircraft travelling at around one hundred and forty miles per hour in a howling gale.

Piece of piss, eh?

With no warning buzzers, no red and green lights, the timing of the jump was completely in the hands of Ryan Beard. He strode from the flight deck, his confidence belying his tender years, clipped himself to a support and began to open the rear door of the aircraft.

What is it like standing at that opening, travelling at 120 knots? Well, imagine trying to stand up in a force nine, then triple it.

The freezing air rushed into the aircraft, almost knocking us off our feet. It rattled the plastic pull down screens over the windows, tearing one from its mountings.

With the cacophony of sound and Ryan's oxygen mask, any attempt at verbal communication was pointless.

We were flying a full twenty thousand feet above the cloud cover. The moon lit the swirling mass of white and grey below us. From above, it was a stunning sight, however, I knew that once we hit that cover, we would be blind until we made the other side. Then, of course, those same clouds would work against us, cutting off any moonlight and we would be forced to navigate the final ten thousand feet, piss wet through and in near total darkness.

I could tell that Ryan was taking instructions from his brother on the flight deck via in-ear comms.

He looked at me and gave me the nod.

We lined up, one behind the other, Me first, Des, Butch, then Si. Once we were in position, Ryan held up three fingers, then two, then one.

I looked out into the tempest that would greet me, and as Ryan's final finger disappeared, I dropped into the night.

Am I an adrenalin junkie?

The answer to that one is difficult. I have spent the vast majority of my life in dangerous and often life threatening situations, so you could call me that. What I will say to you is that being scared is normal, but being in a situation where you have absolutely no control over the outcome, is a whole new ball game.

Exiting the aircraft was like being hit by a battering ram, it knocked the breath from me. For several seconds I had difficulty in working out which way was up and in which direction I was falling. It was only when I saw the shapes of the other three men in my patrol being tossed about in the wake of the aircraft, that I realised where the ground was and that I was upside down.

I had to fight to get into the standard free fall position. It was shockingly cold, and I was terribly disorientated.

I was deaf from the roar of the wind as I ploughed through the thin atmosphere at one hundred and eighty feet per second. Trying to twist my head to see if any of my patrol were still visible, not only caused me to lose balance, but the movement played havoc with my mask, and I gave up rather than see my oxygen source fly off into the night.

What seemed like seconds later, I was in the clouds and blind. For me, this had always been the scariest part of a HALO descent. The feeling of falling at such great speed, the noise, the freezing temperatures all heightened at the moment all vision was lost.

From my exit at thirty thousand feet, to my opening height of two thousand, would take a tad under three minutes. How thick the cloud cover was, and how low it lay to the ground, was a guessing game.

I had been falling for just over two minutes and I was still in dense cover. The moon had long since lost its fight with the mass of moisture in the air and now everything was black, both below and above me.

I felt an almighty gust of wind push me left. it almost flipped me over but as I fought to keep my position I saw the first sparse twinkle of lights below. The aerial photographs, the maps, the plan didn't mean anything at that moment, but I felt a whole lot better. All I could make out was what looked like farm buildings scattered between narrow lanes.

Four seconds later, I pulled the ripcord on my chute and the satisfying tug on my harness snapped me upright as it opened.

Everything slowed, and I pulled away my mask. Feeling instantly back in control of my destiny, my mind began to work as it should. The wind made navigation difficult, but I steered away from the lights of the farms and towards the darkness of the fields. As I got more and more of my shit together, I realised that in the distance off to my right, was the N69 coast road that served the Shannon estuary.

I had been blown about a mile or so off course from our drop zone, but not too far away to be an issue.

The Regiment always used square, RAM parachutes for free fall operations, as they were more manoeuvrable and made for a softer landing providing you got it right.

As my boots touched terra firma, I scanned the sky above to look for Des, Butch and Si, but it was black as pitch, no moon, no stars.

After releasing my harness, I sorted myself out and got all my jump kit together. Easier said than done in a thirty five knot northerly, I'll tell you.

It took me three attempts to deflate the canopy, fold it up and stuff it into a bag that was attached to the parachute harness. Weighing in at 15kgs plus the reserve and breather, there was no way I was lumbering about the Irish countryside looking for an ideal spot to conceal the stuff. So, as my eyes grew accustomed to the lack of ambient light and I spied a large metal trough in the near distance, it was a no brainer. In it went.

Once free of my burden, I made ready my Mp5k and BAP, zipped up my jacket and fired up my UHF comms.

Within ten minutes, all the patrol had called in. We were spread out, but everyone had made it down unscathed and I had to be happy with that.

Just after midnight, we all four stood in near total darkness in the middle of a field.

"Everyone okay?" I asked. "No injuries?"

"Piece of piss," said Butch.

Si shot him a look.

Des lit his pipe. "Let's fuck off," he said.

# Des Cogan's Story:

Our LUP had been pre chosen for us. Rick gave me the point, so I checked my map and compass, and set off tabbing the fifteen k towards Banna beach and our lovely holiday caravan.

The spooks rented all kinds of safe houses in the South. During the eighties there were dozens of undercover operatives working there who needed someplace to stay.

Much later in my life, I was to learn that over twenty of them never returned.

The jump had been a nightmare for me. I'd done dozens of fixed line drops and a good few freefalls, but a HALO in those conditions was just about as hairy as it got, and I was very pleased to be back on the ground.

Our plan was to be at the caravan park within three hours. Carrying only belt kit and standard weapons, and with no Bergen's to slow us down, five k an hour was a piece of cake.

The park was closed for the season, making it an ideal choice for our lying up point, and by 0250hrs Boxing Day, we all sat in a large green static van with the gas heater warming our bones and a brew in hand. It reminded me of being a kid, when the whole family went caravanning. We'd drive all the way to North Wales, to Conway, in our old Vauxhall Victor. Mum, Dad and my two eldest brothers on the bench seat in the front and five of us kids crammed in the back. It was shocking. My Dad chain smoked all the way there with the windows closed. Ne wonder I smoke, eh?

I remember my old man kicking off with the guy on the site one time because the maximum occupancy of each caravan was supposed to be six, and we had seven kids.

Good times? Well at least I didn't need to jump out of a fuckin' plane to get there.

Rick had spread out all the aerial shots we had of where the spooks said the nitrobenzene was being stored.

Now, let me put this into perspective for ye.

Nitrobenzene is an extremely hazardous substance. It's highly toxic and readily absorbed through the skin.

Prolonged exposure causes serious damage to the central nervous system. Even brief inhalation of the vapour causes headaches, nausea, fatigue and dizziness.

For years, the Paddies had used Ammonium Nitrate fertilizer mixed with fuel oil, ANFO, to make improvised explosive devices. But combine this benzene shit with AN and you had one hell of a volatile mixture.

Our problem was, we couldn't just go shooting up some wagon with nitrobenzene on board without risking the health of half of Munster. Even if the gear didn't catch fire or explode, it would still cause a major problem, either airborne, or in the water course.

No, we had to slot these boys in situ, then drive all three hundred plus gallons of the nasty stuff, through bandit country, all the way to an RV just shy of the border.

We got all the best jobs, eh?

Rick read my mind.

"If we let them load, the Provo's will take the gear along the fastest route," he said, tapping the map. "The M7 to Dublin then the N7 to Dundalk, probably six hours in a lorry carrying toxic and flammable goods. But a hard stop on the motorway, is a none starter. Even if they move at night, there will still be traffic, and a risk of a stray round causing a major incident."

Butch was staring at the aerial photograph of the chemical store.

"How far is this place from here?" he asked.

Rick sat back in his seat and sipped his brew.

"The storage area at Muingnatee, is a three hour tab, and looking at the map, other than what looks like some kind of treatment plant, there's fuck all else near it. There's the river Lee to the north and a massive area of bog to the east."

Si leaned in. "We could make some noise there if we had to, no problem."

Rick cocked his head. "Meaning?"

Si twisted the shot around and traced the building with his finger. "Look, this treatment works. It's only small, but I'll bet a pound to a pinch of shite that it's manned during the day."

"Maybe those boys get a backhander for keeping an eye on the gear," offered Butch.

Si shook his head. "Possible, but I'd say the Provos won't make a move whilst there's workers close by. They'll come after dark. And what's more, three hundred and eighty gallons of benzene is what? Seventeen hundred kilos? Two tons? And those buildings are too small to hold a truck big enough for the job."

"Go on," said Rick.

"Well, that means the Provo's still have to load the wagon," said Si. "That won't be done in five minutes, either. Benzene is normally delivered in sixty kilo plastic containers, that's twenty eight to thirty drums, four drums per pallet… let's say seven pallets. That will take a good while. After all, they won't want to spill the fuckin' stuff."

I could see Rick's mind working overtime. He nodded his head and rubbed his chin.

"So, what are you thinking, Si?"

"I say we move now, tonight while it's still dark. We can be there for just after seven. That would give me an hour or so to drop distraction devices around the plot. Nothing major, just enough to disorientate our targets. Then we dig in and wait. When the Paddies turn up with the truck, I blow the devices one by one and we slot the fuckers whilst they still have their fingers in their ears."

Rick looked around the patrol. "Anyone any better ideas?"

There was silence.

"Fair one," said Rick. "Then that's the plan. We'll tab there as a patrol. Any contacts en route are dealt with as civilians until we know otherwise. Once we're on plot and we know who we're dealing with, no one gets away. We take them all in the yard." He picked up the photograph of Connor Gallagher. "Especially this guy… Are we happy?"

There were agreements all around.

What we didn't realise at the time, was quite how wrong we were.

The cupboards in the caravan had revealed a bounty of riches in the form of binos, spare batteries, extra ammunition and warm clothing. Rick had allocated us our positions around the target premises and we were on our way within fifteen minutes. We were dressed for a night operation and despite not having slept, I felt comfortable. This was my theatre. The wind had dropped slightly, but it had begun to rain, and it was bitter.

Cold, wet, dark and windy.

What Scot wouldn't be happy in those conditions?

We crossed the river Brick just south of Abbeydorney and other than having to negotiate the N69 at Leith Cross, we were able to remain off the beaten track and away from prying eyes the whole way there.

We rattled off the miles and just before 0720hrs we were all on plot, and settled in.

Si had brought a small amount of C4 along, together with all the necessary components to make it go bang. As he moved out of cover to plant the small distraction devices, I couldn't help but recall Libya. I'd had a good look in Rick's eyes as Si had suggested his plan. Tiji had gone horribly wrong and we'd lost Frankie Green as he was planting explosive charges under Abdallah Al-Mufti's car.

Rick was in no mood to lose another man under his command and he barked down his radio at Butch and me to keep Si covered as he moved between locations in the half-light.

Ten minutes later, Si was back in the relative safety of his position and we all settled in for the wait. Patience is not something that comes naturally to all men. Personally, I didnea mind sitting and waiting, but Rick was a whole different ball game and I was glad that he was fifty yards east of my position, so I couldn't hear his constant moans and groans.

Despite the public holiday, just before eight the first waterworks employee turned up. A stocky bloke in his fifties got out of his car, stretched himself and walked wearily over to the entrance of the small purification plant. We saw the lights come on inside as he went about making the place ready for business, and minutes later, a second car appeared.

The occupant of this one was younger and leaner. He stood by the side of his car for a few minutes and smoked a fag. Once he'd stubbed it under his foot, he too wandered to the small plant and disappeared inside.

My comms crackled slightly as Rick spoke. "That's the sum total of our Boxing Day workforce, I reckon."

No one replied, because seconds later there was the unmistakable sound of an HGV lumbering its way up the narrow lane towards our position.

"Heads up," said Rick.

The rain had stopped, and the clouds had parted to leave a crisp clean bright morning. Good visibility worked both ways and we all kept our heads down as the truck pulled to a halt in the yard that serviced both the plant and the storage units.

There were two men in the cab of the wagon. The driver was a sandy haired man in his forties and he wore a camouflage army style jacket. In the passenger seat was a younger man with long greasy dark hair. Both jumped down from the vehicle and walked around the back. The wagon was an eighteen tonne, curtain sided rigid, with two large doors and an electrically operated tail lift at the rear.

The moment the rear doors were opened, four more men jumped down from inside. There must have been a fifth because although I couldn't see him, he was tossing ArmaLite rifles out to the lads standing on the ground.

Once everyone was armed, all removed balaclavas from their respective pockets and pulled them over their heads.

Rick was on comms. "Anyone ID Gallagher?"

"Negative," I said.

"They like their balaclavas these Paddies eh?" said Butch.

At that, the seventh man jumped out of the wagon. He too had his face covered.

He spoke to two of his men and pointed over to the water plant. Both nodded and jogged over to the works. We were about to get the answer to one of our questions.

The two Provos kicked in the door of the plant and rushed inside. We could hear raised voices and there was a cry of pain as one of the poor fuckers got a clip for his trouble. Moments later, both workers were dragged out into the yard. They'd been hooded and had their hands tied behind their backs.

Now, the IRA boys could easily have waited for darkness to fall, for the two ordinary Joe's to go home to their wives and kids so they could do their dirty business undisturbed. But no, this was all about power and fear. It was the way that all terrorists and gangsters worked in poor communities. Let the weak know you're there.

It was a statement. No one can stop us. No one will help you.

The younger of the two men was trying to plead with his captors. Through his hood, you could hear him saying something about his kids. One of the two that had dragged him out, a big heavyset bloke was standing behind him. He raised the butt of his rifle and slammed it into the back of the guy's neck. He fell forwards onto his face with a nasty slap and didn't move.

Tough guy, eh?

The Provos were getting organised. Two men stood either side of the roller shuttered entrance to the store. Two covered the road into the yard, two stood guard over the workers. That left the guy whose face we hadn't seen, the guy who had given out the weapons and the orders. He walked towards the store with a bunch of keys in his hand.

"Ye'd think they were expecting bother." I said.

"They're gonna get it," offered Butch.

"Radio discipline now, lads," admonished Rick.

I settled myself and turned down the Ultradot sight clipped to the top of my Mp5k. On its minimal setting, the red dot superimposed on your target is the smallest available, making it easier to fire with both eyes open from distance. I loved the Mp5. Using the iron sights, it was a very accurate wee weapon, but with the Ultradot strapped to it, you could give it your missus and she'd slot this lot ne bother. I clicked off the safety and waited for Rick to give me the nod.

I was just in the mood for these fuckers.

"I have the pair at the yard entrance," said Rick.

"The two by the door," I said.

"The pair with the prisoners are mine," said Si.

"I'll take the boss man then," said Butch.

"Standby," said Rick. "Standby… Go, go, go…"

Si set off the first charge which he'd planted by the entrance. It threw up a fountain of mud and grass, causing the two men standing close by to duck. I heard Rick's Mp5 explode into action and a split second later both were down. The second, third and fourth charges all followed two seconds apart. My pair, standing by the door of the store began firing wildly in the direction of each explosion. I let out a long slow breath and slotted both with a single shot each.

Si had the most awkward shots as his targets were close to the civilians, but as I lifted my head from my weapon, I saw he had already expertly dispatched his pair.

That left the boss man who had rolled under the wagon and was laying down rounds in any direction he could think of.

Butch opened up and fired twice before the guy's ArmaLite fell silent.

"Let's move," shouted Rick into his mic.

With that we were all on our feet and running to our respective targets. As I reached my pair, I put a single round into the skulls of both men. To my left and behind me, I heard the rest of the patrol doing the same.

You may think this brutal. Maybe you think this unfair or against conventions and rules. Well that maybe true, but we hadn't come for prisoners, we'd come to stop innocent people being blown to pieces.

The politicians could argue the rest.

ROBERT WHITE

Rick crawled under the lorry and dragged the lifeless body from under it. He pulled off the guy's balaclava and inspected him. It was Connor Gallagher.

One down...

*Twenty years later, Woodhead Pass, Peak District National Park.*

# Rick Fuller's Story:

Mitch used part of the broken fence we'd ploughed through to lever the ruined front wing of Lauren's Audi away from the nearside front tyre. Then, between us we manhandled the woman's corpse that Al-Mufti had thrown from the back of his Transit van, into the boot.

The car fired first time despite part of the exhaust system being torn from under it. However, the dash lit up like a Christmas tree with every conceivable warning light and the odd Teutonic buzzer sounded to tell us to go straight to the main dealer.

I figured any remainder of Lauren's warranty would be void under the circumstances.

Mitch selected all-wheel drive and slowly reversed the Audi back onto the tarmac as Lauren and I looked down Woodhead Pass with heavy hearts.

"He could be anywhere," she said, half to herself.

I let my arm slip around her shoulders.

"We'll find him, I'm sure of it."

She turned and looked into my face. "I don't think I could bear to lose him."

Des Cogan was the closest thing I had to any kind of family. We had fought alongside each other and carried each other's burdens in times of great sorrow.

"He'll be fine," I said, more in hope than anticipation.

Mitch pulled alongside us, and I dipped my head into the open passenger window.

"Will she run?"

"I reckon so, for a while at least, Mr Fuller."

I nodded, and moments later we moved off in the last known direction of Siddique Al-Mufti and the captured, Des Cogan.

The car spluttered and popped but we made decent progress, each member of the team pensive and silent. As we began the descent into Sheffield we negotiated a sharp left hander and I saw that, just as our Audi had demolished part of the roadside barrier a couple of miles earlier, another vehicle had done the same here.

Mitch had noticed the destruction too and pulled us to a halt.

The big American examined the road, using the torch on his mobile.

"Y'all might have expected to see tyre marks, uh?" he said. "Who ever went through here, didn't get chance to touch the brakes."

We trod gingerly in the darkness towards the break in the fence. As Mitch reached the opening, he stopped and held up his left arm to signal for us to do the same. With his right, he pulled his custom made .44 Magnum from his shoulder holster.

As the moon found a break in the cloud, I saw the reason for his caution.

Lying some one hundred metres away from our position, on its roof, was the Ford Transit Siddique Al-Mufti had used to abduct Des from the Prince O' Wales in Ancoats.

There was the smell of diesel in the air, but other than the odd swooping, screeching owl, the night was silent.

My guts tightened as I considered the scene ahead.

Mitch signalled for Lauren to take the left flank and me the right.

I watched as she drew her Colt and began to move over the uneven ground. I found my Glock 19 in my waistband and began the slow silent approach to the upturned Transit.

The moon had washed all the colour from the landscape, yet it accentuated the ridges in the moorland, aiding our progress.

Minutes later, I found myself peering into the open rear doors of the van. An Mp5 was lying, discarded near the doors and what appeared to be a full clip of empty nine millimetre shells littered the interior. Two bodies were visible through the mesh bulkhead, trapped in the front compartment, both were hanging upside down, suspended by their seatbelts.

Unfortunately, for Al-Mufti's men, seatbelts don't help with a bullet to the back or half a Perkins diesel engine stuck in your nether regions.

Lauren leaned into what had been the driver's window and nodded to confirm my suspicions that both were very dead.

I turned, looked back toward the road and saw Mitch Collins casting a long shadow off to my right. Seconds later, I heard him call out.

"Mr Fuller... Sir, over here. It's Mr Cogan... and he's alive."

I've never been a religious man, so to thank any God would have been hypocritical.

"Thank fuck for that," I said.

Des was lying on his back next to the corpse of Siddique Al-Mufti.

Lauren knelt next to the Scot. She held his hand and spoke quietly to him but got no response. She looked up and caught my eye.

"He's lost a lot of blood, Rick. Looks like a bullet wound to his foot. I think there's some damage to his shoulder too, it may be dislocated, or the collarbone is broken. Either way, he needs fluids, and fast."

Des suddenly coughed and opened his eyes.

"I need a fuckin' pint, that's what I need."

"Always there with the one liners, eh, Des," said Lauren, with a relieved, fleeting smile. "Now hold still, this may hurt."

Des winced as she began to remove his boot and inspect the damage to his foot.

"Steady there, lassie. Where's yer bedside manner when a man needs it?"

Mitch had already sprinted over to the Audi to recover a basic first aid kit and some meds. As he made it back, I hunkered down next to my old pal.

"We'll get you a Guinness before you can say 'Jack Robinson' mate. No problem."

The Scot managed a brief grin at that.

Lauren and Mitch applied pressure and began to stem the flow of claret from his bullet wound.

He screwed his face up in pain under their touch.

"What happened," I asked him.

He took a deep breath. "After the bastard threw Maggie from the van, I lost my rag and I kind of shot mysel' in the foot, eh, pal?"

I shook my head at the Scot's attempt at humour under such tragic circumstances and marvelled at his pain threshold.

"You're a nutter," I said, and turned my attentions to the body of Siddique Al-Mufti.

He was obviously as dead as his men in the van. He'd suffered a compound fracture to his right femur and his blood had soaked through his trousers and into the ground beneath.

It shone black in the moonlight.

At first, I considered that he had simply bled out after the accident. Then I noticed a purple bag next to his body.

It looked like some kind of religious item. The kind of thing a priest might carry to an altar. I lifted it up and found it contained a number of crudely fashioned nails. A dim light came on in my head and I remembered that purple fibres had been found at the scene of Todd Blackman's murder.

Kneeling to take a closer look at the boy, I saw that someone had driven a six inch nail smack bang in the centre of his forehead.

I looked over to Des who was barely conscious. "I thought you were no good at DIY?"

The Scot snorted. "That was for Frankie Green," he said wincing in pain. "...And for Maggie too. We... we need to find her, mate. She's out there somewhere. She may still be..."

I cut him off. No point in prolonging the matter.

"No, mate. Sorry, she's gone. But we've got her in the car. We'll sort it, don't worry."

Des turned his face away. "Fair one," he said.

I stood, found my mobile, walked out of earshot of the team and dialled the number I needed. Cartwright answered on the second ring.

He was silent as I briefed him, then offered, "That's good work, Fuller. Very good work. Can you get Cogan to Sheffield... to the infirmary?"

"I think we'll make it there, yes."

"Good. I'll make a few calls to clear your way... keep the local Constabulary out of your hair. But listen, Fuller. Put Al-Mufti and the woman in the rear of the van, clear any weapons and spent cartridges and fire the whole scene. You understand me?"

"Jesus, Cartwright. The woman deserves better than that. Des and her were..."

"That's not a request, Fuller," snapped the old spy. "This was never a fucking democracy. It ties up some loose ends in your neck of the woods and keeps the Americans happy."

"You mean it removes a connection to Todd Blackman's murder."

"Just do it, Fuller. Enjoy your million dollars... I'll be in touch... sooner than you think."

The million dollars was the fee the CIA had agreed with The Firm and us to solve Todd Blackman's murder without there ever being the need for a trial. Young Todd was outwardly gay and his father, Senator J.E. Blackman, a front running Presidential candidate, couldn't risk that little snippet becoming public knowledge. We were quickly becoming MI6's blunt instrument and I didn't like it one bit.

"I think we need a break," I said.

Cartwright snorted. "Idle hands don't suit you, Fuller."

With that, the old spy closed the call.

We lay Des across the back seats of the Audi and Lauren got a pipet of morphine into him. He muttered Maggie's name under his breath, then within seconds, he was out like a light.

I gestured for Mitch and Lauren to come to me.

"Cartwright wants the whole scene cleaned and torched… Lauren, clear the van of any obvious weapons, ammunition, spent stuff, anything traceable. Mitch, get Al-Mufti's body, pull that fucking nail from his head and drop him in the rear of the van."

I popped the boot and saw Lauren's face change as she realised what I was about to do.

"You can't," she said incredulously. "For fuck's sake, Rick. You promised Des…"

I grabbed Maggie's right wrist and began to move her corpse.

"Orders, Lauren. From the top."

She strode over, her face full of anger.

"And since when did you become Cartwright's lapdog?"

I lifted Maggie from the boot, pulled her body over my shoulder and gave Lauren a sharp look.

"Just sort the weapons, Lauren."

As we pulled away, the Transit burned brightly on the horizon. Mitch drove, Lauren sulked, Des slept.

I knew why Cartwright wanted the scene to look the way it did. Okay, the driver's corpse had taken a single round buried deep in his back and there would be a strange hole in Al- Mufti's skull, but after the ferocious blaze that would burn long into the night before the services arrived, on first sight it would look like a terrible accident. A little gentle persuasion from The Firm, when it came to the post-mortems, and the whole business would be brushed under the carpet, all nice and neat.

The Firm would let the local cops continue their dreary investigation into Todd Blackman's murder, until it eventually petered out without a single arrest, just the way the Yanks wanted it.

With Yunfakh's threat to the UK nullified in a single week's work, and Senator Blackman firmly back in the running for the White House, Cartwright would consider the book closed.

However, our 'friends' across the Atlantic still had the small issue of Mason Carver, their double dealing senior operative to contend with. He was currently lying in a morgue somewhere in Manchester, with half his face missing. As far as I was concerned, Mitch had done us all a favour when he'd put that .44 in his cheek, but I had a sneaky feeling that we hadn't heard the last of it. The boys from Langley, Virginia would have wanted Carver alive. They would have wanted to know what he knew, and just who else was involved in his treachery. I reckoned that any future jobs involving the hunt for Yunfakh, would also involve the CIA.

Of more concern to me, was Abdallah Al-Mufti himself.

We had slotted his son and his gang had been driven from British soil. With them had gone any chance of his boss, Khalid Kulenović winning the billion dollar construction contract in Ancoats. Put those two small events together and it spelled trouble for our team.

The rich and powerful rarely lay down after such setbacks. And I knew we would need to tread carefully until both major players were out of the game.

Twenty minutes later, the Audi's satellite navigation unit announced we were at Sheffield Infirmary. The hospital's surgical team had already been briefed by persons unknown, and, as we pulled up outside A&E, Des was instantly lifted from the back seat by medics who called out his blood pressure and other vital signs as they placed him on a gurney. Within minutes, he was prepped and on his way to theatre.

I stood in the starkly lit waiting room. Two drunken women sat arguing in one corner. Both sported the signs of a recent fist fight and constantly goaded each other. I was forced to step over and read them their horoscope before I lost my rag completely and threw them through the fucking window.

It had been a stressful day.

Mitch struggled bravely with an ageing coffee machine in the corridor.

Lauren stepped in the room, gave the two, now quiet, women a cursory glance and then glared at me. She was pale and drawn. More to the point, she obviously still hadn't forgiven me.

"Is this what we do now, Rick?" she said coldly. "Play politics?"

I shrugged, not quite knowing what to say. Big picture speeches didn't seem appropriate, so I kept my mouth shut.

Lauren had different ideas. "Des cared for Maggie you know?"

"I know."

"But it didn't enter your head that her family, or even Des, may want to see her buried? That they may have wanted to have a funeral, to be able to say their last goodbyes?"

Goodbyes were not on Cartwright's list. The Firm would ensure that no one in the van would ever be identified. Maggie would be reported missing by the staff in her pub, and would join the thousands of adults every year, never to be found. It was a shame, but it was all part of the game we were in. Lauren was upset. Des would be angry with me. Both would just have to suck it up.

Mitch saved me any further awkward questions by walking over balancing three small plastic cups in his hands.

The perfect gentleman, he handed Lauren her cup first. "Ma'am."

"Thanks Mitch," she said quietly.

"Mr Fuller."

"Thanks," I said, taking a sip of the shockingly bad, but welcome brew.

Mitch sniffed his cup, considered it palatable enough and took a drink. "What now, Sir?"

I raised my eyebrows and blew out my cheeks. "Well, believe it or not, Mitch, once we have our Desmond on the mend, we still have a business to run over in Manchester. What about you, pal? We always have room for a good CP guy.""

The American shrugged his massive shoulders. "Well Sir, now that is the question, ain't it? I'd say I'll be answering a few questions about Mason Carver for a piece. But once they get that out of the way, who knows?"

Lauren managed a smile.

"It's been good working with you, Mitch." She turned to me and gave me the evils. "Nice to have a man around who knows how to treat a lady."

If Mitch had been wearing a cowboy hat, I swear he'd have tipped the fucking thing. "Delighted, Ma'am," he said, grinning like a Cheshire cat. "I may even stay a while with the scenery being so pretty an' all."

I swear Lauren fucking blushed.

I checked my Rolex.

"Well, we may as well get some rest until Des is out of theatre," I said. "I say we find a hotel. I know a really nice boutique place not far from here."

Lauren shook her head. "We passed a Travelodge on the way in, didn't we? That will do us for a few hours."

I returned the look she'd been giving me.

"Lauren, in the last forty minutes, one million US Dollars, has been transferred into our business account, and I will not be staying in a hotel that's made from concrete slabs and serves a fucking buffet breakfast."

## Des Cogan's Story:

Maggie sat at the end of my bed, looking wonderful. She smiled at me, her eyes full of affection. To her left was my ex-wife, Anne. She was dressed in a pale pink blouse, one that I'd bought her when we'd been on a rare holiday down south. She had all her hair back, the cancer that had racked her body, seemingly gone... pretty as a picture. As usual though, she looked concerned about me.

To Maggie's right was Frankie Green. He looked fit as a flea and there were no holes in his wrists.

"How you feelin', Jock?" asked Frankie, his voice hoarse.

"This is a dream, ain't it?" I asked.

Frankie shrugged.

"You look pale," said Maggie.

"I'm doin' alright," I said. "Nice of yer all to drop in like. But it's only a flesh wound. I'll be up and about in no time."

"That's not what the surgeon said when he took the bullet out," said Anne, her voice as equally as dry as Frank's.

"Oh aye?" I said. "What did he say, like?"

"Bone damage," said Maggie. "Those little ones that footballers are always breaking just before a World Cup."

"Metatarsals?"

"Aye that's them," said Frankie. That and some ligaments. You've been on the table a while. You'll be on crutches for a good few weeks they reckon."

"And you need to pack that pipe in, too," added Anne. "You ain't getting any younger you know. I mean. Look what happened to me, eh?"

I felt a sudden pang of guilt.

"Don't be like that," scolded Anne. "You were the only one with the guts to help me, and for that, I'll always be grateful."

I didn't know what to say. Finally I asked, "Is it, well... is it nice where you all are?"

"Food's not too good," said Frankie. "And I miss the wife and kids."

"I'm going to miss you," said Maggie quietly. "We didn't have enough time."

"There's never enough time," I said.

As if to prove my point a sharp insistent voice began calling me.

"Mr Cogan! Mr Cogan!"

I opened my eyes and turned my head to see a tall man in a surgical mask.

"Aye, that's me."

"Good, you're awake. Are you in any pain?"

I had a think. Strangely, I wasn't.

"No, I'm fine, Doc."

The guy was Irish, from the south. "You sure? I can give you something if you are. I mean, I've fused some small bones in your foot there."

He pulled down his mask to reveal a handsome smiling face. "It's not every day I get to pull a bullet from someone. A shooting accident they say, uh?"

"Aye," I said, thinking how swiftly The Firm worked when they needed to. "I must remember the safety catch next time. To make matters worse, I banged me shoulder too."

"Ah, yes," said the Doc. "You got away with some severe bruising there. Luckily nothing broken or dislocated. However, there are some small rib fractures from another recent injury. Are you accident prone, Mr Cogan?"

"Riding accident," I said.

"Really?"

I nodded and moved on. "I believe you've fixed some metatarsals in the foot… and a wee bit of ligament damage, too."

The Doc looked at me like I was mad.

"Quite a lot, yes. But I have to say it's the first time I've had a patient tell me what I've just done to them on the table."

He turned to leave the room, his visit at an end.

"But, just press the buzzer if you change your mind about the pain relief, Mr Cogan. A surgery like that causes the body quite some trauma."

"Thanks, Doc," I said. "I will."

He smiled at me again. "And, if you want my advice, Sir. Maybe you should leave this shooting lark to the professionals."

I shook my head.

"Aye, maybe you're right there, eh?"

## Lauren North's Story:

We'd been forced into the Travelodge after all. Rick's posh boutique thingy was booked up, apart from the Honeymoon suite and he'd been as grumpy as I'd ever seen him.

He'd risen at death o'clock and found somewhere to buy a change of underwear for us, but we all still sported the signs of battle, with speckles of Des' and Maggie's blood on our outer clothing.

It drew the odd sideways glance from the various reps and commercial travellers enjoying the unlimited full English.

Rick and Mitch both seemed to follow the same diet regime of masses of grilled protein, fresh fruit and gallons of water.

I opted for porridge, honey and a banana, washed down with three cups of black coffee.

Just before nine o'clock, we all stood in the hotel car park, whilst the nice people from Audi dragged my broken RS6 onto a transporter and a guy in a very shiny suit delivered my replacement car.

Much to Rick's annoyance, it was only the S-line model.

I mentioned the availability of taxis to him, received a glare that would seriously injure most at a thousand yards, and the three of us piled into the jet black rental, with only two of us smiling.

Ten minutes' drive saw us paying the extortionate fee to park the car in the visitor's bays at Sheffield Infirmary. Then, it was a short walk to the reception area where we were directed to Ward 11.

Des occupied a private room.

He was propped up, his left leg raised and heavily bandaged.

As we filed in, he managed a smile.

"Ye took ye time," he said. "Dinnea tell me, the big man's been shopping."

"We needed skids," said Rick sitting next to his only friend. "How you feeling, pal?"

"Aww, I'm okay. Problem is, ma foot's a wee bit of a mess, eh? At least the shoulder isn't dislocated. But I'm turning all the colours of the rainbow from the neck down. I had to tell the Doc that I'd fallen off me horse the week before. I wouldn't mind but my ribs are still killing me from Albania."

"You've been in the wars alright," I said.

Rick grabbed Des' good arm. His eyes dark. He lowered his voice and gave him the bad news.

"We had to torch everything, pal… clean the scene. I mean, everything, including Maggie. I'm sorry mate, Cartwright was insistent."

Des seemed distant for a moment, as if recalling a time he'd tasted something unpleasant.

"No worries," he said. "Ye did what ye had to."

The Scot turned his attention to Mitch, changing what was obviously a painful subject.

"And how are you, big fella?"

Mitch raised his brows. "I had a small issue, Mr Cogan. You remember Mason Carver?"

"Oh yeah," nodded Des. "Slimy fucker if you ask me."

"Well," said Mitch. "Seems y'all were on the perceptive side there. Mr Carver was on Yunfakh's payroll from the beginning."

"And?" questioned the Scot, flinching as he lifted himself against his pillows.

"Mitch slotted him," I said flatly.

I saw a glimmer of a smile from Des.

"So it's all over, the operation I mean?"

"I reckon a trip over the pond may be in order to finish the job," offered Rick.

Des took on a look I'd rarely seen. A man full of hatred. "Abdallah? The father? I'd be up for that, mate."

"Let's see," said Rick. "Get yourself fit and well first, eh?"

"A month, and I'll be back on my feet I reckon," said Des.

Rick's phone buzzed in his jacket. He checked the screen.

"I need to take this," he said.

## Rick Fuller's Story:

"How's Mr Cogan?" asked Cartwright.

"He'll live. Four weeks, they reckon. We don't heal the way we did in our twenties."

"Try being my age, Fuller."

"Keep on like this, Cartwright, and none of us will see your age."

"You'll be a very wealthy corpse, Fuller."

"No pockets in shrouds. That's the saying, isn't it? Anyway, I don't believe you rang me to ask about my colleague's condition."

"True."

"So?"

"So, I'm on this blasted train. The one that ghastly man Branson owns, and it's stopping in a place called, Preston in just over two hours. Not the nicest of towns, all very Catholic. Anyway, I've visited once before when the Provos decided to blow up the army careers office on the main street. There happens to be a good coffee shop just down from the site of the blast, Italian owned, traditional, called Brucciani's. I'll see you there, Fuller… just you. Don't be late."

The line went dead.

I stepped back into Des' room. All three faces examined me.

"Cartwright wants me up in Lancashire for a meeting."

"When?" asked Lauren.

"Now," I said.

"Probably wants a full de-brief eh, pal?" offered Des.

I shrugged. "Maybe, he didn't say."

Des shuffled in his bed as if desperate to be free. "Don't even think about going State side to slot that fucker Al-Mufti without me, pal."

I held up a hand. "Calm down, Des. I'm going to have a chat with the old bugger, that's all. Let's not get over excited."

"Who's this Cartwright dude?" asked Mitch.

"The Firm," said Lauren. "MI5… MI6, you pick."

Mitch let out a long whistle. "Well, I hope you can trust him more than Mason Carver."

"Different era," I said. "This guy's a relic from the Cold War, from The Troubles."

"You want to take my rental?" asked Lauren.

I shook my head. "I'll need to change first. I look like I work in a butcher's shop. A cab will have me in Manchester within the hour. I'll pick up the Aston. It's time she had a run. Seems a nice day for it."

There were no more questions from the team, probably because they realised I wouldn't or couldn't answer them.

The taxi driver was mercifully quiet all journey, and with a clear run to my apartment, made it in just under fifty minutes. I showered and changed into a nice caramel lightweight Hugo Boss suit, dressing it down with a cream Duck and Cover polo, buttoned to the collar, and a pair of chocolate leather loafers by Alfred Dunhill that I picked up for less than £200 in the sales.

I didn't have time to nip to the lock-up and collect my preferred Sig Sauer 1911 Fastback, but, as I was meeting with a spy, and make no mistake, despite his age, a man with dozens of very dangerous enemies, I tucked my Glock 19 into my waistband for good measure.

The Aston fired first turn, I selected sport mode, slipped on my Aviators and turned up The Chilli Peppers on the Linn Hi Fi.

No matter how you earn it, making just over a quarter of a million pounds in less than a week, makes a man feel good. I rolled down the windows and listened to the Aston's exhaust note as she hit the red line.

They say money can't buy you happiness. But some days, it puts a fucking smile on your face.

I parked in a multi-storey above St Georges shopping precinct smack bang in the centre of the city, just a short walk from the coffee shop where Cartwright wanted to meet.

As I stepped through the door into Brucciani's, I checked my Rolex and noted I was on the button.

The place was like walking back into the 1960s, all polished panelled wood walls with dozens of black and white photographs of Hollywood stars filling every space. In keeping with the theme, the waitresses all wore black dresses and white pinafores and there was that delicious smell of freshly ground coffee in the air.

I instantly liked the place, and so did most of Preston by the look of it. It was packed.

Cartwright was sitting at a small round table in one corner. He was sandwiched between a pair of young mothers with pushchairs, and a group of rowdy college kids. He had a face like thunder and it was all I could do not to burst out laughing.

As I approached the table, the old spy stood and held up a palm as if he were a cop on traffic duty.

"Get me out of here, Richard," he said sharply. "I can't bear to hear another flattened vowel."

Feeling somewhat disappointed, I turned on my heels and began my exit with Cartwright shuffling behind me.

"I was looking forward to their speciality malted coffee," I said.

"Bah!" spluttered the old spy. "You'd need a large gin in it, just to be able to withstand the drivel these people talk."

We stepped out into the midday sunshine and I scanned the street for an alternative venue. Down a narrow side street was a pub, 'The Oddfellows.'

"Apt," I offered.

"Can't possibly be any worse," moaned Cartwright.

It turned out to be a nice little boozer, and as it had just opened for the day, was sympathetically quiet.

I bought Cartwright a large Bombay Sapphire and tonic and opted for a sparkling Elderflower water for myself.

"Not down with the kids, then?" I asked, hardly able to keep the mirth from my voice.

Cartwright picked up on my tone instantly. "Richard, there comes a time in a man's life when he values peace and quiet." He took a large gulp of his gin. "If I'd been forced to listen to any more inane hogwash about nappy changing and teething to one side, or fucking Snapchat, whatever that is, to t'other, I may have given you the contract to torch the place."

I sat back in my seat and smiled.

"Social media," I said. "Snapchat is a social media platform."

"Balderdash," spat the spy. "Anyway, as I have a return ticket on the Branson express and intend to be back in the Capital before I feel the need to buy a flat cap and a whippet, we need to get on."

He picked up a menu from the table and examined it.

"But not before luncheon."

I shook my head and waited.

Cartwright drained his G and T and waved his glass in the direction of the barman. The guy nodded and within moments was over with Cartwright's refill and a notepad in hand.

"Would you like to order food, sir," he asked.

Cartwright removed his glasses and eyed the young man. "Where are you from son?"

"Poland, Sir."

"I thought as much, far too efficient for a local… I'll have the chicken and avocado salad." He handed me the menu. "Richard?"

Scanning the single sheet, I couldn't see anything I fancied.

"Do you have a daily special?" I asked.

"Fresh sea bream in lemon sauce, sir."

"I'll have that," I said. "No potatoes, just green salad."

The guy noted our choices and was off to the kitchen.

Cartwright poured tonic into his spirit. "Can't see the bream being fresh," he muttered.

I ignored the cantankerous old git.

Finally, he lay his palms on the table and got on with it.

"So, Richard. With Mr Cogan temporarily incapacitated and Ms North a trifle tired and emotional. I have a small task for you."

"Why do you say Lauren is emotional?" I asked warily.

Cartwright ignored me. "Let's just say, I think it best that she keeps an eye on things back in Manchester for now. That, or helps nurse Desmond back to full health."

"Have you been having us watched?" I said, feeling my hackles rise.

"Not exactly, Richard. But the health of all our operatives is always of great concern to us. We have a duty of care, you know."

I nearly spat my drink out. "Yeah, right. Pull the other one."

Cartwright pursed his lips. "My point is that it has come to my notice that Ms North has become increasingly attached to your good self, and that a cooling off period may be in order."

"What if I don't want a cooling off period?"

"You don't?"

I opened my mouth to speak, but unfortunately left sufficient a gap for Cartwright to fill it.

"As I thought. There will be time for romance when all this is over, Richard… And now is not the time."

"Will this ever be over?"

Cartwright took a breath. "Yes, for you, Mr Cogan and Ms North... of course. In your line of work, operatives have a shelf life, no matter how well preserved they may be."

"And our sell by date is fast approaching, is it?"

Cartwright gave me a fleeting smile.

"Not just yet, old boy."

As was his way, the years of conspiracy and espionage suddenly kicked in and he had one last look around the bar to check his surroundings.

"How's your Irish accent these days, Fuller?"

I'd spent many hours practising the Northern Irish lilt during my time with the Regiment and after so many tours, it had become almost perfect.

"I've not used it in a long time, I'd say rusty at best."

Cartwright waved a hand. "Not a problem. Even a born and bred Belfast boy, who'd been travelling the world for the last ten years would have lost some of his edge, and as this little job involves Johnny Foreigners and working in the South, I don't see a problem."

I raised my eyebrows at that one. Former British soldiers visiting the North at least had the odd supporter. Certain areas of the South were a completely different matter.

"Where exactly is this job?" I asked cautiously.

"The wonderful city of Cork," said Cartwright.

"Jesus H Christ."

"It's a fine spot, Fuller. Nice hotels, good food and the craic, as they say, is mighty."

"It's been a Sinn Fein stronghold for centuries."

"It's not so bad these days, Richard. Tourism is the thing there now. They have thousands of English visitors every month."

"So why do I need to pretend to be from Belfast?"

I detected a twinkle in the old spy's eyes as he looked over my shoulder. "Not exactly Belfast, Richard, more the borders... Ah," he said. "Lunch."

Time must have been of the essence, as during all our previous meetings, when the food had arrived, it was usually complimented by total silence. Not on this occasion.

"I need you to seek out another of our chaps who has been embedded in the South for many years," he said, spearing some chicken. "As you rightly say, Cork has been notorious for harbouring active PIRA members since Adam discovered fruit, and we've had operatives on the ground there for most of that time."

He chewed for a moment and shrugged. "I have to say, with varying levels of success, but this chap is a fine fellow and does a great job. He's a little on the eccentric side, but a good sort. I'm sure you'll get on famously."

Cartwright eyed my plate.

"How's the bream?"

"Fresh," I said, smugly.

He screwed up his nose. "Anyway, once you find Finbarr…"

I nearly choked. "Finbarr?"

Cartwright nodded and kept his poker face. "That's the chap… Finbarr O'Rourke. Once you locate him, you'll play the part of his contact from the North, and complete a deal he's brokered with the person or persons that we really want to speak to."

I crunched my way through some nicely dressed salad.

"And who might they be?"

Cartwright lay down his cutlery and took a long drink of his gin.

"The people who will lead you to Abdallah Al-Mufti, and eventually, we hope… Khalid Kulenović."

"I had a feeling we hadn't seen the last of Yunfakh, but I thought they were contained to the States now?"

Cartwright gave me a withering look. "That may or may not be so, and indeed, you and your little team will no doubt have to travel to that terrible country eventually. But since the demise of Mason Carver last evening, there has been some intelligence sharing taking place between our agencies… at the highest level. Therefore, now that our friends across the pond are aware of Yunfakh's existence, we've been tasked with aiding the Americans in any way possible. This little excursion is a … start… call it a peace offering."

I cocked my head. "And these guys, the ones doing the deal, are Yunfakh?"

Cartwright resumed the consumption of his salad and shrugged. "Unlikely. They do fit the usual profile and hail from one of the former Soviet states, but we think it's more likely that they are just criminals hoping to sell on the goods to Al-Mufti. That's as much as we know."

"And what exactly are these goods that we are selling?"

"Ah," said Cartwright pointing a fully loaded fork in my direction. "That will be the sale of a stockpile of now redundant AK47's"

I felt my chin hit my chest. "You want me to sell stockpiled weapons to people who you think are connected to Kulenović?"

"Correct."

"And just how are we going to obtain these AK's, Cartwright?"

"Finbarr knows where they are."

I'd suddenly lost my appetite.

"Finbarr *knows* where they are?"

"Indeed."

"So he collects these AK's, shows them to the gangsters, takes the cash whilst I follow the boys all the way to Al-Mufti, is that it?"

Cartwright scraped the last of his lunch from his plate.

"Not quite, Richard. Finbarr is insistent that he needs another pair of hands. Apparently, there is a small issue with the chap sitting on the weaponry. He may need some gentle persuasion to part with his cache. And to be frank, both Downing Street and our friends across the Atlantic will sleep far easier knowing we have a second man on the ground. And that man is you, Fuller."

"This sounds like a crock of shit."

"Don't be negative, Richard. The cache isn't needed by the Paddies anymore. The Troubles are behind us. They're only too pleased to have them off their hands."

"Patrick O'Donnell and his crew didn't seem to think so," I said, giving Cartwright a stark reminder of just how well armed his men had been when we travelled to rescue Lauren.

Cartwright sat back in his chair, drained his glass and waved a dismissive hand.

"Real IRA, New IRA or whatever they are calling themselves, are no more than a set of disgruntled gangsters, Richard. They have neither the manpower nor money to cause us an issue. Indeed, once you have the weapons in your possession, that will be your ploy with these chaps from the Balkans."

I shook my head. "What? I'm a skint Provo, please take these assault rifles off my hands so I can buy my missus a new fucking frock?"

"Now there's that negativity showing through again, Richard. Once you find Finbarr, I'm sure everything will become clear."

I felt my temper beginning to get the better of me. Cartwright always managed to wind me up, push all the right buttons.

"Find Finbarr? Why would I need to find him?"

Cartwright looked suddenly sheepish.

"He sometimes, well, he often goes walkabout. As I said, he's a trifle eccentric. A damned good operator, just a little... off the wall."

"So, let me get this straight, because I'm beginning to sense a right royal gang fuck here. You want me to pose as an ex IRA player, travel to Cork, find this Finbarr bloke, who sounds as nutty as a fucking fruitcake, and help him sell a shed load of old AK's to some Russian gangsters?"

Cartwright opened his briefcase and slid an envelope across the table, any hint of mirth gone from his face.

"Passport in the name of Sean Devlin. Air tickets, Liverpool to Cork, leaving in four hours. You need to ditch the designer suit and shoes. At least try to look like you're a bit skint. I'm sure after your last payday, you can afford to nip around town now, and buy something suitable. Oh, and there's a briefing note and the last photograph we have of Finbarr O'Rourke in there. You may need to remind him who you are and what the job is when you find him. But as I say, he's a good sort."

I opened the envelope and examined the picture. The guy's nose was completely flat to his face and he had more scar tissue around his eyes than Henry Cooper.

"Scrapper is he, this Finbarr bloke?" I asked.

"Been known to throw the odd punch," said Cartwright absently as he closed his case.

He stood, smoothed down his suit jacket and nodded towards the envelope.

"Your fee is written on the back of that. Your turn for the bill, I believe. See you in a week or two, old chap."

\* \* \*

After a brief and unsatisfying shopping spree, I drove straight to Speke. Once inside the terminal building, I changed out of my good clothes and pulled on nondescript jeans, a t-shirt and a lightweight casual jacket, all with labels I daren't look at. Checking the departure board didn't improve my mood either. I was travelling on my least favourite airline.

I called Des.

"I'm not supposed to have my phone on ye know," he said. "I've probably switched off half the life support machines in the next ward just answering this."

"You sound chirpy," I said.

"Lauren and Mitch have just nipped out shopping for me and are bringing back some cold cans."

"Your surgeon will have your guts."

"Nah, he's Irish. All Irishmen understand the need for a drink."

"Well, funny you should mention that. I'm on my way to the Emerald Isle as we speak. I'm sitting in John Lennon waiting for the cattle truck to catapult me to Cork."

"I'm all ears," said Des.

I took a deep breath. "Cartwright has lost one of his minions and he wants me to find him. But get this. Once I do, we're going to pose as Provo's and sell a cache of AK's to some Eastern Bloc bandits."

"You're making me jealous, you get all the best jobs."

"Yeah right."

"What's all this got to do with us?" asked Des.

I checked my surroundings. "It's all a bit tenuous, but apparently, these boys from the Balkans or wherever have a connection to Khalid Kulenović. Cartwright thinks he's the end user."

Des dropped his voice. He sounded concerned. "These boys are Yunfakh?"

"Don't reckon so, seems they're simply traders, middle men, out to make a dollar."

"And are you making some?"

"Says ten grand a day on the back of the envelope."

"You'll be gone a while then?"

"I hope not. I was anticipating some R&R whilst you sit on your arse drinking yourself stupid. Anyway, listen up, pal. Get Lauren and Mitch to pay Egghead a visit, will you? I'm looking for anything he can pull up on a guy by the name of Finbarr O'Rourke."

"Good Irish Catholic name."

"Yeah, too Irish for my liking. He's been on the Firm's books for years, a real deep cover merchant, but he's prone to going missing. According to the brief Cartwright has left me, he called in this little job over a week ago and they've not heard from him since. Looking at his picture, I'd say he was mid-forties and a real handful, probably done a stint in the military at some point. Get Simon to look for any chatter that may give me a place to start. I'll get his picture scanned and mailed to you as soon as I land."

"Okay, pal, no problem."

"Good man. Oh and tell Lauren I'll give her a call as soon as."

"You're going to be popular."

"Only the depth varies, mate."

I closed my phone, considered calling Lauren straight away, but thought better of it and went for a wander in duty free.

I cheered myself up somewhat by buying some new aftershaves, then sat in one of those big pub franchises, sipping Evian, awaiting my flight from hell.

Cartwright had paid for what is laughingly called 'speedy boarding.'

All this means is that you get to sit on the fucking plane for half an hour longer than everyone else and watch whilst the great unwashed fight over where to put their oversized hand luggage and Aldi carrier bags.

The old spy had also ensured I had extra legroom. My seat was midway down the plane by the over-wing emergency exits. The downside to purchasing these spaces, is that they tend to be used by the clinically obese or people who insist on flying their three toddlers around the fucking world, purely to irritate the rest of the passengers on the aircraft.

I was blessed with a woman the size of a small country and her stick thin husband who thought he was Frank fucking Carson and didn't stop telling me crap Irish jokes, until I 'accidentally' spilled hot coffee over his leg.

Forty eight hellish minutes later, I landed in Cork.

The City has a small but modern airport. I delved in my carry on for my fake passport, but needn't have bothered, as no one asked to see it.

The wonders of the European Union, eh?

Now, if you were wondering why I had reservations about my visit to the fair city, let me explain a little.

Cork was once fully walled, and held the name, 'the rebel city.' This dated back to its support for the Yorkist cause during the English War of the Roses. There was no doubt, Corkonians liked to fight and often refer to the city as 'the real capital,' Cork having been the centre of forces opposing the Anglo-Irish Treaty during the Irish Civil War. Are you catching my drift here?

Since the nineteenth century, Cork had been an Irish nationalist stronghold, with widespread support for Irish Home Rule.

In the War of Independence, the centre of Cork was attacked by the British Black and Tans, an event known as the 'Burning of Cork'. During the battle, fierce fighting took place between Irish guerrillas and UK forces and the locals took heavy losses.

If you read your history books, that fighting has never really ended. Cork is the centre of pro-Irish independence to this day.

So, I was back. Back to the place that changed my whole life. It was history repeating itself. From those early days as a teenage soldier, right up to the assassination of my archenemy, Patrick O'Donnell, Ireland, North and South, had been part of me.

I knew all about arms caches too, how they worked, and the kind of men who watched over them.

If you recall, I began this part of my story by telling you how my patrol had been dropped into County Kerry to prevent the Southern Brigade moving a large consignment of nitrobenzene to the north and blowing up half of Belfast.

What you don't know, is what happened after we got hold of the gear.

*Boxing Day 1987, The Fane Valley, County Louth.*

# Des Cogan's Story:

It had taken us just under an hour to load the truck with the drums of nitrobenzene and the seven dead players.

The two poor sods that worked in the water plant had been shitting themselves, convinced they were going to get slotted, but we'd led them back into the building and locked them inside, leaving them hooded and tied to give us enough time to get where we were going.

That turned out to be two places.

The first was a small farm just off the N69 at Newtownfane. The place was a bonny spot on the banks of the river. It had a large enclosed yard, two barns and several other smaller outbuildings. The house itself was medium sized and looked in good condition. As we pulled into the drive, I noticed it had a 'For Sale' sign nailed to the gate. Out of my price range though.

We were met by two other patrols from 22 SAS and a suit of debatable origin. The lads helped us unload the drums into one of the outbuildings whilst the bodies were carried into the back of what looked like an old bread van.

What happened to those corpses, I never really found out. Connor Gallagher popped up on the news as missing a couple of times, but there was never any confirmation of his death and there was no mention in the press of any British Special Forces operations in Kerry that year.

However, that couldn't be said for what was about to happen next.

Rick had spent about ten minutes with the suit. I'd heard raised voices coming from the barn where they were talking, and as he walked over to our patrol, I could see he wasn't a happy bunny.

He dropped a brown envelope on the tail of the wagon and opened it up. It contained a map, more aerial photographs of another farm and the same picture of Sean Patrick McMullen we'd had to work with earlier.

"This retard thinks that because we're in the right wagon and that Si has the same colour hair as Connor Gallagher, that we can drive straight up to this fucker's front door, jump out and slot the bastard without an issue," spat Rick.

I studied the map.

"I thought the spook back in Hereford said that McMullen lived in Dundalk."

Rick just gave me a death stare.

"This is much nearer the border." I lifted up the chart for the lads to see. "This is a fuckin' stone's throw from Crossmaglen."

The farm consisted of a small bungalow and a large open fronted barn with an arched roof to one side. From what I could see, access was down a narrow country lane.

"That's single track," said Butch. "If you think this eighteen tonner is going down there without all the village knowing, you've another thing coming."

"And if the village know…" said Si.

"Then the target will know," added Rick. "Look, I told this fuckin' halfwit that McMullen will probably already think that something has gone tits up. This guy is a serious player, one of the top men in the organisation. He won't be sitting in his front room with his turkey sandwiches watching the fuckin' Guns of Naverone."

"Good film that," said Butch. "Greg Peck was awesome."

"Fuck off, Butch," snapped Rick. "Anyway, I reckon he'll already have smelled a rat and he'll have security there."

I lit my pipe just to annoy Rick even further.

Si Garcia scratched his beard and looked at McMullen's photo. "How much AN did the spook say was at this farm?"

"He didnea," I said. "He just said, 'a large stock.'"

"So," said Si. "What would hurt the Provos more, losing the AN or losing McMullen?"

"You're not suggesting blowing the place up are you, Si?" asked Rick.

Our latest recruit shrugged his broad shoulders. "Looks to me the nearest other houses are three to four hundred yards away. They'd need some new glass in their windows, but that would be all if I do it right. We go in across country, I use what's left of the C4 for a detonator, and Bob is your Auntie's lover."

Rick looked over his shoulder as the suit was opening the door to his car.

"Fuck him, let's do it our way."

By the time we'd found a suitable spot to hide the wagon and got kitted up for our tab to McMullen's gaff, it was starting to go dusk.

Our plan was simple enough. ID the target, plant the charge and then fuck off quick sharp.

The farm was in wee place called Colgagh, in County Monaghan, just two miles from the Northern Irish border. Crossmaglen was just a short tab from there, and although it was regularly referred to as 'bandit country,' there were also a good few friendly faces knocking about in the form of 40 Commando and 2 Para.

Under any other circumstances, you might have thought Colgagh picturesque, but tabbing across those fields in the pissing rain and freezing cold, clambering through viciously sharp hawthorn hedgerows and wading through fetid ditches, didn't bolster the holiday spirit.

That said, the tab was mercifully short and by 1800hrs we were in our forward operating position, a shallow drainage ditch in the field opposite the target premises.

I wiped moisture from a pair of small binos and scanned the front of the property. The wee bungalow was off to the left with the barn on the right, set back maybe twenty metres. A large concreted yard had been laid in front of it. There was a small tractor and a couple of bits of ancillary farm machinery dotted about, but what concerned me most was the three men standing around a makeshift brazier at the bottom of the drive.

The old oil drum was well alight, and the three players stood around it, warming their bones and chatting between themselves. Each had automatic rifles slung over their shoulders.

There was no attempt at hiding their weapons. This was a show of strength.

"They're expecting company," said Rick quietly.

"No surprise there," said Si.

Just to confirm what the spooks had said, the front door of the bungalow opened. Silhouetted in the doorway was none other than our man McMullen. He held a pistol in his right hand and sported a bulletproof vest. He shouted to the three men at the brazier, and two of them sloped off into the shadows. They had obviously nipped over for a warm and left their posts, annoying their boss in the process.

"Wish we had NV," muttered Butch.

"Okay, listen up," said Rick. "Target is confirmed. Me and Si will work our way around the back of the barn. The fertilizer has to be in there. I don't see another place to store it. You two stay put here. Once the charge is planted, I'll give two clicks on our comms. If things go to rat shit, take out as many of these boys as you can. Either way, our RV is the reservoir on the Drumboy Road, north of the border. Are we clear?"

There were nods all round and Rick and Si disappeared into the darkness.

## Rick Fuller's Story:

We scrambled out of the ditch that had been our FOP and stayed low, below the hedgerows, giving the barn a wide berth. I'd always found any attempt at silent movement difficult. Being my height and weight didn't lend itself to delicacy. It seemed that every pace, every lungful of air was amplified tenfold and I found myself holding my breath as I took each careful step.

That said, as we crossed the narrow lane and slipped into the field adjacent to the barn, all I could hear was the wind in my ears and the rain splattering on my shoulders.

We used an age old tactic to approach our target. One man goes, the second covers and each leapfrogs the next man until the goal is reached.

We were just shy of fifty metres from the building. I'd just watched Si drop into prone and was about to move, when I saw him raise a hand. One of the players who had been standing by the brazier out front was leaning against the barn in almost total darkness.

Had he not been smoking a cigarette, we would have missed him, and I may even have wandered straight into his grasp.

We waited. Lying on the freezing ground soaked to the skin. Finally, the boy stubbed out his smoke and, his habit temporarily satisfied, began to patrol the perimeter again. Once Si was happy, he tapped the top of his head, a signal for me to join him.

I dropped in alongside.

"We need to slot that fucker," he hissed.

Now, killing a man without making any noise is not as easy as you think. The Regiment drill its troopers in unarmed combat, but there is no training to kill a man in silence. Cutting a man's throat isn't easy, and in my experience, a far from silent operation. Besides, the knife I carried in my belt kit would just about slice my corned beef sandwiches. Where was Butch Stanley and his Kukri when you needed him?

Si seemed to have read my thoughts and produced a garrotte from his webbing. I couldn't hide my surprise.

"You're a proper little boy scout," I whispered.

"It's my Spanish heritage," he said casually, and raised his powerful frame to a crouch. "RV on black face, five minutes."

I lay there for what seemed like an age, waiting to hear screams or shots. When neither came I lifted myself up and trotted to the rear of the barn.

Si was tucked in behind some hay bales. The player with the twenty a day habit was lying at his side with his head at a jaunty angle.

Si pointed off to his right. "Never mind him, check those out."

Parked in a line, out of sight of the road were four Austin Maestro vans, all decked out in yellow British Telecom livery.

"Cover me," said Si, and moved swiftly over to the parked vehicles. He disappeared around the rear of the first van. Moments later he shuffled himself back to my position.

"Looks like we're a bit late for the NA," he said searching in his belt kit.

"Go on."

"Well, I've only looked in the first van, but it's filled to the rafters with ANFO and the detonator's prepped. I reckon all four vans are ready to go. They must already have found out that the benzene is a lost cause and gone with the tried and trusted method. They've already mixed the fertilizer with oil and packed it. We're looking at four massive bombs."

I nodded. "Let's crack on then, son."

Si began to mould a small amount of C4 between his fingers. "I've only got some short fuses left, pal. Better tell the lads to get on their toes... you too."

My mind took me instantly back to the deserts of Libya and Frankie Green. I shook my head. "All you explosive boys are the same," I said. "Go do the business. We'll all fuck off together."

I watched Si crawl under the back of the first van and attach the C4 to the petrol tank.

The science behind ANFO explosions is simple, but the effects are devastating. The fertiliser, mixed 98% AN to 2% diesel was hard to set off, so the Provo bomb maker would have had to manufacture a small explosive charge to achieve his aim. The PIRA often used an organic peroxide explosive known as TATP made by using over the counter chemicals. Once synthesised, this explosive is extremely volatile and evaporates in the open air. Si had seen the det, so we knew these mobile bombs were to be used soon.

We had found our New Year's Eve devices.

As Si rolled from under the van, I hit my pressel twice, the signal for Des and Butch to move. When our youngest team member had said he only had short fuses, he wasn't joking.

The first explosion caused a domino effect, with each van going up in turn. When AN is packed into an enclosed space, like a vehicle or other metal container the explosive shockwave is huge. The four of us lay face down in a field as the night sky was illuminated by towers of flame. I turned my head to see the barn destroyed and the small house ablaze.

We lifted our tired bodies from the sodden ground and headed for bandit country.

*The City of Manchester. Twenty years later.*

# Lauren North's Story:

So, Rick was in Ireland again. I'd waited for him to call me. When he didn't, I brooded in my empty, still part decorated flat with nothing but the radio and a bottle of cheap plonk for company, gawking at the screen of my iPhone, willing it to ring.

I was more disappointed than hurt I suppose. No, fuck it, I'm lying to you. I was devastated.

The fact that he hadn't called to tell me what Cartwright had got him doing was bad enough. Using Des as his go-between, rather than have the balls to call me directly were the actions of a man that didn't care.

Well, not enough, anyway.

And now he couldn't even be arsed to give me a quick phone to say he'd landed.

No, I was good enough to fight alongside him. I was good enough to run his errands and go see Egghead, but not quite sufficiently valued to warrant a telephone call to say, 'hi, I'm okay, how are you?'

I sipped on my wine and changed the station on the radio feeling truly sorry for myself. Finally, I did something terribly vengeful and stupid. I picked up my phone and dialled the one person I shouldn't have.

"Hello Lauren," said Larry. "You okay?"

"I'm fine," I lied. "You?"

"Still suspended, but I detect some movement. I take it your job is over."

"Not really."

"I see, so what have I done to deserve a call from you? I got the distinct impression that you were pissed at me, you and Rick were an item and it was best for me to do the gentlemanly thing and back off."

"I was very hard on you last night in the Ostrich," I said.

"You were right, Lauren. You told the truth. My lack of understanding, my decision to play by the rules, got people killed." I heard him sigh. "At least Henrietta Duvall is out of danger."

"That's good," I offered. "I hadn't heard, we've been... a little busy"

"As ever," he said.

I drained my glass and took the deepest of breaths.

"Take me dancing, Mr Simpson. I need to go dancing. Drinking and dancing."

## Rick Fuller's Story:

I wandered towards the taxi rank with those old war stories still floating around my head, found a cab and slumped into the back seat. A fifteen minute taxi ride later brought me into the city proper and my hotel, just off the south tributary, and walking distance to the centre.

You see, Cork is situated on the River Lee. This splits into two channels at the western end and divides the city centre into islands. They reconverge at the eastern end where the quays and docks lead outwards towards Lough Mahon and one of the largest natural harbours in the world.

Visitors get confused, as when the locals direct you anywhere, they only ever refer to 'the river' and neglect to mention which stretch, the north or south. Probably their idea of a little joke.

My hotel on McCurtain Street was named The Isaacs and nestled in a small cobbled courtyard. It boasted a very nice looking bar and an award winning restaurant named Greens. As I watched some of the clientele enjoying pre-dinner drinks, I began to wonder if Cartwright had been a little over zealous when it came to my Hugo Boss number, as most seemed to be dressed in the latest designer fashions.

The evening was fine, warm and dry, so I decided to get my bearings, explore a little of the city and practice my rusty Belfast drawl.

I wandered across the street, past The Everyman Theatre, and one of the older established pubs, The Dan Lowrey.

A few hundred yards along McCurtain Street, I found a place called The Corner House. As it was just a little after six o'clock, I was surprised to find the place extremely busy and a small group of musicians in full swing.

I pushed my way to the bar, ordered a half of Beamish stout, the local brew and eventually found a seat.

One big difference between the English and the Irish, is that us Anglo Saxons like our own space. If we see a table set for four people in a bar, with one person sitting at it, we leave the solitary chap to his own devices.

I like that.

This is not the way of the residents of Cork city.

Oh no. Within milliseconds, I was joined by three middle aged women who pushed their way into my personal space and surrounded the table with piles of shopping bags.

They then set about interrogating me.

"Ah, are you alright there so?" "He's a fine looking man, is he not, Mable? "Are ye a visitor now?" "The session in here is mighty." "That fella on the fiddle is famous in these parts?

And so it went on.

I did my best with my accent.

None of them could work out where the fuck I was from. In the end, I gave up, wandered up the street, bought myself a burger and went to bed exhausted, no wiser and with no plan of just how I was going to find the elusive Mr Finbarr O'Rourke.

## Des Cogan's Story:

I didnea feel too well. Probably more mental than physical. A mixture of the pain and images of Maggie flying through the air as Al-Mufti pushed her from the moving van, ensured that I'd woke every hour or so through the night, sweating and full of hate.

To make matters worse, the staff had discovered my stash of Guinness, and it had been confiscated.

The Doc arrived just after eight-thirty, had a look at my foot and announced he was pleased with his work. Apparently I would be getting a painful visit from the physiotherapist in an hour or two.

The prognosis was that I could leave hospital as soon as aftercare could be arranged. I would need help with the basics, dressing, bathing, that kind of thing.

I lay in my bed considering who would offer me that kind of help and quickly came to the conclusion that there wasn't anyone.

As it turned out, I was very wrong.

Just after ten, my room door opened and in walked Grace Yakim and her boy, Kaya. The sight of her and the wee chap brought both pangs of sorrow and genuine happiness. It was hard to believe that it had been less than a week since we had laid JJ, her husband and a man who I would always consider a great friend and soldier, to rest.

As I lay, wounded and tired in my bed, the presence of Grace and the boy raised my spirits no end.

"How did you know I was here?" I asked.

"I tried your mobile, but it was off, so I rang your offices in town. Estelle, your secretary, said that you'd been in a car accident."

"Aye kind of," I said, managing a smile.

Kaya ran a toy bus across my bedclothes, making vroom vroom noises. He stopped the red double decker at my bandaged foot.

"Hello, Des," he said, a rather blank expression on his face.

I looked into Grace's eyes. She was as lovely as ever, but the sparkle just wasn't there. Same with the boy, there was something missing. I knew only time could restore that spark, that certain something, and even then, after months or years, it may never fully return.

"How are you bearing up?" I asked, feeling stupid for asking the obvious.

"We're okay, Des, thanks. The house just isn't the same though. I'm thinking of visiting Turkey for a while. You know, get some sun and let Kaya see where his Dad came from? Show the family their Grandson."

I knew that neither their Irish nor Turkish families had been supportive of Grace's and JJ's marriage, and that not one single member of either side had attended the funeral.

"Isn't that going to be a tad on the awkward side there, hen?"

Grace looked at the floor for a moment, then caught my eye. "He's still their blood, Des."

"That he is, hen, but I know how hard it can be with family like."

Grace took a breath. "Anyway, that won't be happening just yet, and we're not here to talk about me, we're here to see you, and get you sorted."

"You are?"

"Aye. I spoke with your Doc on the way in. He's from Kerry, would you believe? My mother and his went to the same chapel for a while. Small world, eh?"

"It is," I said. "I went to Kerry once, just dropped in, like."

Grace smiled at that.

"Anyway, I was askin' after you, and he says that you can come home tonight so long as you have the care, so."

"That's as I understand it, aye, but…"

"But nothing Des. After what you've done for Kaya and me, it's the least we can do."

She found another smile from somewhere and her face lit up.

"I have four brothers so, seven of us in a trailer, can ye imagine that? You won't be the first naked man I've seen in the bath, I'll tell yer."

I knew exactly what it was like growing up in a large family, all crammed into one small space, all fighting for the cleanest bathwater.

The truth was, I must have spent hours in the showers during my first weeks in the Army. The seemingly endless supply of piping hot water was an absolute luxury for the young Private Cogan.

I shook my head.

"That's all well and good, Grace. But seeing yer brothers getting bathed and lifting my bollock naked, ugly mug in and out of the water will be a totally different matter."

"I may be wee, Desmond. But I'm stronger than I look. And anyways, you're not so ugly."

## Lauren North's Story:

I opened my eyes and let my mind work out exactly where I was. I hadn't felt this way since university. I could smell the alcohol in the room, that and the unmistakable aroma of sex.

I cricked my neck to my left and saw Larry dozing away, his usually perfect hair was tousled and the beginnings of a shadow formed on his handsome face.

He looked content.

I felt…well, where do I start with this one?

The night's events began to play back in my head.

Larry had collected me from my apartment and taken me into town. First we'd gone to a bar, the name of which escaped me, but we'd had a few drinks there, definitely. Then we'd walked to The Ritz.

Jesus, it was like stepping into a time warp. It was eighties night and the place was packed. I'd never seen so many pedal pushers and so much big hair since my college days.

I'd asked to go dancing, and that's just what we'd done.

Danced… and drank.

For such a big guy, Larry could move, no doubt. But it wasn't those movements that were bothering me. It was his moves once we'd got back to his place.

I slipped my legs from under the sheets and began to search for my clothes. The only item in the bedroom were my pants.

I racked my brains, did my best to focus, stepped from the bedroom and stood on the landing.

My bra was on the stairs.

The moment I saw it, I had a flashback of it being removed and what was going on at the time.

If I hadn't felt so devastatingly stupid and slutty, I'd have smiled.

The lounge revealed the rest of my clothes, together with my mobile.

I opened the screen to find four missed calls.

One from Estelle at the office. Two from Mitch Collins and one from Rick, time stamped 0052hrs.

I ran to the kitchen and puked.

## Des Cogan's Story:

"Well, that's fine news, Sir," said Mitch. "Home cooked food and a proper bed to sleep in will do you good. That's mighty kind of the lady."

"I reckon you're right there, Mitch," I said, eyeing him and Lauren suspiciously.

"But I have to say, ye both look like ye had a good night the pair of ye. And by the Christ hen, ye smell like it too. What the fuck were ye drinking… petrol?"

Lauren glared at me. All sullen, like a wee bairn that had been caught with their hand in the cookie jar.

Mitch shrugged his shoulders and risked a glance in her direction.

"I'd be guessing my night wasn't as entertaining as Ms North's, Sir. I was summoned to be de-briefed. Seems the guys at the big house wanted to know exactly what occurred in Mr Carver's apartment to cause his demise. They were concerned that Mr Carver was tied to his bed at the time he was shot. Fortunately for myself, your friends in MI5 had traced the young lady that was in his company when we arrived, and she admitted it was her that had restrained Mr Carver, for the purposes of…err, sexual activity."

I had a grin at that one.

"So, you were there a while then, Mitch?"

"Until just after four, Sir, yes."

I turned to the esteemed Ms North. She looked awfully sheepish and green at the gills.

"And where were you being de-briefed, hen?"

"None of your fucking business," she snapped.

Mitch slipped on his diplomatic cowboy hat. "Ms North hasn't been feeling well, Sir. But we are off to see Simon this morning. You know, the guy that talks real funny."

I was surprised at that one. "We? So you're staying on for a while then, Mitch? I thought you'd be back off to The States, soon as?"

The big American gave me a smile. "Seems your Mr Cartwright has pulled some strings, Sir. With you laid up an' all, he was of a mind to let me stay on. At least until you're up and about."

*Lauren went a funny colour, turned on her heels and ran out of the door.*

# Lauren North's Story:

I'd left Larry sleeping.

It was one of those moments where I really wouldn't have known what to say to him. I mean, let's face it, things happen to people that are never meant to happen. But as much as you feel regret, you have to take things on the chin and accept it was your own choice.

You can blame the drink, the emotion, the 'I was caught up in the moment,' anything you like, but the bottom line is, it's down to you.

I felt like shit mentally and physically.

How many times do you think I asked myself why?

Five? Ten? Twenty?

And, of course, I'd doubly fucked up. Not only had I put any kind of relationship with Rick at risk, I'd given Larry, a decent, nice guy, hope.

Hope, and … Oh, I don't know, just fucking hope, and that was bad enough.

I stepped out of the hospital toilets wiping my mouth and immediately wondered if I would need to go back for another round of shouting down the big white telephone.

Mitch caught me trying to make up my mind. "You feeling any better, Ma'am," he asked, a concerned look on his face.

I shook my head. "I think it was the Tequila."

The big American wrinkled his nose. "That would do it, Ma'am, for sure."

I did my best not to think about the other shots I'd consumed. "I think you'd better drive to Eggheads."

Mitch checked his watch. "We're late," he offered.

I gave him a look. "The boy sleeps late, don't worry."

We arrived at Simon's house, a little after eleven-thirty. Mitch had me at a disadvantage, as I'd never visited the place before and he knew what to expect.

The dwelling had once been a working farm, but Simon's father, knowing that he was terminally ill, had sold off the land around the main house to pay off his crippling mortgage and leave his wife and the then, baby Simon, with a roof over their heads.

The area that was left around the gaff could hardly be described as a garden, more a jungle of overgrown grass, brambles and bushes. Add various discarded kitchen appliances, rusting away in the weeds, and you get the picture.

The front door had once been gloss painted, but all that was left of the peeling colour, were two thin strips down the centre.

I knew how much Simon charged for his services, and I also knew we were far from his only customers. As I knocked on the door, I considered what exactly the lad did with his six figure annual income.

"Why are you standing back there?" I asked, eyeing Mitch suspiciously as I stood on the step.

The American looked at me over the top of his Ray Bans and shrugged, making no comment.

After what seemed like an age, and three sets of fervent knocks, the door was opened by a woman in her fifties.

She wore a pink housecoat and matching slippers, all of which appeared to have been dragged around the muddy garden for a week or so.

In the corner of her mouth was an unlit roll-up.

Seconds later, I understood why Mitch had taken a step away from the door.

From inside the house came the eye watering smell of cat pee, mixed with frying bacon. Moments later, I was assaulted by the animals responsible for the stench, and what appeared to be dozens of the feline terrors ran past me and out into the open.

I cupped my hand over my mouth, but it was no use. Twisting my body to the left, I just managed to miss Simon's mother with a stream of Tequila induced projectile vomit.

The woman didn't even flinch. She simply turned away and bawled, "Simon… company… and yer bacon sandwich is ready."

Mitch and I stepped inside. My stomach was doing cartwheels as we avoided what could only be the more solid of the two bodily functions that came from a cat, on the stair carpet.

As we reached halfway, a cheery looking chap in his thirties appeared on the landing above.

"Ah, Mr Collins," he said with a smile. "Nice to see you again."

After further careful negotiation, we reached the top of the stairs.

Mitch took Simon's hand and shook it. "Hi there, I hope you're well, Simon. Not been flying on any of our satellites recently, I hope?"

"Not since we last spoke, Mr Collins, no. I've been far too busy with the Russians of late. They seem to be getting very interested in other countries politics."

"Oh my," said Mitch, looking like he didn't know what else to say. He turned to me. "May I introduce you to Ms North? She's a colleague of Mr Fuller's"

Simon's already red cheeks turned crimson and he gave me a big beaming smile.

"You certainly can, Mr Collins. As much as I appreciate Mr Fuller's visits and sense of humour. He's not as easy on the eye as Ms North here."

I raised my brows in surprise at Simon's belief in Rick's comic timing and held out a sweaty palm. "Yes, he's a laugh a minute is our Rick. Still, nice to meet you, Simon… err… can we talk somewhere?"

Our pet computer whizz theatrically swept his arm towards an open door at the end of the landing. "Please, Ms North, this way, take a seat and I'll be with you in two shakes. I just need to nip downstairs. The old girl has done me a bacon sarnie and I don't want it to go cold."

We stepped into the mercifully clean and tidy workroom. Sturdy desks held powerful servers that blinked rapidly. Various monitors and keyboards were dotted about the room, all showing nothing but screensavers.

It was as ordered and impressive as the downstairs was chaotic and putrid.

Minutes later, Simon stepped into the room rubbing his stomach.

"The old crone does a fair bacon butty, I'll tell you that. She threw a couple of slices of black pudding on there for good measure. Bloody lovely." He threw a thumb over his shoulder.

"I can get her to do you two one an' all if you fancy? She's been to Bury market and bought a shed load. They sell the best black pudding in the country there, Mr Collins."

We shook our heads and in unison gave a polite, "No thanks."

Mitch turned to me. "What's black pudding?"

I swallowed bile. "You really don't want to know."

Unfortunately Simon overheard.

"It's a delicacy, Mr Collins. Particularly up here in Lancashire. It's made with pig's blood. Bloomin' fantastic it is, sliced and fried in the bacon fat."

I held up a hand before I threw up again. "Can we just move on please, Simon?"

Egghead plonked himself on a chair, gave me another smile and, elbows on knees, clasped his hands together in front of him.

"Course we can, my lovely'. Anything to please. So, what's the problem this time?"

"Well," I offered. "The bottom line is, Rick is currently in the South of Ireland looking for a man by the name of Finbarr O'Rourke. It's imperative that he finds him quickly... within days if possible."

Mitch handed Egghead a copy of the picture Cartwright had given to Rick. "This is the guy," he said. "We ain't too sure how old the picture is though."

Simon studied the image. "Looks a rum fucker to me," he said. "What's he done, like? I mean, Mr Fuller wouldn't be looking for this guy unless he'd been a naughty boy. I know what business he's in, see?"

I shook my head. "No, Simon, it's not that kind of job. This guy works for MI6. He's an undercover operative."

Simon sat back in his seat and blew out his cheeks.

"Oh, bloody hell, love. I'm not sure I need to be getting involved in that kind of cloak and dagger stuff. Dangerous game that. I mean, gangsters and drug dealers are one thing, but spies, well..."

He gave another beaming smile. "That comes expensive... Do-able, but expensive."

Mitch was intrigued. "So how exactly will you go about tracing this gentleman, Simon?"

Egghead rubbed his chin, stood and wandered over to a monitor. He tapped away at the keys for a moment or two, then plugged in what looked like a small radio into the back of a nearby tower.

"This Finbarr chap," he said. "I'm presuming that isn't his real name, but the one he's been using to get close to the Paddies."

I shrugged.

"Well, I'm guessing what you aren't telling old Simon here, is that he's been snooping around the IRA." He turned and wagged a finger. "And they are fuckin' nutters."

Simon tapped some more.

"Now, nutters, tend not to be too savvy when it comes to technology. They normally buy people in, like myself. Not that I would work for the IRA, you understand, but that is what they do. So, if this Finbarr mush was caught using some fancy gadgetry, phone encryption, that kind of thing, it might have got him kneecapped. Also, the telephone systems in the South are a little on the old fashioned side and about as secure as Jordan's underwear. Up until recently, they still had things called party lines. You remember those Ms North?"

I nodded. We'd had one back home in Leeds until the mid-eighties. It was where more than one household shared the same line to keep the cost down.

"I do," I said.

"Cool," smiled Simon. "So, you'll understand why this mush would be unlikely to use a home phone then?"

I agreed with the logic. Mitch looked puzzled.

Simon was on a roll. "And as telephone boxes are as rare as hen's teeth over there... he would use a mobile. Probably a pay as you go job."

"You're going to hack his provider?" I asked.

"Got it in one, my lovely," said Egghead as he rubbed his hands together like an excited child. "But that isn't where we are going to start, not just yet. Oh no, first, we're going to have a look at Canary Wharf."

"The Firm's HQ?" I said, somewhat impressed.

"Oh aye, well, kind of." Simon began typing furiously, line after line of code filling the screen.

"Now," he explained. "The bods in the Firm, have one of the most complex and secure communication systems in the world. However, Her Majesty's government, the politicians, haven't always trusted the boys in Canary Wharf, so they use the boffins at GCHQ as their safety net. Do you get my drift?"

I didn't. Simon ploughed on.

"You see, GCHQ monitor calls in and out of MI5 and MI6. Even the so called secure stuff is recorded. They, in turn, report any unusual patterns of behaviour, back to Downing Street. They use speech recognition software to highlight any regular callers, particular names or terms, like bomb, or terror or whatever"

Simon raised his eyebrows and stuck out his chin. "You following me there, Mr Collins?"

"I think so, Sir."

"Good," smiled Simon. "Now, with a name like Finbarr O'Rourke..."

"Their system would highlight it, because it's unusual," I offered triumphantly.

"Bonne de Douche," pointed Simon.

Mitch looked totally confused.

Egghead turned back to his screen and began to type furiously. "Now, it will take me a minute or two to get in and have a look, but…"

"You're hacking into GCHQ?" I asked incredulously.

Simon turned. "Better than sniffing charlie and crashing cars for a living, eh?"

Mitch gave me a concerned stare. I knew that Simon had a chequered history as a car thief amongst other things. I could see that he wore unusual devices in each ear. Apparently they were to aid his balance and were fitted by doctors after a major car crash had left him with a severely fractured skull.

We waited.

Simon pulled a face. "Hmmm, bit slow today," he said, as if hacking into one of the most secure establishments in the world were as normal as searching Google for your favourite film star.

He sat back and put his hands behind his head.

"Okay, so the system is searching for this mush's name now. Once it finds him, it should come up with the mobile number he's used to call the spies at the Wharf. Then we can trace the area he's called from."

"How accurate will that be?" I asked.

Simon shrugged. "If he's been using a modern phone with GPS, within ten metres."

## Rick Fuller's Story:

I'd woken early and checked my phone to find the screen blank of messages. Pulling on Cartwright's suggested nondescript joggers, I went for a run.

My route took me out of the city, along the south tributary, then the river proper towards the coast. I found that I wasn't alone in my quest to get some miles into my legs and quickly realised that the roads leading to Blackrock castle and observatory were a popular circuit for the fitness freaks of Cork.

My head was full of muddled thoughts that I desperately needed to clear.

Things had been full on. No sooner had Lauren and I regained our fitness after the Irish job, Spiros Makris had been murdered and we'd begun the dangerous search for his killers. That had resulted in a trip to Corfu and then on to Albania.

Avenging Spiros' murder in the lawless north of the country had resulted in the demise of an old adversary, Stephan Goldsmith, but also the death of a member of our team, JJ Yakim. He had given his life to save mine and Lauren's and I would never forget him.

However, there had been no time to grieve.

Even before we'd had the opportunity to celebrate JJ's life, we'd found ourselves chasing a whole new enemy. A man who had been very much a part of my past, in the shape of Abdallah Al-Mufti.

We had learned that he and his vicious criminal gang, Yunfakh were aligned with an American multi billionaire and supporter of terrorist activity, Khalid Kulenović.

We had killed Al-Mufti's son, his first lieutenant, Siddique and made a massive dent in his empire, but it was far from over.

Now, here I was in Cork, looking for a man, who may eventually lead us to Kulenović and therefore the head and creator of Yunfakh, Abdallah Al-Mufti.

My head swam. I dug in and powered myself forward, feeling the burn.

I couldn't and wouldn't rest until both men were in the ground.

As I stepped out of the shower, my phone was doing a dance on the bed-side cabinet. It was Lauren.

"Hi," she said quietly. I thought I detected a strange tone in her voice.

"Hello," I said. "I called you last night, but it went to voicemail. It was late, I'm sorry."

"Yes, I saw," she said. "I… I was dead to the world."

Yes, definitely a strange tone.

"You okay?" I asked.

"I'm fine…you?"

"A little frustrated, but I got a good night's sleep and I've just got back from a run, so…"

"Good…good. Maybe I should do the same myself later."

"Clears the head," I said, wondering why we were dancing around each other.

Lauren pushed on. "We went to see Egghead."

"And?"

"And he just called us back with the last three locations that Finbarr O'Rourke called Cartwright from."

"That's good work."

"Cost us five bags of sand."

I laughed at that. "The boy could open his own beach, the amount he's had off us recently."

"He's a character, alright. You could have warned me about the cats."

"Sorry… so?"

I heard Lauren shuffle paper.

"Well, Simon is pretty certain he has the locations nailed to within ten to twenty metres. All three are in the same area. Des and I had a look on Google maps, and we're both of the same mind. They're three pubs."

Now I knew what Cartwright meant when he said O'Rourke was eccentric. What he meant was he was a piss head.

Lauren listed the pubs and I noted them down.

"How's Des?" I asked.

"He's good. He had some physiotherapy this morning. He's being discharged tonight."

"That's quick."

"Yes, they seem happy with him and he's going to be staying at Grace Yakim's place until he's up and about."

I knew that Des had stayed at JJ's gaff in Manchester, whilst Lauren and I were in rehab after the Irish debacle. He'd grown close to JJ's boy, Kaya. I also knew that on the day of the Turk's funeral, he'd handed Grace an envelope with the deeds to his beautiful holiday cottage in Scotland. He'd promised JJ, as he lay dying, that he would look out for the boy, and that was his way of doing just that.

"That's kind of her," I said.

"I think it will do all of them good. Give Grace something to do."

"Maybe you're right… you sound tired, you sure you're okay?"

There was a short silence, then I heard her take a breath.

"I miss you," she said.

## Des Cogan's Story:

Big Mitch helped me upstairs and lay my newly acquired crutches against the bed. Grace had organised for me to stay in the bedroom that had once been hers and JJ's, as it had an en suite bathroom.

I wasn't sure how I felt about that, but the wee boy, Kaya seemed pleased that I was there. And that was a bonus as I'd figured it could go either way.

Mitch gave Grace the run down on my meds and when my next physio-therapy sessions would be. The big man sat on the end of my bed.

"I think you will be comfortable here, Mr Cogan."

"I reckon," I said. "She's a fine woman is Grace. Tough as they come. She's needed to be of late."

Mitch nodded. He knew the history. "Well, get well soon, Mr Cogan. I'll be along to visit if I may?"

"Of course, you big lump. Be good to see you."

With that, he gave me a tap on the shoulder, and was gone.

There were cardboard boxes on the floor of the bedroom, some with their lids on, some half full. Grace caught me looking at them.

"I wasn't too sure what to do with his clothes," she said. "I know some folks never throw away anything, but I've made up my mind that I'll only keep the things that he loved."

I touched my wedding ring absently. Grace saw me.

"Oh, I'm sorry, Des. I forgot. You lost your wife recently too, eh? How long has it been?"

"Not long... We weren't together, though. Anne, well, she'd re-married."

"Yes, I remember, you told me once."

"Aye, well. She was a big smoker, eh? Liked her fags, she did. Doctors said that's what did for her, like."

"And you were with her in the end?"

I felt the same old churning in my gut. "Aye," I said. "I was, she asked for me."

"That's nice," said Grace.

I had no answer for that one, so I changed the subject.

"This is awful good of you, hen."

She waved a dismissive hand. "It's no bother at all. Kaya loves having you here. I think it will be good for him, you know, to have a man around the house."

"Well," I said, smiling. "I won't be playing footie with him any time soon."

Grace nodded and continued the heart breaking task of boxing up her dead husband's possessions.

"I'll put a few things to one side," she said. "You know, t-shirts and some joggers. I can cut one leg off them, make it easier for you to get dressed."

As she pushed the lid closed on another box, her mobile rang. She pulled it from her jeans pocket, looked at the screen and ended the call without speaking. I didnea know Grace too well, but I knew enough to know she wouldn't scare easy. She did her best to hide that fear, but it was there and it was real.

"Bloody PPI calls. Damned nuisance, eh?" she lied.

"Aye," I said, watching the anxiety in her eyes. "They are so."

\* \* \*

I spent a great deal of time sleeping, the first few days. The body repairs itself better when you sleep, and I felt that I hadn't done that for months.

Grace fussed around me like a mother hen, and when I was awake, fed me mountains of home cooked food. It was a really strange feeling for me. Yes, I'd been married, but you have to understand, that during those years, I was away for much of the time.

Probably why I'm single.

After Anne and I split, and I left the Regiment, I'd found a wee place up on Loch Lomond and became pretty reclusive. Fishing, hunting, shooting and keeping fit were my friends. Despite the loneliness, I'd felt comfortable, happy even. Then, of course, Rick called with the Amsterdam job offer, and everything was turned on its head.

Meeting Maggie had been a breath of fresh air and she'd filled my dreams the last days and nights. My heart ached for her and I couldn't help but feel guilty that I had caused her death by association.

I was, however, far more concerned for the living. For Grace. Despite her tough exterior, I could see that she was struggling. Kaya was as good as could be expected, but he was too young to understand that his frustrated outbursts hurt his mother so much.

I was also concerned about the phone calls. Not just the one Grace had taken on the day I'd arrived, but the four or five since. I'd known that she'd closed the calls without responding most of the time, but on the one occasion she had answered, I'd heard tension, maybe even fear in her voice.

On my sixth day, I think we were all getting a wee bit stir crazy and Grace announced that, as it was such a nice warm morning, we were going out to the park.

The three of us piled into her wee car and she drove us the short hop.

One of the wonderful things about the city of Manchester is its abundance of green spaces.

Alexandra Park is sixty acres of peace and tranquillity that sit in the none too salubrious, Whalley Range district.

It was designed by Alexander Hennell, who, in his words said it would, 'deter the working men of Manchester from the alehouses during their day off.'

Fat chance of that, eh?

The park was also famous for being the venue for the great Manchester Women's Suffragette Demonstration of 1908. One such women's rights campaigner, Kitty Marion, planted a bomb in the park to make her point. It destroyed the cactus house and killed a family of ducks.

Thankfully, the loudest noises these days are those of music, as the park annually plays host to the city's Caribbean Festival.

We'd parked the car and I hobbled along on my crutches taking in the fresh air. The sun was bright and the sky cloudless. Wee Kaya ran about like a headless chicken until we reached the lake. Once he'd seen the now, very much alive ducks, he was in his element and sat cross-legged on a wooden pontoon throwing bread to them and howling with laughter as they fought over each scrap.

Grace and I sat together on a metal bench watching the boy.

I felt myself smiling. "He's a good kid," I said.

"He is, but I'm worried for him."

"Understandable, Grace. Who wouldn't be."

She rested her hand on my arm and looked up into my face. "I spoke to

Lauren," she said quietly. "She told me about Maggie, the lady you met... I'm sorry, Des."

"Aye," I said. "I'm sure you are, hen. But ye have enough on your plate with yersel' and the wee one here without worrying about me. I'd only just met her, but we'd sort of clicked straight off."

"That Siddique was a right bastard," she offered.

"He was, so. But his father had filled his head with hate, and that mustn't happen with wee Kaya here. JJ was a good man, and a great soldier, he wouldn't want the boy brought up hating one race or another for what happened to him."

"I won't ever let that happen, Des. Why do you think I've tried so hard recently to bring both sides of the family together?"

"There were none at the funeral, I noticed."

Grace looked at the floor and let out a long sigh.

"I went to Turkey on holiday. The whole of my family was up in arms. Not one of them has ever been out of Ireland. They'd travel from the South to the North without as much as a birth certificate, no danger. But abroad? Never...so much for calling themselves travellers... ye know that's what I am, eh? A traveller?"

"Aye, I gathered as much hen."

"Well, that's a laugh, isn't it? They call themselves by that name, and proud of it they are, but they never feckin' go anywhere."

She blew out her cheeks. "Anyways, off I went with a friend of mine, Janet Mary. We were so excited."

"And ye met JJ?"

"I did so. But heavens above it was a disaster. His family called me a white whore, and mine were convinced all JJ wanted was an EU passport, even though they'd never seen the likes of one."

I shrugged my shoulders. "Well to be fair hen, it wouldn't be the first time a holiday romance went wrong, eh?"

Grace managed a smile as she looked out across the shimmering water.

"I loved him from the moment I met him," she said. "I knew, and there was no changing my mind."

"It must have been hard for your folks, mind?"

"It was, but we'd hoped that when Kaya came along, that both sides would mellow."

"Not so far then, eh?"

Grace looked in my eyes.

"Des, I'm determined to travel to see my in-laws and try and build that bridge."

"What about yer own, hen?"

She swallowed hard.

"Ye know the phone calls I said were PPI and the like?"

"Aye."

"It's my Da. Well my Da and my eldest brother. They're talkin crazy, Des. They're sayin' that if I go through with taking Kaya to Turkey, they'll come here and steal him away."

I shook my head.

"Do you really believe that, hen? I mean, that's daft talk."

"Aye," she said, her mind elsewhere. "I suppose it is."

## Rick Fuller's Story:

I'd spent almost a week in Cork and visited the three bars that Simon had identified on dozens of occasions. There had been no sign of the elusive Finbarr and I was getting concerned that time was running out on the deal with the Balkan boys.

On my sixth day, I walked around the city, feeling frustrated and more than just a little sorry for myself.

That said, it was a beautiful morning and the crowds were out in force.

The English Market is a popular attraction in Cork, selling fresh produce, meat and fish, and so I spent an hour in there, practising my accent and hoping against hope to bump into my man.

With no luck and feeling even more irritated, I stepped back out into the sunshine with the smell of fish in my nostrils and made an executive decision.

I was going to rattle some cages.

The three drinking establishments that were on my list nestled close to the south tributary.

I'd decided that I was going to make my mark in one of them, cause a stir and flush out the boy I was looking for. A dangerous ploy, but one I was getting ten grand a day to carry out.

Most folks would think that it would take a while for these pubs to open and get busy.

Not in this part of the world. Being on the river and so close to the coast, Cork, as with many dock towns up and down Europe, had bars that opened unusually early or late. This was originally done to accommodate the thirsty harbour workers who toiled during unsociable hours and were glad of a pint at whatever ungodly time they may finish.

Most of these 'early' bars had long gone, their licences revoked. Not just because of the demise of the docks, but because the hardy imbibers of Cork quickly discovered, that with careful planning, you could walk a route of pubs around the town and drink for twenty four hours, straight.

Add the Irishman's love of a fist fight to this heady mix and you could understand why few of these bars remained.

However, one such relic was the Welcome Inn.

Walking inside just after one o'clock, I was met by a crowd of drinkers who had been sampling the establishment's wares since before breakfast.

The place was bouncing.

The front door opened straight into a room not much bigger than the average lounge. The bar was on the right. To the left were a few tables, a fireplace and what was laughingly described as a stage. The venue obviously never had more than one performer.

However, it being early in the day, and due to the lack of space, a solitary table and chair had been placed up there for good measure. I watched as an old boy teetered precariously on the edge of the wooden structure, drunk as a skunk, likely to cause himself a mischief. No one else seemed to mind him.

I pushed my way through the melee and ordered a Beamish. I'd grown used to the locals indulging me in conversation in these places. Before I had the pint to my lips, I felt a nudge in my ribs and a voice ravaged by thousands of roll ups asked me, "You'll be a visitor there so?"

I'd quickly realised the good folk of Cork don't call tourists, tourists. They refer to you as visitors.

"I am that," I said, using my best Belfast brogue.

"Ye from the north then?" asked the guy.

"Aye, but I've spent a wee while in London and Manchester for my sins."

"I can hear that in yer tone, for sure," said the man.

I'd have put him somewhere between fifty and sixty. Lithe built with pure white hair and plenty of it too, all brushed back, curling at his collar. Despite the season, he wore a heavy black leather jacket that, although I was unaware of the maker, I reckoned cost far more than the average weekly wage of the drinkers in the establishment.

He held out a hand. "Paddy," he offered. "A cliché, I know, but my name all the same."

I shook. "Sean," I said. "Sean Devlin."

The man nodded. "So what brings you to the mighty city of Cork then, Sean?"

I shrugged. "Like you say there, Paddy, I'm just visiting."

The guy watched my every movement with sharp green eyes. My hackles rose instantly and, for the first time in six long days, I knew I had a bite. Being the grey man and being questioned by curious Provos had been a regular occurrence back in the day in Belfast or South Armagh. Posing as a local back then was one thing, part of the game, but all these years later, I suddenly found it disconcerting. I was out of practice and off my guard.

Paddy jutted his chin. "Ye don't seem the type to be here to enjoy the scenery, there. Am I right, Sean?"

Now, in these situations, you have a good idea who you are dealing with. I didn't think for a moment that the man was full blown IRA, but he was a sympathiser, a Sinn Fein boy through and through. And, if he didn't get the right answers to his questions, I knew there'd be a possibility that I'd find myself answering some more, to other less salubrious characters, and I wouldn't have a fucking pint in my hand.

When I found myself with my back to the wall, I always used the same tactic.

I got in his face. Best, I always think.

"You ask a lot of questions there, Paddy. What are ye? A fucking newspaperman?"

He took a step away, either concerned for his own welfare, or to give himself room to fight if things didn't go well. That said, he didn't look too worried and gave me a smile that revealed American made teeth. At that moment, my suspicions turned into nailed on certainty.

"Steady on there, big man. I was just being friendly, so."

I figured I'd finally dropped lucky and my wait was over. I was in the right place, and talking to the right player, so I went for goal.

"If you must know there, Paddy, I'm here to look up and old friend. And from what I can see of your good self, I'd reckon you may know of his whereabouts."

Now I knew my question would put old Paddy on the back foot. He'd have to ask who I was in town to see, and more importantly, decide to tell me if he knew him or not.

He eyeballed me, despite his diminutive size, and I began to feel that uneasiness that went with undercover work. Who was this guy? Finally he spoke.

"And who would the man be yer after, so?"

I took a sip of my stout. "Big daft lad, by the name of Finbarr."

Paddy snorted. "Dozens of blokes by that name in this town there, son. You got his last?"

"O'Rourke," I said, examining the guy's face for any signs of recognition.

He was good, but not good enough. I read his expression in an instant. He knew the name, nailed on.

"I never heard of himself," he said, doing his best to be casual, showing those teeth again.

It was my turn to press the matter. I leaned in.

"Listen Paddy, you may have had all yer nice shiny teeth fixed in Chicago or wherever our boys sent yer to collect the fund, but I'm of a mind to knock them clean out for yer. You come over askin' stupid fucking questions of a man who has done more for the cause than most, and when I ask yer a simple favour, you go all fuckin' girly on me."

I pushed my hand into his jacket pocket. Inside were around a dozen Sinn Fein badges all wrapped up in cellophane, ready for the boy to dish out to the tourists.

I held them under his nose.

"This what yer do these days, is it Paddy? Pick these up from yer office up the hill did ye? So ye can hand them out to anyone who'll listen? Give them all the spiel about a united Ireland, eh?"

I stuffed them back in his pocket.

"Fuck off and leave a man to his pint."

Paddy retreated out the door quicker than the French at Alsace. I was left wondering if I'd done the right thing.

One or two drinkers around us had noticed the change in tone to my voice, but other than that, life went on as normal. What I did see though, was the landlord nip into the back to use his phone.

I ordered another stout and waited for the inevitable.

Halfway down my second Beamish, the door of the bar opened, and in walked two players. These boys were younger and taller than Paddy. All shaved heads and tats. They reminded me of the boys back in Manchester. Bad taste, big bling. One was fatter than the woman who sat next to me on my fuckin' flight in.

As they walked to the bar, the drinkers parted like the Red Sea. The landlord looked to the boys, and then to me, just enough to give me away. He may as well have put a sign on my fucking head.

I gave him a knowing wink.

The two boys sidled up, one either side. Fat boy let his humongous jacket fall open to reveal a semi-automatic pistol that almost disappeared into his gut. Having flown in, of course, I was unarmed.

"Would you be Devlin?" he asked, knowing the answer.

I took another sip of my beer and held onto my glass. "I am so."

"We weren't expecting visitors," he said.

I turned and curled my lip. "That's because, I'm not here to visit you, you fat fuck, and if you as much as move toward that pistol of yours, you'll be wearing this pint pot so you will."

I felt movement from the boy behind, so reached backwards with my free hand, found his crotch and squeezed his bollocks like a lemon on Pancake Day.

As boy two let out a scream. Fat boy stupidly took his chance. I held true to my word and caught him across the temple with the barrel of the glass. As it shattered, I released boy two's bollocks, stepped left and stripped Fatty of his Browning.

The big lad was bleeding like a stuck pig and holding his head. I caught him with the butt of the pistol, slicing open his cheek and he went down like a sack of shit.

Boy two had both his hands on his nuts and was being sick on the tiled floor. I put the British Army issue pistol to his head.

"Tell Finbarr O'Rourke, Sean Devlin wants to see him," I said. "Tell him I'll be in the Grocer's, so I will."

I grabbed the boy by his coat and stood him straight. "And I don't want to see you pair again, are we clear there, sonny?"

The landlord caught my eye. This time, he gave me a slow knowing nod.

That told me everything. I'd made my point. I was in business.

Stepping out into the sunshine, I pushed the Browning into my jeans and felt much, much better.

The Grocer's was actually called The Poor Relation Grocery and Pub. I'd no idea why, and never asked. The place wasn't a grocers and nobody looked that poor. It just seemed to be a pub with an odd name. It was a much larger and much quieter establishment than The Welcome Inn, with a stage at the back sporting a PA system that Wembley would have been proud of.

Where the previous establishment had been aimed at the early drinkers, this was definitely the opposite.

Posters adorned the walls, boasting everything from transgendered Brazilian salsa nights, to Can Can dancers. It was not my preferred drinking establishment.

Two young couples played pool in one corner and the long bar was dotted with the odd silent drinker. Even so, I felt I needed to keep my wits about me, so lay off the Beamish and ordered a sparkling water.

The barman raised his plucked eyebrows at my choice, but remained tight lipped, and I sat with my back to the wall, my eyes on the front door, and waited.

An hour passed, and I was beginning to think my little ruse hadn't worked. That was until a young guy of no more than nineteen barrelled through the door, seemingly out of breath.

He was a skinny runt of a kid, with bad acne and an even worse barber. He stood in the middle of the pub breathing hard, scanning the room until his eyes set on me.

The boy did his best to look confident as he walked over, but I could see he was bricking it.

As he got closer, I noticed he had a pierced eyebrow with a single gold stud in it. He could have fastened the whole of fucking Ratner's to that face and he'd still have been pug ugly.

He stood in front of me smelling vaguely of cheese.

"What you want, kid?" I asked.

"Will yees be, Mr Devlin?"

"Who's askin', so?"

This threw the lad, as he'd obviously been told not to give his name. "Err, well that, err…is a secret like."

I almost smiled. Sharp, this boy wasn't.

"A secret, you say? Well, in that case, you'd better not say then, Peter."

The kid screwed his face up so tight, I thought one of his pukes might explode. "I'm not Peter, so. That's me brother, I'm Paul."

I felt like an extra in Father Ted.

"What do you want kid?" I said, my fun over for the day.

He took a deep breath and his rehearsed spiel came flowing out of his dumb mouth.

"If you'll be wanting to see Finbarr O'Rourke, he's in Costigans now."

I pulled fifty euro from my jeans and gave it the lad. He looked like he'd won the fuckin' lottery.

"Oh thanks there, Mister," he gushed. Turned on his heels and legged it.

Costigans was not on my list of venues. It sat on the edge of town, looking out onto the docks. It seemed a tidy sort of boozer with an outside seating area and a few parasols advertising Italian lager. As the sun shone and the day was balmy, there were a few drinkers taking advantage of it, none of whom looked like Finbarr, or anyone connected to him.

Checking the pavement opposite for a lookout, I found it clear, so strolled towards the front door.

As I gripped the handle, an almighty crash came from my right.

Ducking instinctively and covering my head with one hand to protect my face from flying shards of glass, I took two steps back and pulled my newly acquired Browning Hi Power from my belt.

I needn't have bothered.

The cause of the carnage was none other than Finbarr O'Rourke himself. The right hand window of the pub was decimated and the man I had travelled to Ireland to meet, the man who I was to put my trust in, the man who would have control over whether I lived or died, lay on his back between two wooden tables with a tennis ball sized lump on his head, covered in broken glass.

As he'd exited the window, he'd also destroyed two of the very nice umbrellas donated by the Italian drinks giant and flattened one of the lunchtime patrons, who sat rubbing his elbow next to the prostrate Irishman.

Surprisingly, Finbarr opened his eyes, pulled himself to his feet, brushed a few shards from his clothing, cricked his neck and launched himself back through the broken window from whence he'd came, shouting 'Geronimo!' at the top of his fuckin' voice.

I pushed my SLP back into my belt and shook my head.

*Fucking eccentric ain't the word, Cartwright.*

Deciding that discretion is sometimes the better part of valour, I took a seat at a sunny table and waited for the fun to recommence. It didn't take long at all.

Some ten seconds later, a guy in his thirties with the reddest hair I'd ever seen, exited the already broken window and crashed onto a table outside, flattening it in the process. He lay face down, and didn't move. There were the unmistakable sounds of punches being thrown from inside the bar, then a second man of similar age and size was ejected via the same window and joined his mate outside on the flags.

This one was conscious and managed to drag himself to a sitting position. Blood poured from his ruined nose and he had a real shiner developing under his left eye.

Finbarr appeared at the broken pane, his shirt ripped from his back, blood seeping from numerous cuts and grazes.

"Have yees had enough now, there, ye bastards?" he bawled.

It appeared the two had.

Some unseen punter handed Finbarr a pint of stout, slapped him on the back and he disappeared back inside the pub.

As I walked into the bar, Finbarr was counting out euros into the hand of a man I presumed was the landlord.

"That's the third time this year, there, Fin," said the man shaking his head. "I'll tell yees now so, if yees cause anymore commotion, I'm going to have to bar yees."

Finbarr gave the man a dark look. He was a big unit alright. He didn't look the sort to have ever seen the inside of a gym, he was just a naturally powerful guy. About my height, pushing eighteen stone with a shock of sandy hair that was as wayward as its owner was short tempered. He had hands like shovels, his knuckles damaged beyond repair from hundreds of scraps like the one I'd just witnessed.

"I always pay for the damage there, Arthur. Do I not?"

"Aye, yees do," offered the landlord, re-counting what looked like several hundred euros in cash. "I'll give yees that, Fin. But like I say, yees have to think of me other customers like. Yees keep punching fuck out of them."

Fin turned down his mouth and shrugged. "Come on now there, Arthur. It was himself and his mate that started it."

The landlord shook his head. "Aye, that's as maybe. But yees did take the Mick out of the boys hair colour for over an hour."

I stepped over. "If ye can't take a joke, ye shouldn't have joined," I said.

Fin turned his head and eyeballed me straight off. He'd had a drink or two, no doubt, but his eyes were sharp, inquiring, demanding.

"Who the feck are yous?" he asked.

I held out a conciliatory hand. "Sean Devlin," I said.

Fin took my palm. I was like shaking with a rhino. He lifted his chin and looked down his flattened nose at me.

"You're the chap from the early bar then? The one who gave the two boys a slap?"

I nodded.

Fin squared himself.

"And what would yees be wanting with my good self? Do I owe yees money?"

Now, Cartwright did mention that I may have to remind Finbarr who I was and what the job was about. I was beginning to think the whole idea was a big mistake.

"I need to talk to you, Fin… in private, like."

As the guy didn't have a shirt that wasn't ripped to shreds and he sported several cuts that looked like they may need a stitch or two, I suggested, he go to the infirmary and we reconvene over some food once he was cleaned up.

"Feck that," he said. Dabbing at one nasty looking slice on his shoulder with what was left of his upper clothing.

"We'll nip to my place."

A cab took us to a small terrace off South Main Street, and to a quaint, tiny cottage, brightly painted in keeping with the rest of the properties in the row, close to what remained of the original city walls. We stepped inside to what appeared to be an unoccupied room.

No furniture, bare wooden floor.

"I like what you've done with the place," I offered.

"Ye think I'm going to take you to my home, there son?"

I shrugged. "Fair one."

Finbarr turned his back and began to rummage in a cardboard box pushed in one corner. He removed a first aid kit, turned again and pointed at me.

"I take it Cartwright sent yees?"

"He did."

"Well, as we're both batting for the same side, yees can take that feckin Hi Power out of yer belt there and lay it on the mantle. Yees makin' me nervous."

I pulled out the Browning and did as he asked.

Fin began to sort himself out, dabbing his cuts with antiseptic and humming an unidentifiable tune as he did so.

"If yees is going to be playing the part of a man from the borders, yees need to work on that crap accent son," he said.

"The job came in at short notice," I offered.

Fin examined me, cocking his head like a confused parrot.

"Well, that's as maybe, but it don't help my good self there now, does it?"

He found a needle and some suture.

"Right, there's a pub called The High B Bar," he began. "It's on Oliver Plunket Street. Go and get yourself a beer with the rest of the tourists, you'll fit right in with your tone. I'll see you there in an hour. I need to stitch myself up a wee bit. Oh, and leave the HI Power where it is, son. The fat lad will be needing that back."

Forty-five minutes later, he walked into the packed bar.

The High B was smack bang in the middle of the tourist trap. I'd figured that Fin had chosen it, as there were virtually no locals in the place and I wouldn't stand out too much. Then again, it may just have been that he hadn't been barred from that particular establishment for being thrown from the fucking window.

He sat in front of me gripping a pint of Guinness. Clean shirt, hair still looking like birds were nesting in it.

"Fuller," he nodded. "That's yees proper name so, is it not?"

"It is, Fin," I said.

He took a look at my Evian and screwed up his nose.

"You do realise, fish fuck in that, don't yees?"

"It's an old joke," I said. "One I've heard many times."

"Not a drinker then?"

"I've had my moments."

He looked about him.

"What on earth made yees cause a ruck in the Welcome? Do yees not understand how many eyes and ears are about in this town? That kind of behaviour can get a man killed."

I waited until the waiter had collected the empties from the next table.

"Well, as much as I like the place, I'd been in Cork almost a week, and I figured asking around was a good way of getting hold of you. Especially as you seem to have forgotten I was on my way. Maybe I should have just waited for you to be thrown out of the right pub, eh? Anyway, I thought people in your game were supposed to keep a low profile?"

He took a long drink and wiped his mouth. "The way I saw it was if I was going to be here a month or two, then aye, that would work. But if I was going to be here longer, then I would have to blend in, like."

"What? By fighting every red head in town?"

He smiled at that one.

"The Irish respect a man who likes to fight. Win or lose, just so long as he has the bottle to stand his ground, that's enough. Now, is yees passport in the name of Devlin?"

I nodded.

"Good, and where is it the now?"

"The hotel kept it."

"Aye, well okay, I suppose yees may get away with it for a day or two longer."

I wasn't sure what he meant by that, so cracked on.

"How long have you been here, Fin?" I asked.

He shook his head. "Not a clue, son."

I detected a glassy look in his eyes. There was little doubt in my mind that Fin was a man on the edge.

"I've been Finbarr O'Rourke fer so long, it doesn't matter anymore... I ain't going back to England, that's fer sure."

"You don't get tired of looking over your shoulder?"

He eyeballed me. "Do yous?"

It was a fair comment, I suppose. I pursed my lips.

"I don't sleep with a gun under my pillow, if that's what you mean?"

He rested his elbows on the table.

"Me either, Fuller. Things have changed. It's not like the old days where yees had a chain of command and the Provos were up and down from the north every day, hunting fer spies and traitors. Now, it's New this, Real that. Feck me, all that's left are a few bitter gangsters, pissed off that they don't earn as much cash as they used to. No, mainly it's down to fools like those two in the early bar, Fat Lad and his pal... They'll do anythin' fer a few euro"

"So, who sent them?"

"I did. Terry, the landlord gave me a bell, said some stranger was askin' after me. It's the way of the world here."

"You sent them to beat me up?"

"Like you said. I'd forgotten you were coming."

"That happen a lot?"

He shrugged. "Don't worry about me, Fuller. I don't drink on the job."

I drained my water.

"You say the Provo's aren't a threat anymore, but they're still slotting people up north."

"Aye true, they are. But it's just a few hot heads, arguments between rival gangs, and it's over drugs and whores, not religion or politics. The people want peace so they do."

"So, you're almost redundant then?"

He finished his pint on the second attempt and shook his head.

"Yees could say that. It's a whole new ball game these days. Just like yous over the water, Ireland has the whole of the EU underworld to contend with now. The Eastern Bloc boys, the ones looking to buy the AK's are just the tip of the iceberg. The Russians are here, buying up the big houses, washing their money. So are the Albanians, nasty little fuckers. After this deal, I'm about ready to retire, head off into the sunset."

"So, there's a market for the old PIRA stockpiles?"

Fin nodded. "Aye, and the boys are only too willing to sell. The stock we are interested in is held by a guy by the name of Tommy Brannigan. He's a real old school PIRA boy… Big drinking buddy of mine."

"So why do you need me?"

"All will be revealed Fuller. All that matters is I get paid and you get to go on a nice trip to the Balkans or wherever."

"So, you and this Brannigan bloke split the cash and that's you done, finished with the Firm?"

Fin shook his head and revealed a missing tooth.

"Who said anything about splitting the cash me old son? Those AK's are just sitting there."

Now I knew why I was in Cork.

"You're not telling me you intend to steal the guns? That's madness. Why not just broker the deal as planned?"

Fin stood. "A man cannot live on bread alone, Fuller. He has to make a decent living somehow. Now…" he tapped the side of his nose. "Mum's the word… you just play visitor for a piece, and I'll be in touch."

* * *

I wandered Oliver Plunket Street, pondered what the fuck was going on and decided I would just have to live with the situation. Cartwright obviously knew about Fin's little money making scheme, hence my presence so early in the game. But our main concern was the final destination of the guns, not who got paid for the deal.

There was no doubting Fin had been covert for way too long. I'd heard of men going off the rails in deep cover situations before, but I had to admit, his local scrapper routine worked well for him. He could call on the local muscle to do his bidding, and the Sinn Fein boys all seemed to have his back.

To all intents and purposes, he was one of them. A trusted sympathiser. A paid up member of the PIRA, and that made him a very valuable asset to the Firm.

My only concern was his determination to bite the hand that fed him. Once those AK's went missing, there would be an outcry from the quartermaster general that had been tasked with their safekeeping. And as I've told you, I know all about those guys.

The subsequent investigation into the theft would reveal that a visitor had been in town at the time, purporting to be from the North, and that visitor, yours truly, was connected to Finbarr O'Rourke.

Our deep cover merchant was playing a very dangerous game and I was a little concerned just how he was going to play it out.

I made a note, never to be unarmed in his presence again.

Just before five o'clock I returned back to my hotel. As I stepped into the lobby, the receptionist smiled in my direction.

"You have a parcel, Mr Devlin," she said, pointing to a heavily wrapped box nestled in the luggage rack.

Despite my concerns that I was about to take delivery of a fucking bomb, I collected it, squeezed myself and the said item into the small lift and took it to my room for further examination.

I lay it on the bed and gave it the once over. Just as I was about to start slicing at the packing tape, my mobile rang.

"I take it you have my present," said Cartwright.

"I was just checking it wasn't ticking," I countered.

"Just a few toys that you may need in your endeavours, Fuller. Things we couldn't transport on a domestic aircraft."

"I'll take a look," I said. "Will they help with the theft of Mr Kalashnikovs finest invention?"

"Quite possibly... by that comment, I take it you've finally found Mr O'Rourke?"

"Oh yes. You do realise, he's as mad as a March hare?"

"Nonsense, Fuller. He's just a little high spirited."

"Yeah, right."

"Anyway, keep me informed of your progress, won't you, old chap?"

"If I don't find myself with a bullet in the back of my head, yes."

"It's why you have such an impressive hourly rate, Fuller," he said, and closed the call.

Feeling far more at ease with my mystery package, I began to open it.

Rummaging into the filling, I removed the components of a stripped MAC10 light machine gun. Further delving found its noise suppressor. The MAC10 was an old weapon, first made in the early '60s by Ingram.

They were a cheap 1000 round per minute room clearer, challenging to master, but really useful.

It took me less than a minute to reassemble the weapon. Once the suppressor was fitted, the Mac10 was so quiet, the bolt action was louder than the round exiting the breech. At .45 calibre it made a real mess too, but as it delivered over sixteen rounds per second, you were changing the magazine every couple of minutes.

Thankfully, four fully loaded mags came with the old girl.

I rooted further into the box, and found none other than the exact same weapon I'd stripped from Fat Boy in the Welcome Inn. A Browning Hi Power SLP. The old faithful had been named the P35 by some, but to me, and nearly all the lads who'd spent time over the water back in the day, the gun was the BAP, the Browning Automatic Pistol.

Not the most accurate SLP ever made, but what it lacked in precision, it more than made up for with capacity. It had a thirteen round mag. Compared to any other SLP it almost doubled your ammunition, in fact you had fourteen shots without a reload, if you counted the one in the spout.

Two, one-hundred-round boxes of nine mil completed my gift from The Firm.

I loaded the BAP and stuffed it into the back of my jeans. Then I pushed the Mac10, the spare mags, and the boxes of nine mil into my day sack and dropped the bag inside my wardrobe.

I felt better again.

Time for dinner.

## Lauren North's Story:

Estelle had done a good job whilst we'd been otherwise engaged, and with Rick away and Des on the mend at Grace's, there was nothing else for me to do than try and run our business. As I sat at my desk, reading through new job applications from various ex-military and other service personnel, I considered just how little time we'd spent in the building since we opened the doors.

Thankfully, the hard work we'd put in after returning from Abu Dhabi had stood us in good stead and we still had enough contracts and operatives to keep the place afloat.

However, it wouldn't last forever.

Mitch sat at Rick's desk twiddling his thumbs and making the place look untidy.

"Why don't you go and acquaint yourself with the delights of Manchester, Mitch?" I asked, unable to hide the irritation in my voice.

He shrugged his broad shoulders and gave me a smile.

"Would you care to accompany me, Ma'am? My stomach tells me it's time to eat."

I gestured towards the pile of paper on my desk.

"And who will see to these?"

"Why not drop them over to Mr Cogan? I'm sure he'd be glad of something to keep him occupied right now?"

He had a point... after six days of being pampered, I reckoned the cantankerous Scot would have been climbing the walls.

So was I to be fair, but I resisted.

"Anyway, I need to find us a new drill site. The old infirmary buildings, where we trained our first people, are being demolished."

Mitch was nothing if not persistent.

"The agent's will be closed now, Ma'am... maybe in the morning, uh?"

He'd just about persuaded me, when Estelle popped her head around the door.

"Visitor," she said.

I gave her a look that asked who and why.

"Oh," she said meekly. "A lady called Victoria. She applied for some CP work a couple of months ago. This is her interview day."

Estelle pulled an embarrassed face. "We've had to cancel twice already."

I scrabbled for my diary and sure enough, there it was. 1800hrs, Victoria Sellers.

I pulled her CV and scanned it. She'd travelled from London. Postponing for a third time was not only unprofessional, but downright rude.

"Okay," I said. "Send her in."

As the woman stepped through the door, she scanned the room, acknowledged Mitch with a pan-faced nod, turned to me, gave me a warm but unconvincing smile and held out a perfectly manicured hand.

"Sellers," she said.

Her accent was terribly English. She didn't just have a plum in her mouth, I figured she had another wedged in a far more intimate location. From her CV, I'd noted that she'd been educated at a private all-girls school in Buckinghamshire. Then, she'd joined the army, attended Sandhurst and had served in both Iraq and Afghanistan, leaving the military with the rank of Captain and a medal for gallantry.

On parting from her military career, she'd immediately returned to the Middle East, travelling to Kurdistan on the Iraq border where she'd taught defensive driving to the local militias.

On paper, she had all the tools in her box.

I returned her smile and gestured for her to sit. "Please, Victoria."

She slipped her slim frame into the chair and rested both palms on her thighs. "Thank you," she said. "It's nice to meet you, Ms North... finally."

She had dark chocolate coloured eyes, sallow skin and raven hair that shone almost as much as her nail polish. I'd have put her in the attractive, rather than stunning category.

However, from the expression on Mitch's face, I was alone in that assessment.

"Quite," I countered. "We have a busy office here, Victoria and all of us, including myself, have been required in the field of late. Hence the regrettable need to postpone your interview."

She gave me that smile again. "Really? That's comforting. I like to keep a full diary."

I managed a smile of my own. "So, CP is what you're looking for, I see?

Of course you will need the civvy qualification to work for us. Crazy, I know, but the rules... "

"I have it," said Victoria, removing a document from her serviceable but ever so expensive handbag and holding it at arm's length. "I completed the course whilst waiting for you to... fit me in."

Obviously, the private girl's school didn't have warmth or charm on the curriculum.

"Well, you're here now," I said through slightly gritted teeth. "That's all that matters."

Sellers sat in silence, plucked eyebrows raised, waiting.

I though Mitch was about to burst into fits of laughter.

I took a breath. "We have work available in the UK at the moment... "

"I'd prefer to work abroad," she interrupted.

"I'm sure," I said, managing another smile. "A girl likes to travel. But unfortunately, most of our offshore work is in the Middle East and, as you are well aware, Arabic men tend not to employ female close protection officers."

She shrugged those ever so delicate but toned shoulders. "The former Yugoslav states will do, or Eastern Bloc. I don't mind, so long as I'm not a babysitting service."

Mitch couldn't hold his water any longer.

"That can happen to the best of us, Ma'am."

Victoria turned her head and took a long look at the American. For a moment, I thought she would pounce on him.

"Well, it won't happen to me," she said flatly.

Mitch sat back in his seat. "It must be nice to be so... special, Ma'am."

Sellers let a breath out through her nose and dropped her ramrod straight position. She gave me a look, turned to Mitch, then back to me.

"I'm not doing too well, am I?" she said, screwing up her face.

I shook my head.

Mitch stood, picked up his chair and sat alongside the woman.

"Close protection, Ma'am. Well, scuse me for sayin', but the clue is in the title... close. You have to get on with folks a piece."

Victoria regained some of her composure.

"I suppose I'm used to getting what I want."

Mitch smiled. "And I'm sure most folks, particularly men folks, will give it to you, Ma'am. But your ways ain't gonna work with Ms North here, and sure as hell won't go well with Mr Fuller or Mr Cogan."

She popped some wayward hair behind her ears and looked me in the eye. "I suppose the truth is, I'm finding it hard to adapt to life outside the army."

I leaned forward.

"My background is medical, Victoria, so I understand the difficulties some people face once they return to civilian life. Most, if not all our employees have gone through the same thing. Hence the reason they work for us."

"I'm not a basket case," said Victoria, defensively.

I considered my own issues over the last months.

"I wasn't suggesting you were... look," I checked my watch. "Do you drink?"

Seller's face softened for the first time. "I've been known to down the odd glass of wine."

I looked at Mitch.

He nodded. "I'll call us a cab," he said, then pointed at me. "No Tequila for you, though, uh?"

The taxi dropped us outside the Thirsty Scholar. The place was busy with students and the outdoor area was full of customers taking advantage of the warm evening.

We sidled up to the bar. Sellers squeezed in alongside me. "I'll get these," she offered. "What'll it be?"

I blew out my cheeks. "I'll just have half of lager. We're playing catch up with the CP business at the moment, and to be honest, I had a bit of a heavy one earlier in the week and still feel a bit dodgy."

Sellers raised those brows again. "Really? I didn't have you down as a party animal."

"Long story," I said. "Mitch will have a Dr Pepper. He's a real badass."

Finding a small table on the raised area by the dartboard, we sat and chatted about Victoria's career in the army and what she wanted from her life.

Victoria, never Vic or Vicky, by the way, was actually alright. Once you got past the posh totty routine and her natural defensiveness, inside was a straight up decent girl. Well, at twenty-eight, she was a girl to me.

Mitch played his usual polite cowboy routine and fussed around her like a dog on heat. Victoria was having none of it, and took the piss mercilessly. She was an excellent mimic, with a quick wit. Mitch didn't stand a chance.

Finally, the American gave in.

"Hey, I know when I'm beat... Anyways, I'm of a mind to find somethin' to eat. I reckon I'll leave you two ladies to your own devices."

Victoria gave him a knowing smile. "Saddle up there cowboy."

Mitch looked at me and smiled. "I'm hoping you can find Ms Sellers here a nice posting somewhere… cold and lonely… say the Baltic."

"See you in the morning, Mitch," I said.

He nodded. "Goodnight there, y'all."

He walked away, edging his way through the punters, excusing himself as he went.

"Nice guy," said Victoria.

"Don't be fooled," I said. "He's a real tough one."

Sellers sipped her wine. "So, if Mitch is only here temporarily, when are your partners due to return?"

I sat back and considered what to say. "Well, Des… Des Cogan, he's laid up at the moment. He was involved in a car accident a week ago, he'll be another month or so before he's back in full training. Rick is over the water, Cork actually. He's meeting with some people who need our kind of expertise, he could be another week, maybe more."

"So you have the helm?"

"In one."

"And what is your team's… expertise exactly?"

I gave Victoria a look. "Same as yours, I reckon."

"Rick and Des, they're ex- regiment aren't they? 22 SAS?"

I nodded slowly.

"But you are straight out of Civvy Street?"

I shrugged. "You have a problem with that?"

"Not at all, it's just, well… an unusual combination."

"If it ain't broke, as they say."

Victoria raised her glass. "I'll drink to that."

I felt my phone vibrate in my pocket.

It was Des and my mood changed in an instant. His voice was sharp, demanding and breathless. I could hear his pain in it.

"Listen hen, I need you here, at Grace's gaff, now. But swing by the lockup, eh? Get us some kit… for the three of us… is Mitch with you?"

"No, he just left."

"I'll call him. You just get what we need."

"We? Des you're bed ridden."

"Bring plenty of meds too," he said.

"Des, what's happening?"

He paused for a moment. I could hear him swallow.

"They've taken Kaya," he said.

# Des Cogan's Story:

I'd been sleeping, a mixture of being out in the fresh air and the drugs making me drowsy. Grace had cooked wonderful food and she'd sat at the end of my bed as we ate. We'd talked for a while, before she excused herself. Kaya needed to get ready for bed.

It was shortly after that, I must have fallen asleep.

What woke me was the sound of the front door being kicked in by someone very strong. The door splintered on the third blow. I heard Grace scream, as heavy footsteps trampled the hallway.

I rolled out of my bed and landed on my arse, the shock sending sharp needles of pain through my left side.

I hadn't a clue what I could do. It was a pure, natural reaction.

Tearing at the bedroom door with my good arm, I shuffled along on my backside to the top of the landing. Looking up at me from the bottom of the stairs was a man. He pointed a sawn-off in my direction. He didn't speak, he simply shook his head slowly and put a finger to his lips.

I eyeballed him and took in every detail of his face.

It wasn't one I was ever going to forget.

Moments later, a second man twice the age of the first, but of similar size carried Kaya out of the door and along the hall. The boy was sobbing for his mother. Heartbreakingly, he called out for me, too.

The guy with the sawn-off followed after him, and seconds later, I heard car doors slamming. Dragging myself upright and using the banister for balance, I managed to look out of the landing window onto the street below.

A dark saloon, either a VW or Skoda was pulling from the kerb. I clocked the registration and fell back on my arse breathing hard.

As I sat, feeling useless on the carpet, all I could hear were Grace's quiet sobs from below me. I lifted my damaged foot as high as I could and bounced down the stairs on my backside. Once I reached the bottom, I pulled myself upright once again.

As I hopped into the lounge, there she was, sitting on a chair, staring at the floor. Finally, she looked up.

"They said they would," she said, her voice trembling with fear. "I told you they said they'd take him."

"Do you know who they are, hen. Was that yer Da?"

She shook her head. "No, I've never seen them before. They'll have been hired, or they owe my Da money."

"We'll get the boy back, hen," I said finding my phone. "I promise you."

## Lauren North's Story:

"I need to go, now," I said.

Victoria examined me. "What's wrong, Lauren? You look pale."

I didn't quite know what to say.

"There's been an abduction… a child. His father was killed recently."

Victoria cocked her head knowingly. "Working for you?"

I nodded.

"Aren't you going to call police?" she offered.

I shook my head and began to call a cab. "If the mother feels the need, she'll do it," I said as I hit the buttons on my phone.

Sellers stood alongside me. "Well, if you need another pair of hands?"

"Probably best you don't involve yourself in this one."

Her expression turned cold, her eyes darkened. "If you pay the rate, I'll do the job."

I examined her face. No nerves, no fear, calm as you like.

"This will get messy," I said, watching her reaction.

There was the merest flicker of a smile. "I can do messy, darling."

My phone bleeped.

"Cab's here," I said.

We were dropped at our offices, where I collected the S-Line rental. I didn't know Victoria well enough to take her to our lock-up, there would be time enough for that if she proved herself. So, I left her in the warmth of the Manchester evening, standing on a corner, two blocks away, with a puzzled look on her face.

I drove as fast as I dare towards our lock-up, checking and re-checking that Sellers or any other sudden new arrivals in my life weren't tailing me, parked a couple of hundred yards from the doors and walked.

Once inside I grabbed four pre-packed bags. Each contained an SLP, a machine pistol, spare mags, a knife, a torch, balaclava, Plasticuffs and Gaffatape. Next, I went to our medical cabinet, took a deep, worried breath and selected anti-inflammatory and pain killing shots together with a standard battleground first aid kit.

Finally, I found Des' locker and picked up a pair of his boots.

I humped all the gear into the S-Line and fired up the engine. Three minutes later, I pulled alongside Victoria Sellers.

She bent slightly to check who was in the car, nodded at me, had a cautious, but cursory look in the back seat and slipped herself in front.

She eyed the four bags on the back seat. "Did you get what you came for?"

"One of those is yours," I said, hitting the gas.

Sellers reached over, dropped one bag between her feet and unzipped it.

She let out a long whistle.

"When you said messy, I didn't consider I'd be breaking so many laws on my first day."

There was no time for fucking around. "I can drop you here if you like," I said.

I turned and eyeballed her. "If it's too much for you, you know? You can just nip in and see Estelle at the office in the morning. She'll find you something more... legal."

Sellers pulled a SIG from the bag and made it ready. It was like watching a magician at work. Slick and quick. Something she had obviously done thousands of times before.

Pushing the brand new weapon into her handbag, she licked her highly glossed lips and raised those plucked brows.

"This seems much more fun, darling," she said.

As we pulled up outside Grace's house, Mitch was already at the gate. Together we unloaded the bags of kit and meds and dropped them on the floor of the lounge.

It felt like a wake.

Des was sitting in an armchair, on the phone to Egghead. He'd clocked the registration plate of the car used to take the kid and was hoping for a result. Grace sat with her head in her hands, she barely acknowledged us.

Des killed his call, took a long look at Sellers and turned to me. He was not his usual jovial self.

"Who the fuck is this?" he asked.

Our latest recruit held out a confident hand. "Victoria... Victoria Sellers."

Her eyes flashed. "You can call me Captain, Ma'am, Sellers, or Victoria... it's up to you, Cogan. Just not fucking Vicky."

Des didn't take the offered palm, he just glared.

"Which Regiment?" he spat.

"Intelligence Corps."

"Served where?"

"Afghanistan, two tours, Iraq three, then here and there."

Her eyes darted over to Grace who had begun to sob quietly. "And while you've been asking me about my dim and distant, that car has travelled another two miles further away."

Des looked at me. "Is this your doing?"

"My call, yes."

He nodded and finally took Sellers' hand.

"Welcome aboard, Victoria," he said. "Okay… the car is a VW Passat, black, registered to a leasing company in Bristol and has no markers, more than likely a hire car, Simon is working on which fleet and from where it was rented. The good news is, Egghead says he can track the car by hacking into the various camera systems around the city and beyond. So far, we know it has travelled out of town and is heading towards the M62 as we speak. He'll give us live updates once we're on the road."

Sellers shot another glance at Grace, then back to Des.

"Is this a kidnap? Are we expecting a ransom demand?"

Grace raised her head, eyes bloodshot, her lips trembling.

"No. They want my boy, not money. A few days ago, my Daddy called me and demanded I go home and bring Kaya with me."

Grace snorted her derision at that.

"Funny, eh? They didn't want to know me because I was married to a Turk, to a sand nigger, as they called him."

I saw pain fall across her face.

"But now JJ's dead… well, their doors are open wide again, eh?"

She drew herself upward.

"Stupidly, I'd told them that I was going to take Kaya to Istanbul… to show him where his Dad came from, try and make amends with his side of the family. Only for a couple of weeks, you know? Obviously they figured that I wouldn't come back."

Grace cleared her throat.

"They never agreed with me and JJ getting together in the first place, never mind, having a child. They wanted me in Ireland where they could keep an eye on me. Make sure I married into the right family, that kind of thing."

You could see Grace mentally getting her shit together as she spoke.

"Their biggest fear was that I would go back to Turkey and never return. Funny, they have never seen their grandson, but were always desperate to know where he was. It's as if they've been waiting for this to happen, for me to lose JJ."

She curled her lip. "I hate them for that."

Grace wiped her eyes.

"They wanted their Grandson in Ireland, but they were scared of JJ. They knew they'd have to kill him to take me or Kaya. And they knew he would cause the family a great deal of damage if they tried."

I nodded. "We can vouch for that."

Sellers was in.

"So, they are using your son to make sure that you return to Ireland, is that it?"

Grace took a deep breath.

"They gave me that option, yes. But now it's Kaya they want."

I could see Victoria's mind working overtime. "And you didn't take that option, because?"

Grace shook her head. "God forgive me, no. Because, I didn't think that they'd really… y'know, steal him."

She looked at Des for support. "We'll find him, hen. I promise."

Mitch had been taking it all in.

"'Scuse me for sayin', Ma'am, but why don't you just wait for your boy to reach his Grandparents, and then take it from there. Make your peace with them. I mean, they ain't going to do him no harm."

Grace took another deep breath. "If Kaya reaches Ireland, I'll never see him again."

Mitch screwed up his face. "I don't catch your drift there, Ma'am."

Des shuffled to the edge of his seat.

"They're travellers, Mitch. What you may call, Gypsies. There are thousands of them in Ireland, in hundreds of locations. They move around in trailers. Most are off the radar, some are born and die without ever officially existing. They trade between themselves, fight between themselves, but they are a closed community. Strangers stand out like a sore thumb and if you kick one of them, they all fuckin' limp."

Des pulled a syringe from the bag I'd dropped at his side and began prepping it.

"What wee Grace here is sayin', is that once the boy is over the water, there are literally hundreds of locations that they could take him to. Thousands of people who would gladly hide him, and a good few, who would kill to keep him there. The travellers are just that, a mobile community. If they don't want you to find someone, you won't."

Grace stood. She addressed us all.

"My family gave me the choice, take Kaya to them, or face the consequences. I turned them down. They told me, I was no longer their blood, no longer their daughter, and that they would take my child away from me forever. Now, I know my JJ fought and died alongside you guys. So I'm asking you, begging you, for your help, like he helped you. For me, for JJ… please, get my boy back."

## Rick Fuller's Story:

After a leisurely walk back from a very pleasant early dinner, I lay on my bed watching the news with the sound down. I'd quickly realised, in my line of work, if you had the opportunity to rest you took it.

Just before the BBC re-ran its daily headlines, I fell asleep.

It was not to be. Moments later a call woke me. It was O'Rourke.

"Walk over the river, do a left until you reach the bus station. Turn your next right. I'll be in the red Ford… ten minutes."

The phone went dead. As I peered at the screen, two things struck me. One, I hadn't given him my mobile number, and two, his thick Cork accent had all but disappeared.

Cartwright, what are you up to?

I pulled on my jeans, rinsed my face in the sink and took a long look in the mirror. The flecks of grey in my hair were spreading from my temples and silver sparkles around my stubble told me my beard, should I ever grow one again, would be in the same condition. The star shaped scar on my cheek that I'd received courtesy of Stephan Goldsmith's bullet stood out, pale against my tanned face, the Greek and Albanian sun, unable to blend in the damage. I felt an involuntary shiver as I recalled how Goldsmith had poured boiling water over my legs to obtain the location of Des Cogan's house in Scotland, and how, on the second kettle, I had given up my only living friend.

I felt the sudden urge for some more sun on my back, sun that didn't involve chasing gangsters and getting shot at. It had been full on since Amsterdam, and I was feeling a little battle weary. I traced the lines around my eyes with my finger.

You're getting old pal.

I'd just finished feeling my age, when my phone rang for a second time.

Lauren briefed me expertly on the abduction of Kaya Yakim. There was little emotion in her voice, she was matter of fact and business-like. However, she voiced her concerns for Des, and the lasting damage he may do to his foot. She explained the Scot had been adamant that he wouldn't stay behind and I knew there would be nothing she could say to him to make him do so. Whoever had taken JJ's boy would have to put Des in the ground to stop him, and that would take some doing, even with one good leg.

So, for the first time, we would be fighting on two fronts, and I would be alone.

Once she closed the call, I texted her Cartwright's mobile number. With Des half crippled, it was Lauren's team.

She would lead.

I knew nothing of the new face, Sellers, but I trusted Lauren's judgement. After all, it had been her that had ensured JJ Yakim had worked alongside us and I had rarely fought with anyone braver or better. The job to find JJ's boy was a no-brainer. The Turk had given his life to save ours and that was a debt that could never be fully repaid.

Mitch was reliable, tough and a cool operator. He would have Lauren's back and hopefully talk some sense into the cantankerous Scot.

Should Lauren use the number, I just hoped that the old spy would give her his support, but of course nothing in our game was guaranteed.

I lifted my day sack from the wardrobe, removed the Mac10 and mags from it, wrapped the weapon and spare ammunition in two of my t-shirts and stuffed the whole lot back inside. Happy that my bag didn't appear to be holding a machine gun, I slipped the Browning into my belt and strode out into the last of the evening sunshine, head clear and ready to rock and roll.

Finbarr was where he said he would be. I did a full circle of the car before I opened the passenger door and sat beside him.

"Cautious," he said. "You're behaving like a man who doesn't trust me."

I looked into his battered and bruised face. "I trust one guy in the whole world mate. And it ain't you."

I opened my day sack between my knees, pulled the Mac10 and made it ready. Fin watched, emotionless.

"Expecting trouble?"

"Always," I said. "It tends to follow me around. Especially when I'm about to steal guns from terrorists."

Fin shook his head, put the car in gear and we made steady progress out of the city.

"I take it you are going to tell me what the plan is at some point?" I asked.

"We'll talk as we go," he said.

Now that Fin had decided to lose his full on Irish accent, I could detect a northern twang. It reminded me of Frankie Green, a guy I'd fought alongside in Libya. Frankie was tortured and killed by Abdallah Al-Mufti, the man I hoped was at the end of this particular line of enquiry.

Along with the accent, the eccentricity, the manic eyes and the man on the edge of insanity, had disappeared, too.

"So how long have you played the crazy gang act?" I asked.

He shrugged and pulled us onto the road towards Dublin.

"It just developed over the years. Like I told you, a man can't stay in the shadows forever. At some point, he has to stand in the light and be seen. I figured that the best form of disguise was the Finbarr you met earlier. Fin spends his whole life in the spotlight... except on a night like tonight."

"So, Fin isn't your real name?"

"Its best you know nothing of me, Fuller. It's bad enough I know yours. You're Regiment, I can see that right now. Well, you were once, anyways. So you know all about torture. What I said about the PIRA boys is true. They don't have the power anymore. The new breed have no real support or direction, and no strong leadership. But I'll tell you this, the old timers, they'd all turn out in numbers to grab your scalp. They'd string you up and laugh while they tore you limb from limb. You'd hold out for a while, for sure. But you'd give them my true identity if you knew it... in the end, any man would do the same."

Once again, I recalled Goldsmith, his kettle and my only true friend.

"Fair one," I said.

"Has Cartwright given you a back story, just in case we do get compromised?

"You're in disgrace. Thrown out of the SAS. Fell off the perch, a dangerous drunk with a bad attitude. Ye work for a gangster called Davies, you're a leg breaker. Ye will do anything fer money. How's that?"

I couldn't really argue with that.

"So where are we going?"

"First we're going to pick up some kit we need at a place I have just outside Dublin. The target itself is a farm, just north of the city."

"Aren't they all?"

Fin smiled. "I suppose so, yeah, but we need camouflage on this job. The approach to the stash is wide open land, flat, no cover. But no worries, I've got two sets of sniper gear. They won't see us."

"And the players?"

"Tommy Brannigan has lived there all his life. He's getting a bit long in the tooth, but he has two sons. Big mean sons of bitches who think they are real badass gangsters. They'll gladly shoot on sight at the first sign of strangers snooping around. There are guns and ammunition all over the house, and other kit hidden in various other outbuildings. If we were to be compromised in the open…"

I finished his sentence. "We'd be in the shit."

"Exactly," pointed Fin. "The two boys would take us down in minutes. They're both young, fit and switched on. We'll need to dig in and wait for them to leave the plot before we approach."

I wasn't liking the sound of digging in. Indeed, I thought Fin's whole tactic stank.

"Sounds like this could go tits up too easily," I said. "I've been here before, similar job, but with a four man team, and it still got to be a total gang fuck."

Fin shrugged. "I can turn around if you like. Cartwright will send me another guy. These Balkan boys are important to all concerned, I hear."

So, Fin knew at least some of the tale, which meant he knew that pulling out wasn't an option for me.

"I take it Cartwright doesn't care how you obtain the AK's? And doesn't mind that you're keeping the cash?"

"It isn't his cash, is it? And like I said, the Firm are more interested in the end users than me or the IRA's money… Look, this is my last job for The Firm, I've served my time… and my country."

"How much are these Balkan's or whoever paying for the AK's?"

"Bosnians actually. The two boys we'll be dealing with are Hamza and Imran and the price is four hundred euro each, so three hundred and twenty K."

That woke me up.

"There are eight hundred AK's?"

He nodded.

"And how much were you supposed to give Brannigan?"

"The deal was a three way split, me, Tommy and the quartermaster in Belfast.

As with all the PIRA boys, neither of them was keen to meet our buyers face to face. They expected yours truly to do all the leg work, stick his ugly mug in front of a boat load of fucking jihadists and bring them their lump. That was a sticking point with the Bosnians. Their boss was insistent they meet the quartermaster general on the handover. Probably with half an eye on the next load of kit. Finally, I told them, 'no problem,' I'll bring him, his name is Sean Devlin."

Fin gave me that smile. "That's where you and your suspect accent come in."

"That and my abilities for stealing stuff from known terrorists?"

"Come on, Fuller. I never met a SAS bloke yet who wasn't a dodgy fucker."

Well, there was dodgy and there was downright insane. This job was suspect on both sides. There was no doubt, Bosnia Herzegovina was becoming a breeding ground for Islamic fundamentalists, a perfect place for Yunfakh to recruit their boys. I'd fought alongside local militias in Srebrenica, where more than 8,000 Bosnian Muslim men and boys were slaughtered by the Serbs. It was a horrible conflict and I met some of the bravest and toughest men on the planet there. One thing was for certain, the Bosnian boys would be no mugs.

"You're going to make some serious enemies, Fin. You won't be drinking Guinness in Kerry any time soon, that's for sure."

Fin turned, and I was certain I saw just a glimpse of that madness return to his eyes.

"I won't tell, if you won't."

I really didn't give a fuck who got the money, and a couple of dead Provo's, New, Real or same old same old wouldn't cause me any loss of sleep, either.

I turned down my mouth.

"Well, it's your head, pal. What if the Firm come knocking on your Thai beach hut in five years' time?"

Fin let out a small laugh.

"If the Firm fell in a barrel of tits, they'd come out sucking their thumb. The only reason you found me is because I wanted you to. Once this deal is done, I'm out. Out of the business and out of the country. I will disappear like smoke in the fucking wind, pal."

I shrugged. It was his party and it didn't change my life any. But I still wasn't keen on his plan to obtain the cache.

"Maybe there's another way of getting to what we want," I said. "You know… that isn't so… suicidal."

"Such as?"

"Well, I mean Tommy is your drinking buddy, eh?"

"Nailed on piss artist."

"Well, what about his lads?"

"I have a beer or three with them on occasions."

"And when is the deal scheduled?"

"Midnight tomorrow."

"So why not drop them a call, you know? Do they fancy a beer or ten? Celebrate their good fortune. I mean, fuck me, it's what you're famous for, eh?"

"Tommy won't come into Dublin, he's a tight old fucker."

"Well just the lads then. Invite them to a boozer in town… you're paying. You pick them up from the farm and we do it dirty in the car. We take them out where they sit, away from their weapons. Once we have them slotted, we go back to the farm, deal with Tommy, and do the business."

Fin looked over into my face. I saw another flicker of that hysterical smile.

"Sounds like a plan to me."

I felt better.

"Just one other thing Fin… How are we going to move the fucking things?"

This time he did smile, a self-satisfied grin spreading across his battle scarred face.

"They're already in a truck, loaded and fuelled. This cache was always meant to be for a big push, an all out assault on the British Army or the RUC. Ready and waiting to be delivered at a moment's notice… But Good Friday came along."

"Not a bad thing," I mused.

Fin turned dark. "Unless your family were killed by the fuckers."

I knew how that felt, but kept my counsel. This would be a cool head operation. If you let vengeance into your heart on a job like this, you got sloppy. It clouded your judgement. Take it from me, I know.

Twenty minutes later, we pulled into a services and Fin made the call.

The boys were home and the bait was taken.

## Lauren North's Story:

Just speaking to Rick had made me uncomfortable. I have never liked secrets and lies, no matter how good the reason, especially if it was just to spare hurt feelings. My guilty heart harassed my head and I knew that until I told him the truth, I would have no peace.

However, I had to put personal matters to one side and deal with the issues at hand. The first of which was Des.

I'd watched him inject his foot and shoulder with two powerful localised pain killers, then drop two anti-inflammatory pills down his neck, just for good measure.

I'd selected a type of pain relief that had a similar effect to the drugs dentist's use, where it anesthetises the area but, unlike morphine or codeine based meds, doesn't affect your mental capabilities. I knew the strong anti-inflammatories would give him bad guts, so I'd thrown in some antacids to help him there, too.

He winced as he pulled on his boot, laces fully open.

I offered to help. But he gave me a look that told me to mind my own.

I'd already made my thoughts clear on what Des should and shouldn't be doing, and he'd given me short shrift. Mitch had been his usual diplomatic self. Sellers, being the new girl, sensibly remained tight-lipped.

With herculean effort, Des finally stood and stamped his injured foot firmly into his boot. Hopefully, he wouldn't feel a thing for a few hours, after that, he would be in agony.

He gave me a 'told you so' look.

"Right then," he said. "A quick re-cap. We are looking for two white males. One is mid-twenties, six-two heavy set. He's a carrot top but cuts it to the wood, green eyes. He has a scar or cleft in his chin that is quite evident and makes him easily identifiable. When I saw him he was carrying what looked like a Berretta pump, sawn short. Guy two is older, maybe double guy one, similar height, paunchy. Balding. Blue eyes. Looks a proper handful though. He was holding Kaya when I clocked him. I didn't see a weapon, but that doesn't mean anything. Grace has copied a current shot of the boy on her printer. Mitch, Victoria, have a good look… Now, let's get on our way and sort these boys, eh?"

Moments later, Des had said his goodbyes to a very tearful Grace and we piled in the Audi, the Scot in front, leg extended, Mitch at the wheel and we girls relegated to the back seat. Sellers got busy immediately, going through all the kit bags individually, making each weapon ready and safe. She worked methodically, with a professional air. From our very bad start, I began to warm to her very quickly indeed.

That said, it seemed that the moment her work head was on, all familiarity went out the window. As she handed out each bag, she referred to each of the team by surname only.

"Cogan," she said handing Des' bag over the seat. She glanced at me, expressionless and slid mine over. "North…" she said. "…and Collins, I'll keep yours behind your seat. I've left the SLP's action forward, safety on. Mp5k is action back, safety off. Are we all okay with that?"

"Yes, Ma'am," offered Mitch, unable to stop himself smiling.

Des turned to the American. I'd never seen him so dark. "Get yer foot down son. Ye can flirt when we have the boy back, eh?"

Des' phone was connected via Bluetooth to the car's system and when it rang, I jumped involuntarily.

Simon's voice boomed through the speakers.

"These mushes have just stopped at Birch, Mr Cogan. The service's ANPR system flagged it up three minutes ago. I'll call you back when they pull off."

Except, he didn't.

Mitch drove us quickly, without drawing attention to the fact, and we made good progress out of the city and onto the North West's busiest motorway network.

Once we hit the M62 we were forced to slow due to the obligatory roadworks, but finally, with the phone still silent, we pulled into the tired looking service station.

As with most of the UK's motorway establishments, parking is limited to two hours, or the driver is subjected to a hefty fine, hence the ANPR system. This is connected to a main server which in turn speaks to a separate site that dishes out the tickets to the unfortunate driver. No doubt it was the ticketing site that Egghead had hacked into, giving us our heads up. Clever, eh?

Birch is a relatively small service area, but still had capacity for over two hundred cars.

It took us just over five minutes to find the Passat we wanted... empty.

I stepped out of the back seat of our Audi with Sellers in tow. We walked to the rear of the target vehicle. I tapped the boot with my fingers and put my ear to the metal. Des was down in his seat, SLP in hand, keeping his eyes firmly on the car. I looked to him and shook my head.

Mitch had taken up a spot by the main doors of the services which gave him a view of the VW and eyes on anyone leaving the food court.

Happy that Kaya wasn't trussed up in the trunk, we girls trawled the various American takeaways and coffee shops inside the services for any sign of our two targets or Kaya himself. After checking the ladies, we called on Mitch to do the same with the gents.

Ten minutes on, we were pretty sure our targets had got away on their toes.

We returned to the Audi full of frustration.

Des was on the phone to Simon in an instant. I could see him nodding and hear his muffled voice from inside the car. Finally, he rolled down the window.

"Egghead says that the camera systems that cover the inside of the building and the car parks themselves are not connected to a server... he can't access them remotely. We're going to have to ask the duty manager nicely."

"I'll do that, Cogan," offered Sellers. "I'm a persuasive kind of girl."

"Knock yourself out, kid," said Des. "Just be quick about it."

Sellers shot the Scot a look, checked herself in the reflection of the Audi's windows and strode off in the direction of the main building.

Des turned to me. "Keep an eye on her, hen. I'm not convinced."

I nodded and scuttled after our new employee. As I reached Sellers' shoulder, she smiled. "He doesn't trust me, does he?"

"You surprised?"

She shook her head. "Not at all... but he will, soon."

We strode into WH Smiths. Sellers' smile disappeared from her face as she approached the middle aged man at the counter. The Queen herself would have been proud of her accent.

"Good evening, would you call your duty manager as a matter of urgency, please?"

The guy looked Sellers up and down. "What's the problem, love?"

Sellers cocked her head. "Are you the duty manager?"

"No, I'm just saying..."

"Well, don't just say," spat Sellers. "I want the duty manager. I've told you it's urgent. And I'm certainly not your love."

The guy took on a look that told me he'd dealt with many irate customers in his time. I guessed he was the late-night guy, too. Just started his ten hour slog. That meant he drew the short straw. He had the pissed up coach trips, the stag and hen do's and all the crazies that roamed the motorway networks in the wee small hours to deal with.

He was unimpressed.

The guy was short and stocky. His work shirt had the sleeves rolled down, trying to hide a mixture of professional and self-inflicted tattoos. Company policy, no doubt. His manager probably bent the rules to employ him in the first place, it being hard to find anyone who would work through the night for the money on offer.

He was a Manc, maybe making the trip out each night from Stretford or Hulme, or one of the other less salubrious areas of the city.

He offered a thin sarcastic smile. "Well, as you ask so nicely, I'll call her for you. But she'll ask me what the problem is before she even moves her arse from her office, so it would help if you could give me a clue as to what your issue is… love."

Sellers leaned forward, resting her chin on her palm, one elbow on Mr Tattoo's counter, eyes dark. "Then you'd better call security."

The guy looked puzzled.

Sellers's explained. "Look, old chap, if your Duty Manager isn't standing in front of me in two minutes flat, I'm going to… now what do you Mancunians call it? … Kick off big time."

Sellers' 'off' sounded more like 'ourf.'

The guy's smile widened. "Yeah right, I'm terrified."

He should have been.

Victoria reached out and grabbed the guy by the wrist. Her left, his left. It was a flashing movement. She took one step, twisted her body so her right hip was against the counter, brought her free arm around at a right angle and, using all the kinetic energy of her twisting torso, connected her palm with Mr Tattoo's elbow.

The guy found himself, bent at the waist, his arm flat to his counter, palm up, unable to move.

"Want me to break it?" asked Sellers quietly.

The guy shook his head.

She released him and checked her watch.

"Two fucking minutes," she said.

I did my best to hide my smile as I gazed at the rows of monthly magazines on the shelves.

Mr Tattoos rubbed his elbow and spoke into his headset.

Sellers re-applied her lipstick in a nearby mirror as if nothing had happened. In under a minute, we had a Duty Manager and a very overweight security guard eyeing us suspiciously.

Sellers got in my ear. "We are in luck, darling. The stars are shining upon us."

"Patricia!" announced Sellers, stepping forward, arm outstretched.

"Ma'am? My God. That you?" offered the Duty Manager, seemingly delighted to see Sellers.

The pair shook heartily.

Patricia turned to the fat security guy. "I won't be needing you, Colin. This is my old CO from my army days… I'll deal with this from here."

Sellers gestured in my direction. "Lauren North… Lance Corporal Pat Murphy."

The woman smiled at me. She was around my height, a few pounds heavier, but trim and fit. Her hair was cut short and coloured a deep burgundy. She spoke with a north eastern accent. Sunderland, Middlesbrough, maybe. "Ex Corporal, Ms North. I'm a civvy now, as you can see."

I smiled and kept my mouth shut.

Sellers pressed on. "Now Pat, I'd love to catch up, and now I know where you are, we most definitely will, but we need a quick look at your CCTV. It's very urgent… sorry."

Pat looked unsure for a moment. "Is this official business, Ma'am?"

Sellers was flat calm. "Of course it is."

Pat nodded. "This way, Ma'am."

And off we went, no ID, no questions. I was learning a great deal about Victoria Sellers in a short space of time.

She commanded respect and I could see why. More importantly, she could handle herself and I had a feeling we would all need to be at our best in that department in the coming days.

The CCTV room was small and cramped. It doubled as an office for the guards working the service area. Various items of hi-viz clothing, dangled from hooks screwed to the back of the door, a small fridge had been pushed in one corner, a tray, four mugs and other brewing kit sat alongside a grubby kettle.

"Brew?" offered Pat Murphy.

We both declined.

Sellers seemed to know her way around the CCTV system and as Murphy looked on, quickly flicked through the couple of dozen cameras located both on the East and Westbound areas. Moments later, she had a clear shot of the Passat.

She stood. "Okay, Corporal, I need to know what has happened to the occupants of this vehicle. We believe two adult males, and one young boy. Are they still on the services? Or have they changed to another car? Quick as you like."

Pat Murphy immediately took Sellers' place and began searching the system. An alarm sounded as the car's registration appeared on a separate screen with a time stamp underneath it.

"Time of arrival," said Murphy, typing rapidly.

"We had that," said Sellers.

Murphy eyed her old CO. "I suppose you would," she said perceptively. "But the rest of the system is local. It's not connected to the internet so can't be… accessed."

Sellers nodded knowingly and waited.

Moments later, we had the first pictures of our targets. The two men Des had described so accurately slipped from the VW and went around to the boot.

They popped it and removed a large suitcase. It took both of them to lift it out and they were very careful to sit it on its wheels before moving off on foot, the youngest pulling it alongside him.

Sellers was strident, challenging. "Where do they go from there?"

Murphy was on the ball, too. She turned to Sellers, horrified. "You think the kid is in the case?"

Sellers was impassive. She shrugged. "We won't know unless we find them, eh, Corporal?"

"One moment, Ma'am," nodded Murphy, working the system.

"There," I said." "Camera nine."

Sure enough, there they were, dragging the case with them. Then they were gone.

For almost a full minute, the men were out of shot. No amount of searching would trace them.

"Blackspots," announced, Murphy. "The whole area is covered in them. We complain, but…"

Then Murphy found them again, and it wasn't good news.

## Rick Fuller's Story:

When Fin had described the land as flat and open around the target, he hadn't been exaggerating. As we closed in, I could see a huge barn behind the main house and several other smaller outbuildings dotted around a large floodlit yard. There were three vehicles visible, one Shogun 4 x 4, a small saloon that looked like a Hyundai or some such Far Eastern offering and a big black 7 series BMW.

"Nice motor," I said.

"They've got company," said Fin with a frown on his face. "The Beamer ain't theirs."

There were no signs of any goods vehicles, so I presumed the truck and the AK's were nestled safely in the barn.

As we drove past the farm, just two hundred yards from the road, lights burned in both the downstairs and upper rooms.

I imagined our boys buttoning their Ben Sherman's and splashing on the Old Spice in anticipation of their pub crawl in the fair city.

It wasn't going to be their night.

We drove steadily for about two miles before we came to a suitable place to execute our 'dirty' plan.

Our chosen plot was a small layby, large enough for two cars, but only just. It didn't seem well used. The solitary litter bin was almost empty and the usual plastic cartons and bottles didn't decorate the trees that lined the edge. There was a small post and rail fence bordering the land beyond.

I kicked the top rail off one section making it a simple stride over to get myself out of cover and alongside the Ford when the time came.

The expression of taking someone 'dirty,' is an American one, often used by Delta Force and Recon Marines. Delta used the ploy in Iraq and Afghanistan to great effect, managing to kidnap or kill dozens of known Taliban or Al Qaeda in the process.

Basically, your target believes that they are in a safe vehicle with a trusted occupant, usually the driver. However, the driver is primed to pull up at an agreed location. He ensures the doors of the vehicle are unlocked. His co-conspirator, then appears from nowhere, opens the door, slides in either alongside or behind the target and either slots them, usually a double tap, spine shot, or takes them prisoner. The vehicle then drives away with its living or dead cargo and either dumps the corpse or hands over its shiny new prisoner at a safe location.

This ploy can be used anywhere, from a busy city street to a quiet country lane and was given the nickname 'dirty' as it often involved shooting an unarmed enemy in the back.

I'd never been to Iraq or Afghanistan, but I'd fought in Africa, the former Yugoslavia and in South America. Believe me, you didn't give a shit where you shot the fuckers.

As we had two targets, Fin had agreed to take the front passenger, whereas I would take the guy in the rear. The beauty of the plan was its simplicity.

I was to wait in the treeline whilst Fin collected our players. Shortly after leaving the farm, Fin would announce that he needed a piss. He would pull over in our layby, I would step out from the darkness, slide in the back seat and it would all be over in seconds.

Piece of piss, eh?

Yeah, right.

I watched the tail lights of the Ford disappear into the night, then listened as the engine note grew quieter until the only sounds were those of the night creatures living in the woods around me.

As my eyes grew accustomed to the darkness, I was just able to make out the shadows of the trees opposite as they rocked in the breeze.

This was a lonely spot. The chances of anyone hearing four sharp cracks from two pistols fired at point blank inside a car was almost nil.

I stepped over the fence and tucked myself into cover. Dropping my day sack that contained the MAC10 at my feet, I checked over my Browning and waited.

Fin had been gone less than ten minutes when I heard the sound of a vehicle approaching.

As it was way too soon for his return, I took a step backwards and settled myself further into the undergrowth away from the car's headlights.

The vehicle in question was a Nissan people carrier of some sort. As it approached my position, it slowed and without indicating, pulled over into the layby. The driver instantly killed the engine and lights and I was plunged into total darkness.

Once again my eyes began the slow process of making the best of any ambient light, but within moments, they were saved the job and all became clear.

The male occupant of the Nissan began checking his phone and the car's interior was lit up like a Christmas tree.

I could see the driver was a guy in his late forties with a shock of greying hair that fell across his forehead. The phone also gave me a fair view of his passenger. Female, much younger, pretty, and as far as I could make out, quickly becoming naked.

As he lay down his phone I could hear the tinny muffled sounds of music.

I shook my head in dismay and cursed my luck. To add insult to injury, Lionel Richie and Three Times a fucking Lady drifted from the car.

I always hated that song.

The pair locked in an embrace for a few moments, as the guy began the age old ritual of trying to recline the girl's seat, whilst vainly attempting to keep the romantic feel to the whole proceedings.

In my limited experience of these things, nigh on impossible.

With Fin now minutes away, the only thing I could hope for, was that the guy suffered from premature ejaculation.

As Lionel gave way to Westlife, it didn't look good.

I'd seen operations compromised in many different ways over the years, but a copulating couple was not a problem I'd encountered before.

I ran the previous few minutes through in my head. What exactly had I seen and heard?

The guy, older, suit jacket, shirt unbuttoned at the collar.

*Just finished work?*

The girl, half his age, keen to indulge in some early evening sexual activity, peeling off her clothes.

*Rushed for time maybe?*

What else? The phone, the cheesy music and… a child seat in the back.

Of course, hence the reason they had not climbed over into the far more comfortable rear.

I took a few steps towards the fence, pulled my own phone from my pocket and selected the camera function.

Then, walking as quickly as my eyes allowed me, I made my way around to the passenger side of the car, gave the front window a sharp rap with my knuckles and fired the camera for the first time.

The flash bathed the whole layby in light and I saw the guy twist his head in shock. He was red faced from his exertions, eyes wide in surprise. The girl however, appeared non-plussed and simply looked straight at me with a knowing smile on her face. I took a second and third shot then made a show of capturing the registration plate of the Nissan.

The guy began to bark at the girl to cover herself. He was struggling to roll into the driver's seat. With his trousers around his ankles and his bare arse like a shiny pink moon in full view through the windscreen, he began to curse me.

"Who the fuck is yees, ye bastard?"

I continued to shoot frame after frame, all angles, striding around the car, knees bent like a deranged paparazzi. The girl hadn't moved. She lay naked, displaying all she had to offer on the reclined seat as the guy struggled to pull up his trousers and fire the engine.

"Smithson's Private Investigators," I shouted using my best Belfast drawl. "Would ye, like my card so? Yees wife already has it."

"Fuck that," shouted the guy. "And fuck yees, too."

Finally, he got the Nissan's engine to fire and I was bathed in the red of brake lights. The front drive wheels squealed as the guy hit the gas and I was showered with pebbles as the Japanese marque snaked into the gloom.

Within minutes I was back in darkness and silence, shaking my head in disbelief.

Slipping my phone back into my pocket, I considered what I had just witnessed.

Deceit is a terrible thing. Lies and treachery hurt as much as any bullet. I saw it in Des' face when he found out that Anne was seeing another man.

As I turned my attentions back to the task of assassinating two members of what was left of the PIRA, I considered myself lucky that I'd never had my heart broken by betrayal.

Well, not so far.

# Des Cogan's Story:

Lauren, Mitch, and the new girl Sellers, all arrived back at the car together. I'd been sitting in the passenger seat with my foot up on the dash, muttering the odd Hail Mary and hoping for a miracle or two. As the big American dropped his frame into the driver's seat, my leg jarred with the car's motion and I instantly felt needles of pain shoot through my nervous system.

As I was three hours away from a second pain killing injection, I reckoned that the chances of the big man upstairs being about to work his magic in that department were slim to none.

I twisted my frame to look into Lauren's face and instantly saw that my second prayer wasn't high on the Almighty's list of priorities, either.

She swallowed hard. "They've had him in a suitcase," she began. "A solid type, you know the kind I mean."

"Go on, hen," I offered, my guts churning. "Spit it out."

She looked into my eyes and I thought I detected tears forming.

"We saw them lift the case from the Passat, then we lost them for a while. Then… well then, we picked them up again standing by a Mercedes van with a large caravan attached. They…"

Lauren's voice faltered, but Sellers was in. No emotion, detached.

"We saw them pull the child from the case, but the boy appeared lifeless. The two players were shaking him. A woman came into shot. Young, early twenties, fair haired. We think from the van. She took the child from the two males and started CPR. She looked like she knew what she was doing but the CCTV frames per second here is poor, hence the guesswork. It's impossible to say if the kid was alive or dead but he was definitely carried into the Merc."

Sellers checked her watch. "That was exactly twenty two minutes ago."

I looked into our latest recruit's face. She had no connection to Grace or Kaya, no emotional attachment to anyone involved in the whole sordid mess, but even so, she was a cold fish.

"You think the kid is dead, don't ye?" I said flatly.

Sellers shrugged. "Like I said… impossible to say. But if you put me on the spot, that would be my prognosis."

I felt my blood run cold. My anger threatened to engulf me. My hands were shaking as I felt for my phone.

"Registration?"

"Irish plates," said Lauren quietly. "5534DAZ."

I turned to Mitch. "Let's go, big man. We're going to find these fuckers. And when we do, they'll wish they'd never been born."

## Rick Fuller's Story:

Satisfied that the husband of the year and his bit on the side were long gone, I settled back into my spot and waited for Fin to arrive with our targets.

No sooner had I found cover, then I heard the sounds of a vehicle approaching, its headlights flashing through the trees.

The change in engine note as the vehicle slowed was obvious.

The last thing Fin needed was my big boat race looming large from the undergrowth, so I couldn't risk a look see. I just had to wait for the car to draw to a halt.

Leaving the MAC10 in my bag, I pulled my Browning from my belt, slipped off the safety and took a deep breath. For this job to work, timing was everything.

The second the car stopped, I had to be at the rear passenger door, gripping the handle, ready to dish out the good news.

As the crunch of rubber on gravel filled my ears, I saw it was Fin's red Ford.

Stepping forward, I lifted my left leg over the broken fence and planted it firmly before raising my right. As I twisted my frame, I saw that Fin had missed our agreed stop and pulled the car some ten strides further up the layby.

My hackles rose, and all my bells and whistles went off. This was either the work of a fucking amateur, or the shit had hit the fan.

I was out in the open so had no choice but to stride forward, my path lit by the tail lights of the Ford.

Ten paces, four seconds. Four precious seconds. Four seconds as a sitting duck.

I was six feet from the boot, when the rear door flew open. In one swift motion, a long leg slid out, one hand gripping the door pillar, and a bull of a man with a shiny shaved head pulled himself into view. He had blood on his shirt and a big fuck off Desert Eagle in his fist.

He instantly raised the weapon to fire.

I stepped to my right and dipped my frame to make his target smaller and harder to hit. As I bent my knees, I saw the tremendous muzzle flash from the Israeli weapon and felt the intense heat from the massive .50 round as it flashed past my face and buried itself into one of the trees behind me.

Baldy had most of his body hidden by the car. He had cover, I did not. And, just to add to my woes, the driver, who was most definitely not Finbarr O'Rourke, was stepping out of his door waving what looked suspiciously like a Mini Uzi machine gun.

These boys meant business.

I was in the proverbial brown stuff and this was no time for fancy shooting.

Launching myself right, back over the fence and into the trees, I attempted a forward roll that went horribly wrong. I caught the right leg of my jeans in some brambles which meant I found myself lying on my back rather than standing on my own two feet.

My follicly challenged friend opened up good style with the Eagle and rounds slammed into the ground around me.

I rolled to my left, found my footing, took three steps back and tucked myself behind a nice sturdy tree.

Now, it was a different ball game. I had darkness and cover and it was the two players who had a big fucking problem.

I raised the BAP two handed, cupped the grip with my left hand and got off three rounds the way I had practised many thousands of times. A double tap to Baldie's chest and one to his head.

The boy's legs folded underneath him and he disappeared from view behind Fin's Ford.

The driver instantly opened up with the Uzi.

Stupidly, he had the thing switched to fully automatic. Its impressive rate of fire makes the Uzi a very useful weapon if you want to hit lots of targets in a short space of time. But, just like the MAC10 I had sitting somewhere in the woods, it's an up close and personal weapon on full auto. Lethal in an enclosed space, dangerous in a drive-by, but with the shooter standing ten yards away, pointing it one handed, and with me tucked nicely behind a mature oak, he may as well have thrown the fucking thing at me.

Less than three seconds later, there came the unmistakeable click of an empty weapon.

I stepped forward, Browning in the aim, and eyeballed the guy.

ROBERT WHITE

"Drop it."

"Fuck you," he spat. "You've just killed my brother, ye bastard."

The boy had a thick Southern Irish brogue, was my height, but at least twenty years younger, with broad shoulders and powerful arms. His right hand still held the Uzi, in his left jeans pocket was a spare mag.

I could almost hear his mind working.

His best chance was to spin his body around and back vault over the bonnet of the car, fall behind the engine block and reload.

If he'd been facing a bank robber, or a street thug, that may have been a safe option, but if he tried it with me, I'd slot him before you could say, Fosbury flop.

My Browning was pointed directly in the centre of his chest.

"I'm only going to ask once more son. Lay the Uzi on the roof of the car... nice and slow."

The boy stayed where he was and curled his lip.

"You deaf, ye hun bastard ye?" he said. "I told yees to fuck off."

I dropped the Browning a couple of inches and put a round smack bang in the middle of his right kneecap.

I never was one for patience.

Three strides and I was back over the fence. The boy had dropped the empty Uzi and was screaming all kinds of obscenities at me. I picked up his weapon, rested it on the roof of the Ford where I'd wanted it, walked around to where his pal had fallen and dragged him between the Ford and the trees. Once he was out of sight of any further lovers of outdoor sexual activity, I tore off his blood stained shirt, stepped over to screaming boy, stuffed a good chunk of it in his mouth and gave him a crack with the butt of the Browning.

He was instantly away with the fairies and the night was once again blissfully quiet.

Turning my attention to the car, I could now see that the front seat passenger was indeed Finbarr O'Rourke. He was slumped forward, his seatbelt holding him in place. He had three obvious bullet wounds, two, all having been fired from behind him, one exiting each kneecap and a third embedded in the back of his skull.

Textbook PIRA punishment.

Years of dealing with the Provos made you extra careful, and as there was obviously nothing I could do for the poor sod, I left him where he was.

Something had gone horribly wrong. Fin had been a deep cover operative for many years. His persona had worked for him all that time, but somehow, he'd been compromised within twenty four hours of meeting yours truly.

Now, call me old fashioned, but that smacks of people in very high places telling tales where they shouldn't, and I couldn't help but wonder if Fin's decision to steal the AK's rather than broker the deal, hadn't rattled a few highly placed cages.

Fin had been kneecapped, a vicious and unbelievably painful experience, and therefore, as we'd only recently discussed, he could easily have told these boys all he knew. I needed to know exactly what that was, particularly the location of the handover of the AK's. That, and if the numbers back at the ranch had increased any.

Brannigan Junior appeared to be coming around some and began clawing at his makeshift gag, his body needing big lumps of oxygen to try and sort out his pain receptors. I stepped over to where he lay, pulled the Uzi's spare mag from his pocket and increased his problems ten-fold by giving his injured knee a good whack with it.

Bullets and the magazines that hold them are heavy. It was like being cracked with a small crowbar.

The boy screamed into his gag and rolled about the floor like a Premiership striker in the penalty box, blood seeping through his fingers as he gripped his ruined knee.

I got in his face. "Who's at the farm now? How many?"

The boy did some shouting and questioned my parentage, but nothing more. Figuring that time was on my side at this particular moment, I waited for his pain to subside enough for him to remove the gag of his own accord.

Finally, he managed it and lifted himself up on his hands so his back rested against the Ford's front wheel.

He examined his outstretched leg, as blood pooled around it, shimmering in the moonlight.

"I need the hospital," he said.

"True," I offered. "And I need a wagon load of AK's."

The boy snorted his derision. "Fuck you… not a hope. They'll be gone… long before you can get to them."

I nodded slowly. "And in about twenty minutes, so will most of your bodily fluids."

He winced in pain as he shuffled himself further upright. "And if I ain't back at the farm soon, my Dad will come lookin'. Him and plenty more. You're a dead man. Just like that treacherous cunt in the car."

I shrugged. "I've heard it said before."

The boy's left eye was closing from the belt with the Browning. Even in the limited light he looked pale. Yet he didn't look scared.

I changed all that by putting a second round into his right ankle.

"How many at the farm?" I bawled.

The Irishman was convulsing with the pain, shaking involuntarily. Shock, blood loss, fear, all conspiring against his undoubted bravery. His lips trembled, mouth open, eyes wide, but no words came.

I pointed the Browning at his left ankle.

"How… fucking… many?"

"No… no… don't," he stammered. "Fucks sake… Five… six, maybe."

With things moving on apace now, I tried a different approach. Let him talk about a subject we all love. Money.

"Why do you boys want to sell the IRA's crown jewels, eh? What do you want with all that cash?"

The boy swallowed.

"It ain't my money. It's going to my old man and his mates from back in the day, the old guard. They've been talking about selling those guns ever since Good Friday. The IRA have had enough."

The boy threw up, spat out some remnants of food and looked me in the eye.

"Look, Cork, Dublin and Belfast are all full of tourists these days. And tourists want to have fun. They want the good things in life, not fuckin' bombs and bullets."

"Such as?"

He screwed up his face.

"Come on. What do you think? Paddy O'Donnell had it right, until some fuckers topped him, eh? The face of the people, and all the time making millions on the side. My Dad did Paddy's bidding for years. He says it's his turn now."

I pricked my ears up at the mention of O'Donnells name. I don't know why I was surprised. All these fuckers pissed in the same pot.

I shook my head.

"So now he's dead, you guys are going to fill the gap, is that it? Street hookers, cocaine, heroin. Just what Ireland needs more of."

The boy snorted.

"Who are you, fucking Mother Theresa? My Dad took the chance of hiding those guns… took the risk, for years. He figured it was our turn. O'Donnell would have done the same, for sure. Turn them into cash, turn them into real assets."

"But O'Donnell paid the price."

"So, there's a gap in the fuckin' market… Look, I need the hospital."

The boy was a proper little entrepreneur, eh? It seemed Lauren's good work on the streets of Belfast had changed the face of the city's criminal community. That was no surprise. I'd seen it happen often enough in Manchester. Slot one dealer and before you can say Ecstasy, another one is up and running. That said, I did wonder if Cartwright already knew that O'Donnell was connected with Tommy Brannigan… but time was ticking, so I ploughed on.

"How did you know Fin was going to double cross you?" I said.

"Dad got a visit. Some bloke in a fancy car… and you can shoot me all yees want, but I can't tell yees who he was, cos I don't know. I ain't never seen him before."

"Was it you who killed him? Did his kneecaps?"

The boy pulled his face. "What does it matter? Look, we needed answers. How would you have got them?"

"Like this," I said, and put a third round in his left ankle.

The body's tolerance to pain works in unusual ways. It reaches a certain level, then peaks. The boy lay there breathing heavily. His systems all closing down inside. He was alive… but it wouldn't be long.

I knelt by him.

"I want the location of the handover, son. Give it me and you go quick."

He mumbled something incoherent, then finally focused on me.

Now, I've stood in all kinds of places, from jungles to stinking ditches interrogating prisoners of all colours and nationalities. In the field there is no time for finesse, no time for niceties. This was no different. I didn't enjoy the process, it was pure necessity.

Moments later, the boy gave me what he knew, and it was all over in a heartbeat.

He didn't even beg.

I rolled him over the fence on top of his brother. Then, after checking for any signs of a boobytrap, I pulled Fin from the car, dropped him in the same spot and covered the three corpses with branches and leaves. It would be a while before they were discovered. The creatures of the night would begin to uncover them eventually.

Maybe the next time my favourite courting couple came to this lonely spot, they might notice the unpleasant fragrance in the air.

So, this job was about drugs and money and my nemesis, Patrick O'Donnell, had once again reared his ugly head. Criminals and their wares never seemed to be too far away from any conflict.

One phrase the boy used rattled around in my head. It wouldn't let me go. It sat there as if on a loop of tape and it made my guts churn. 'My Dad did Paddy O'Donnell's bidding for years,' he'd said.

The big question was, just how many years, and exactly what bidding?

I leaned against Fin's old car and did the maths. Back in 1996, the brothers would have been children, but the father would have been in his thirties or older. I knew that the team that travelled to England and murdered my wife back then, were at least three strong. The investigators found two sets of spent cartridges at the scene and witnesses reported a woman sitting in a car at the end of our road. O'Donnell had paid his price, but what if the man sitting in his front room right now was one of the others?

I did my best to put that to the back of my mind, but if I got the chance, I was definitely going to ask the question.

## Lauren North's Story:

The mood in the car was solemn. I couldn't get those jerky images of Kaya being carried into the van out of my mind.

I spoke almost to myself.

"Why would they put him in a case?"

"German car," offered Seller.

I looked across at her inquisitively.

"The boots can all be opened from the inside these days," she said.

I nodded and fell back into a troubled silence.

Des had called Simon with the registration number of the Merc and we had set off East at a steady pace, waiting for information. I looked over to my right and could just about make out the outline of the moors. They sent a shiver through me. Stephan Goldsmith had left Rick up there, presuming him dead, but even more chilling, was the fact that Hindley and Brady had plied their horrific trade up on those lonely hills. Somewhere up there was a murdered child that had never been found.

I pushed my dark thoughts away, just as Simon's voice filled the car once more.

"This van, Mr Cogan... well it was registered to some building firm in Salford, but they've informed DVLA that they sold it, so we've no registered keeper."

"Any signs of them passing the motorway cameras?" asked Des, his voice sharp, irritable.

Simon was tapping keys. "No, sir... and as these mushes have been on the move for over thirty minutes now, I'd be thinking they are on the minor roads. Either out towards Rochdale, or maybe Saddleworth."

The mere mention of the moor sent another shudder down my spine.

"Okay," said Des. "What about traveller's sites in the area? Can you have a look? I want all of them in a twenty mile radius."

"I'm on it, Mr Cogan... give me five."

Des closed the call. "Pull off at the next junction, Mitch," he said. "We're going to upset the locals."

Now, upsetting the locals, in Des speak was a pretty unpleasant experience for those concerned. I gave Sellers a look that told her so. She just shrugged and settled back in her seat, nonplussed.

Minutes later, Simon was back on with the list of traveller's encampments. However, he had one further snippet of information.

"The only other thing is, Mr Cogan," added Simon, after he'd read the address of the final site. "Is that our local rag has been reporting an unofficial camp, not far from my gaff. It's on Tesco's car park in Haslingden. The locals have been up in arms about it for a week or two. They want them off there quick sharp, but them Pikes ain't for moving."

Des made a note. "Thanks, Simon. Good work, pal, we'll have a look-see."

Sellers was already on her phone. "Haslingden is seven miles back the way we came, but it's all motorway or dual carriageway. We can be there is under ten minutes."

Des turned to Mitch. "Put yer foot down, son. Let's make it five."

## Rick Fuller's Story:

With my head full of questions and the old feelings of guilt and loss tumbling around in my guts, I'd collected my MAC10 from the bushes and confiscated the two dead boy's weapons. Not knowing exactly how many bodies were now at the target premises, I figured I couldn't have too much firepower.

According to the dead boy, the handover with the Bosnians was at Kinsale, a small coastal town, thirty miles south of Cork. The AK's were to be driven there by the Irish and loaded onto a boat by the foreign crew, no doubt bound for the European coast. Payment was to be in cash.

From there, I figured that our arms dealers would sail under cover of darkness and make land in northern France, maybe somewhere around San Malo. They could then head unchecked across country, through Belgium and Germany and, if they chose Austria rather than the Swiss alternative, make it all the way to Italy without a single border crossing. From there they had a myriad of choices of how to arrive in their homeland.

Personally, if I were taking the trip, I would head through the Italian lakes. It was then a leisurely day's drive to the Autostrada Adriatica. Along that five hundred mile coastal road, it would be easy to find a quiet cove and have a boat waiting for the short hop over to the former Yugoslavia.

I did a drive-by of the farm and sure enough, there were two extra vehicles there, but no black 7 series. It would be interesting to know exactly what our friend in the black Beamer had told Brannigan. But that could wait.

In addition to the Shogun and the Hyundai, the yard now boasted a dark blue or black A4 and a Land Rover Defender that had seen better days. So, I had anywhere between the six guys young Brannigan had eluded to, up to a possible eight, plus Tommy.

And I couldn't wait to chat with him.

Of course, now that all my plans had gone to the dogs, this was very much a fly by the seat of your pants job.

Tommy would be expecting his two strapping lads home for supper, so technically, it would be no problem driving the old Ford straight up to the front door if I chose to.

All very well, but from there, it would get too messy for my liking. An all-out assault on the main house, single-handed was not something I relished no matter how many guns I had.

Pulling over far enough away from the farm, so as not to concern our pillars of the Irish community, I considered how there might be a better solution to my sticky situation.

I popped the tailgate of the old car and had a proper rummage in the boot. Pushing a tow rope and jump cables to one side, I had a good root in the toolbox and removed a sturdy rubber torch and a Stanley knife. Then, lifting what had been Fin's waterproof coat from the floor, I discovered a very handy five litres of unleaded, held in a bright green plastic container. As luck would have it, in his coat pocket was a disposable lighter.

Happy days.

I'd never been one for making improvised explosive devices. I'd always left that to the likes of Frankie Green and Si Garcia, who made blowing things up their life's work, but I knew how to start a fire.

It took me ten minutes to cut up the rear bench seat of the old Escort, then twist and knot five strips of fabric into metre-long lengths. Then, I loaded the MAC10 and the Uzi and pushed two spare mags into my jeans. Baldy's Desert Eagle only had one round in the spout, and as I was bereft of any .50 shells, I threw it. It's a heavy and cumbersome weapon, and if it won't go bang, it's as much use as a fucking chocolate fireguard.

The trusty BAP went in the front of my waistband and I was off, on foot across the darkened fields, the two light machine guns on straps around my neck, my strips of cloth in one hand and petrol can in the other.

Showtime.

## Des Cogan's Story:

Tesco's supermarket, Haslingden was situated a couple of miles outside the town, just off a dual carriageway that feeds the M56. It was a weird approach and was accessed via a long sweeping slip road that gave the driver a good look at the main building and petrol filling station.

As Mitch pointed the Audi at the entry slip, I could clearly see the traveller's temporary encampment nestled in the far corner of the car park.

Even with such a brief recce I noticed the black Merc van was not included, however there was a lone trailer without a tow vehicle alongside it and as the registration plate had been removed from it, I felt my spirits rise.

"Could that be the caravan?" I asked.

Mitch shrugged. "I lived most of my boyhood in a trailer, Mr Cogan, but none looked like these."

"Looks similar," offered Lauren.

Sellers remained tight lipped.

We pulled up in a parking space and stepped out into the warm night air. The supermarket was a twenty four hour a day job and shoppers still wandered about the place, although none ventured towards the encampment or parked their cars nearby.

Travellers had a bad reputation, warranted or not.

I did my best to keep my weight off my injured foot, but even so, I felt like I'd been run over with a bus. All of Grace's good work had been ruined in a matter of an hour.

Big Mitch leaned in the rear passenger door, pulled an Mp5k from the day sack Sellers had prepared for him, tucked it under his arm, zipped his jacket and strode off in front.

As we approached the camp, I could see tell-tale lights flickering in the trailers as the occupants enjoyed their evening TV. However, the caravan we were most interested in, remained stubbornly in darkness.

We were less than twenty yards away when a small terrier type dog ran out from under a tipper and gave us a sniff. The camp was littered with all manner of vehicles and plant. Battered pickups towing generators rubbed shoulders with shiny new Mercs. These were surrounded by all manner of shite, from kid's toys to piles of scrap metal. The wee dog did his job and began to yap. Soon, the first trailer door opened and out stepped a guy with a far less friendly animal, a large angry looking Doberman on a chain.

The dog had its ears clipped, so they sat upright like a fox's. This was an American or German fashion, very much against the law in the UK, but it gave the breed an even more aggressive look.

The guy was burly, with a beer drinker's belly. He wore a once white vest; a pair of grubby looking tracksuit bottoms and those awful plastic shoes people wear for the beach.

"Nice Crocs," muttered Sellers.

"What the feck does yees cunts want?" bawled the guy.

"Friendly, too," added Sellers.

His dog issued a low menacing growl for good measure.

I got straight to the point.

"We're looking for a wee boy."

The man whistled, a single high-pitched shriek, and seconds later, the occupants of several other trailers appeared, to see what the fuss was about. To my disappointment, we suddenly had much more company that I'd hoped for.

"Well, there's no boy here that ain't our own," shouted the guy, looking around at his fellow travellers for support. "So why don't you just feck off were ye came from before I let Fritz here have a chew on ye legs."

The dog barked at the sound of its name, and hopped from foot to foot, as if eager to sink its teeth into something. As I was already bleeding like a stuck pig, I didnea fancy being Fritz's next meal.

Big Mitch unzipped his bomber and produced his Mp5k. He knocked the action forward with the heel of his hand, but I heard him click the safety on for good measure. I knew why Sellers had prepared the weapon the way she had, but this scenario didnea call for it, not quite yet. There were instant mutterings of concern from the gathered travellers, fat boy in the vest went a wee bit wide eyed.

"Now sir," said Mitch, his low Southern drawl filling the night air. "I, too, owned a Doberman Pincher like Fritz there. They are a fine animal and I loved him very much. At his best he could run at over thirty miles per hour and his bite pressure was over three hundred pounds, enough to break a man's arm." He pointed to the H and K. "But you see, this little baby has a muzzle velocity of 1230 feet per second. So, I'm of a mind, that should you let old Fritz try his luck, tonight would be his last on God's green earth."

The guy looked worried but not convinced. "You can all feck off with ye fancy talk. There's just shy of twenty men here who will all fight ye till they drop."

He turned to me.

"And you… ye Jock bastard, well you don't look too good. If ye ask me, you look like ye should be in the hospital."

The dog started to whine, sensing trouble in the air.

The guy jutted his chin defiantly. "So… we'll take our chances."

I was about to read him his horoscope, when a voice sounded off to my right.

I turned to see the man with the scar on his chin, the carrot top, the one who had hushed me as he'd left Grace's house. He held the same sawn-off pump in his fist. It was pointed at Mitch Collins' back.

"Aye," he shouted. "We'll take our chance, so we will. I could blow the kidneys out of yer big Yank friend from here, no danger. Then what? You and two women will take us on? You're dreaming son"

"How's the boy?" I asked, barely able to keep my anger at bay. "Is he alive?"

The guy fuckin' smiled at me. Can you believe it? I could feel my self control slipping.

"He's not your problem, son," he bawled. "He's none of your fuckin' business."

I let my head fall for a second. I could feel my heart in my chest. I hadn't felt this way since the day I fought Tam McCullagh, the school bully at St Johns all those years ago in Glasgow. I looked down at my footwear, almost expecting to see my brother Patrick's steel toe capped work boots on my feet.

Except all I saw was my Timberlands, and one of those was leaking my claret onto the tarmac.

I lifted my head. I felt like I had the devil himself inside me.

My voice was low. I didnae do it on purpose. It just came out that way. It was almost like it wasnea me talkin'.

"But Kaya is my problem, pal. He is my business, and I want him back where he should be… with his mother, Grace. Now, I've been a soldier most of my life. I've always played the game, listened to orders, obeyed them and taken the consequences. But no tonight… tonight, there's no rules, no here, not with you, son. Now, I know what you're thinking. You think I'm fucked and can't fight, eh?"

"I know it," he said. "I seen yees in the house, ye couldn't walk."

I straightened myself. "Well, you're mistaken, son. I'm takin' the boy, like it or not. Taking him where he needs to go, home. Now, if that means shooting you dead where you stand, then… so be it."

He gave me a look that told me I was talking shite.

In a way, he was correct. My SLP was tucked in the front of my jeans. I was in considerable pain. He was maybe fifteen metres away. It was dark, and I would have to take the shot one-handed. Not easy. In fact, it was the shot of a lifetime. Draw, twist, aim, fire. All before he could pull the trigger on his pump.

There was a wee commotion in the crowd, and a woman appeared at the guy's side. I wondered if she was the one the girls had seen on the CCTV back at the services. She was slim, fair haired, pretty, twenties.

"The boy's not here," she shouted. "He's at the hospital."

So it was her.

The guy with the pump turned, taking his eyes from me.

"Shut the fuck up, woman. Who told ye to stick yer nose in."

She ignored him and set her eyes on me.

"Look, Mister, the kid's sick. It wasn't our fault, he kept opening the boot, and we thought he'd be fine in the case. We… well we couldn't wake him up."

I took the deepest of breaths. I don't think I'd ever felt such rage. Everyone has a breaking point, and I was close to mine. The sequence of recent events, Anne's death, JJ, Maggie and now maybe Kaya all piled on top of me like a great weight. I'd carried burdens most of my adult life, seen and done things no man should ever see, but standing there, in that car park, I knew I was out of control.

I eyed the red head. "Where's your pal? Where's the other guy?"

Right on cue, there was movement and the man I desperately wanted to see, pushed his way through the crowd. He still looked a proper tough nut, same age as me, but a few stone heavier. He, too, had a shogun in his grasp. He lifted it into the aim.

"Fuck off," he said.

It was my turn to smile.

I shook my head.

"Fuck off? Is that it? Is that the sum total of your vocabulary, pal? Let me get this in ma head. You take a wee boy from his mother, ye stuff him in a suitcase until he suffocates, and when ye pull him out, ye have a wee panic on, so ye drop him at the nearest casualty. Am I right? I'm pretty much on the money there?"

I turned to the woman.

"That's the way it went down, isn't it, hen?"

She looked at carrot top and nodded.

I let my right hand fall to my side and turned back to the bruiser.

"Ye know what sticks in ma craw there, pal? Ye know what has really pissed me right off? The thing that means I can't walk away and leave ye here? It's that ye didnea care. Ye just sauntered back to ye wee cosy vans to watch the fuckin re-run of EastEnders… didn't ye? Ye left that wee boy alone and scared. Not knowing if ye'd killed him or no. And now, all ye can say to me is… fuck off?"

I drew, twisted and aimed at carrot top first. Double tap, one handed. I was a little high, but considering the circumstances, it was on the money. The first round caught him in the shoulder, the second in his throat. I didnea hear the screams of the massed travellers as they dove for cover, sheltering their own kids. I didnea even hear the rounds exiting the breech. It was if I was in a dream. A silent, bloody nightmare.

I'd expected the hard nut to fire on us, but he didnea.

He was too busy pushing his way through the panicking hoards, heading for a silver BMW.

I couldn't run, but I didn't need to. The big lad was hampered by his own.

He tried to batter his way through to his car, swiping at his fellow travellers with the sawn off. I just walked, took steady paces, limping slightly, right arm extended, the foresight of my SLP in focus, the centre of the boy's back in the relative fog ahead.

I pulled the trigger and saw the round find its target. The guy fell, dropping the shotgun as he did so. The crowd had parted like the red sea. People were scrambling in all directions, not knowing who would be next.

But they, of course, were safe.

My man was crawling along the tarmac, screaming for help, but none was coming. Two more paces and I stood over him.

As he began to plead, I put a round in his head.

They say that a man gets the smell of blood in his nostrils the same way a wild animal does. Once he begins to kill, it can become a frenzy of death and destruction. I'd seen it in massacres in Africa. Unchecked aggression from poorly trained troops or militias - but me? I'd been taught to display self control, yet it had deserted me.

I could feel my legs moving as I walked towards the woman. I knew I still held my handgun in the aim. As I drew closer, once again, I formed my sight picture.

The girl didnea move.

She looked me straight in the face. I saw tears in her eyes and wondered if they were for Kaya or herself. Tears of guilt and sorrow all look the same, don't they?

Somewhere behind me I heard my name called, but it wasn't enough to break the spell that had set me on my murderous course.

As I drew ever closer, the woman sank to her knees and crossed herself.

Shaking with anger and pain, I touched the barrel of the gun to her forehead. She closed her eyes and began to pray. It was the Lord's Prayer, but it passed me by.

"Des!"

The voice was close. It was Lauren.

"Des come on. We need to move… now. Leave her. Des, please."

"Look at me," I said to the lassie. "Open your eyes. I want to see your eyes."

She did as she was told.

What was in there? Fear? Definitely. Regret? Certainly.

"What's your name, hen?" I asked.

She swallowed, sniffed, "Bernadette," she said.

I nodded. "And are you a good Catholic girl, Bernadette?"

She pressed her lips together and more tears fell. "I used to be, honest sir, I did."

"Des!" Lauren's voice was insistent.

I swallowed once more, ignoring her plea. I cocked my head and looked closely at the girl.

"Well, you listen to me, hen. You'd better get some practice in and pray for that wee boy you took from his mother. Pray with all your might that he lives. Or as your God is my witness, I will come back and find you."

I turned away and I heard the girl burst into tears.

It was a pitiful wailing sound.

"Let's move," I said.

## Rick Fuller's Story:

I dropped down into a shallow gully some fifty metres from the main house. It hadn't been noticeable from the road, and I was glad of the cover. Slipping off the two machine guns, I sat, watched and listened.

From my position I could see movement through the windows of the building. The lights blazed, and I could hear the faint sound of music playing.

Now, don't think for a moment that I'm tarring all the Irish with the same brush here, because I don't mean to. Over the years, I've met many charming, intelligent and appealing folks from the Emerald Isle and I've fought alongside many a brave Irelander. That said, the Provo's, like many terrorist organisations, drew their fighters from the disgruntled poor, most of whom aren't blessed with greatest intellect.

If you cast your mind back to the very beginning of this tale, when I stole Patrick O'Donnell's cocaine, you'll recall that he'd left his back door open and the key for the bloody safe was on a hook in the kitchen.

I rest my case.

Now, forgive me for my candour, but if you'd recently discovered that one of your fellow IRA chums had been about to rip you off, you'd slotted him and then sent both your sons out into the night to deal with his accomplice, but neither had returned as expected, you might be somewhat on your guard.

Not these fuckers.

As my breathing returned to normal and my ears and eyes tuned in to their surroundings, there was no doubt that the dumb bastards were having a little party to celebrate their good fortune of now only having to split their ill-gotten gains two ways.

I'll be the first to admit, that traditional Irish music does nothing for me, but at that very moment, as the jigs and reels wafted out into the night air, I shook my head and managed a wry smile.

I laid out the strips of cloth that I'd fashioned from the old car seat and steadily soaked them in petrol from the can.

Happy with my work, I slipped the MAC and the Uzi over my shoulders, picked up my mobile firestarter kit, and set off towards the happy gathering.

As I got closer, I could see that the last five metres around the house were laid to gravel. There wasn't anything I could do about it. For my plan to work, I had to get up close to the doors and windows. I just had to tread quietly and hope that the boys had Black Velvet Band turned up to the maximum.

I started at the rear of the gaff, laying the first length of cloth across the bottom of the back door. I hadn't enough strips to cover every opening of the house, so I concentrated on the kitchen, where from what I could gather, the party was in full swing.

I'd just laid the second strip on the sill of the biggest window, when I heard the kitchen door open. Cursing my luck, I dropped down with my back against a chimney breast and swung the MAC10 forwards, gritting my teeth, holding my breath.

Seconds later I heard the unmistakable sound of a man pissing on gravel. He farted loudly and let out a long sigh of relief. I heard him sniff, once, twice.

"Stinks of fuckin' petrol out here, Tommy," he bawled over his shoulder to the massed guests. He began zipping himself and sniffed again.

Turning the cocking handle through 90 degrees, I made the MAC10 ready and tucked my legs under my body, ready to spring forwards. If it was going to go to rat shit, at least the back door was open, and with the MAC10 and Uzi at my disposal, I figured I had a fair chance of slotting the whole gathering.

"Probably that fuckin' old mower out back," came the reply, presumably from Brannigan, and doubtless the man I wanted to talk to before I left.

"Been leakin' for months," he added.

The pisser seemed happy with this explanation and I heard the door slam shut and a bolt slide into place.

Once again, I could breathe.

I made safe the MAC10 and returned to my incendiary responsibilities. Each time I lay a strip of petrol soaked cloth on a window sill, I risked a sneaky peak inside.

I counted six guys, including the father of the two unfortunate boys currently decomposing in the layby. Even with all the advantages I had, six was a big ask.

Once I'd done, I returned to the back door and poured the remainder of British Petroleum's best down the paintwork.

Now, here was the gamble. One of two things was going to happen. The boy's currently doing shots in the kitchen, would either run away from the flames and exit through the front door of the farmhouse, or come flying out the back with all manner of makeshift firefighting equipment to douse the flames.

*Eeny, meeny, miny, moe.*

I fired the first bit of old Ford Escort that I'd dropped below some patio doors. It instantly illuminated a section of the rear yard and I got on my toes before it lit me up with it. The second strip, sitting on one of the kitchen windows, must have had more fuel soaked in it and it went up with a satisfying whoosh. Keeping my head down, I made the third incendiary a couple of seconds later followed by the back door, which went up like a Roman candle on bonfire night. As I sprinted in the crouch to the final window, I heard the first shouts from inside the house, so once I'd fired the last device, I dropped myself into prone off to the right of the back door and watched the fruits of my labour unfold.

Moments later, I had the answer to my riddle and one of the boys came barrelling to the back door with a pan of water.

If things hadn't been so fucking serious, I would have laughed my bollocks off. The pissed up player pulled the back door open, drawing the flames upwards and towards him. At this, he tripped over backwards in shock, his pan of water drenching his upper body, but leaving his bone dry legs firmly in the flames.

He began to shout for help as his jeans caught fire, but rather than withdrawing his feet from the heat, for some unknown reason, he lifted them upwards, as if he was doing some kind of fucking sit up and then wiggled them about, yelling for his mates to look sharp.

Player two was next. He sees his pal's Wranglers doing a fair impression of a bonfire night Guy, panics, and chucks his glass of Jamesons or whatever inflammable spirit he's drinking on there for good measure. The fire engulfing player one, turns a blue colour for a minute and the shouts get louder.

You couldn't have made it up.

A third face then takes some semblance of control, pushes player two out of the way and pulls number one out of the flames.

Panic over.

Then, an older guy came into view.

I just knew he was my man. I felt my guts churn just at the sight of him.

He seemed calmer than the others, more in control and he was armed.

Holding an AK in his right hand, he stepped over the burning cloth on his back doorstep and looked out into the night.

It took all my self-control not to slot him there and then, but I knew the other boys would have to come out and deal with the increasing problem of the fire before it took hold proper.

Sure enough, out they came, all except charred legs. They stood behind the older guy on the gravel, unsure if it was safe to move. After all, even in their pissed up state, it was obvious they were the subject of an attack.

The players began arguing between themselves as to who would tackle the blaze.

My man, the old school player, had heard enough of their squabbles.

He turned and handed his AK to his nearest guest.

"Cover me whilst I get me hose, fer fuck's sake," he said, and strode away abusing the lot of them as he went.

I waited and watched.

Less than a minute later, he was back with the pipe and began dousing the flames. That moment was as close to perfect as I could have hoped for.

Four players, all bunched together at the back door, as the fifth nursed his burns on the floor of the kitchen. And now, Paddy O'Donnell's old soldier, Tommy Brannigan, the guy I desperately wanted to chat with, was separated and vulnerable.

I'd rarely fired an Uzi, an Israeli weapon first used by IDF special forces in the 50s. The model I'd stolen from the dead Irishman was a Mini. It spat out 950 rounds every minute. Its far smaller than the standard gun, and weighing in at just six pounds, it felt more like a pistol.

It was allegedly accurate to 100 metres, but in the dark, with multiple targets and with me on the move as I fired, I couldn't rely on that statistic.

The Ingram was on a sling around my neck. A far less well made weapon, and even less accurate than its Israeli counterpart. But at .45 calibre, a devastating firearm up close.

Once the Uzi was empty, it would be a simple task to swing the MAC10 around my body and finish the job.

I hunkered down on my haunches eyeing the player with the AK. He looked like he'd forgotten the reason he was holding the weapon in the first place and was too busy watching his older mate spraying his window frames.

Not one of them even saw me coming.

I must have been less than ten yards away when I opened up.

The twenty round mag in the Uzi didn't last long. Its rate of fire equates to just under sixteen rounds per second. Even so, it took care of the player with the AK, and the two men closest to him were cut to pieces in the process. I let the smoking Israeli weapon fall to the floor and grabbed the Ingram.

The last man standing at the back door got the full brunt of the MAC10. The bigger calibre rounds punched into his body, slamming him against the farmhouse wall.

Before he hit the floor, I was on the doorstep.

The guy with the burns, was in the middle of the kitchen cowering behind a sturdy looking table. He looked at me with a mixture of surprise and fear. The slightest squeeze of the Ingram's trigger put three rounds in his chest and he fell back, eyes wide open, legs twitching.

Danny Boy played mournfully in the background.

Apt really.

Two steps back took me into the open again.

I let the MAC10 swing against my hip and collected the AK from the dead man's hands.

The final player, and the man I wanted to speak to, was on his toes, running across the flat open ground that had been so troublesome to us in the first place.

I lifted up Mr Kalashnikov's most lethal invention and found my sight picture. The fire selector on the AK47 is a large lever that sits on the right side of the rifle. I always found it weird that it's operated by the shooter's right fore-fingers, meaning you have to take your hand from the business end of the weapon to select the fire mode. The selector was in the 'up' position, meaning the safety was engaged. One notch down gave the shooter fully auto, so I clicked it twice, to semi and steadied myself.

The crack of a 7.62 round is unmistakable. The sonic noise of a projectile travelling at over two thousand feet per second, is something you never forget, especially if it's being fired in your direction.

However, I didn't want to kill my target, well, not immediately at least, so I'd aimed at his legs, something alien to anyone who shoots at another human being.

Unsurprisingly, my effort missed, and my target veered off sharply to his left, disappearing into the darkness.

I had no choice but to run after the bastard.

I dropped the AK47 and sprinted off. Now, I'm a big bloke, not exactly built for speed, but the army and particularly the Regiment gave me something precious. It instilled me with discipline and a desire to get from one place to another using nothing but my own two feet.

That might sound simple, and most things in the forces are, they have to be, so that your average bloke can understand what he has to do. But the Regiment took that principal to the eighth degree and although most men were of a slighter build than me, I'd always found the determination to succeed where others found their resolve lacking.

Within a minute, I was just ten yards behind my prey.

I could hear him blowing hard, and as I grew ever closer, saw his head rocking from side to side. A sure sign that he was fucked.

He made the mistake of turning to look where I was, and as he did so, tripped and fell, knocking the wind out of him. I stood there, looking down at the guy, more pissed off about having to run, than tired from it.

Drawing my BAP from my waistband, I pointed it at his head.

"Who the fuck are you?" he said, rolling on his back and gasping for air.

I looked into his eyes for a moment before I spoke. I don't quite know why I said what I did, but I just knew. I just fucking knew.

"I'm the husband of the woman you killed. Hereford, 1996."

He screwed up his face.

"I don't know what you're talking about, son."

I eyeballed him some more.

He was lying.

He studied me for a moment and decided to bring us back to the present day.

"You'll be the one that treacherous bastard Finbarr was working with then?"

I nodded.

"That's right, the one you sent your boys to kill."

His eyes grew wide and the realisation hit him.

"My two boys are?"

"Dead? Yes… Yes, they are. I killed them both."

He flew into a rage at that. His grief empowering him. I couldn't blame him for that, but as he lifted himself from the ground, I kicked him square in the chest, sending him back to his prone position.

"Stay the fuck where you are, pal," I said. "I ain't done with you yet."

I looked in his face again, studying it for his reactions.

"Do you remember her?" I asked. "My wife? She was young… beautiful."

He stayed quiet but there was a change in his eyes, a change he couldn't hide. I don't care who you are, you remember taking a life. It stays with you, no matter who, why or how many.

Whether it was his way of getting back at me for slotting his sons, or just bravado, I had no way of knowing, but he sneered at me, turned his head and spat on the floor.

"It was business," he said. "Paddy and me came for you. She was just in the way."

I rubbed my face with my palm. My head swam. When we slotted O'Donnell, I drew a line under Cathy's murder. I figured that after ten years, it was the best outcome that I could hope for. I'd never considered that I'd stumble across the second shooter. I took the deepest of breaths.

"Tommy… that's your name, eh?"

"What if it is?"

"Get up… come on, now, on your feet."

He rolled over and managed to stand. He was older than me, early fifties, with thinning curly hair. He had the look of a farmer about him. The ruddy complexion, the calloused hands. He swayed slightly, maybe the booze, maybe his situation.

I waved the Browning. "Go on… back to the house."

"I'll not help yees, ye'll get nothing from me," he said.

I jutted my chin. "Walk."

A couple of silent minutes later, we made the gravel path that surrounded the house. Brannigan was heading for the back door, where his dead pals lay.

"Not this way," I said. "The front… walk to the front door."

He looked over his shoulder and shrugged. "Why don't yees just get on with it, soldier boy."

I gave him a swift shove to make my point. "The front," I said.

Finally, we stood at the entrance. A security light sat over the large double wooden doors and illuminated us. For the first time I had a really good look at the guy. He was sweating and there was fear in his eyes.

"Stand on the step and face me," I said.

He did as he was told, and I saw him swallow hard.

"Is this what it was like?" I asked, not wanting a reply. "That day? I mean, I know it wasn't dark like this, it was daylight. I know it wasn't calm, it was windy. It was me who found her, see? At *our* front door, lying on her back."

It was my turn to swallow; my mouth was dry, and I felt my legs start to shake. The Irishman didn't take his eyes from me.

I looked back into his face and felt my hatred bubble up inside.

"You used an AK that day, too, didn't you? … Her wounds were horrific."

"Like I told yees. It was business," he said flatly. "Nothing personal. Paddy wanted you murdered. He had this connection who gave us your address, your picture. It was meant to be you, not the girl. But she'd seen our faces."

My heart was breaking all over again. I could see Cathy lying there, torn to shreds. I heard my voice crack as I spoke.

"You killed me that day, Brannigan. You killed me as sure as any bullet could ever do. When Cathy took her last breath, mine went along with it. I don't live anymore. I don't feel. I don't care. Compassion, sympathy, mercy… they've all deserted me.  So, in a way, you did your job. On the other hand, it makes what I'm about to do, a whole lot easier."

I felt my finger on the trigger. I took two steps forward, slipped my left hand behind the boy's neck and pulled him to me. I pointed the muzzle downwards, just above his navel and let go two rounds.

His legs gave way and he began to scream in agony.

It would take him a while to die.  A hole in the stomach or the intestines causes stomach acid and intestinal bacteria to contaminate the peritoneum. The pain is horrendous, and peritonitis quickly takes hold. Even if he lived the night out, he'd die in agony of the infection next morning.

A quick search of the house gave me Fin's mobile and the cash from his pocket. The bastards couldn't resist taking his last few euro.

I switched on the phone and waited for it to start up. There in his contacts were the two names I needed. Hamza and Imran. All nice and easy.

That said, it took me an hour to find the keys for the barn and the truck.

As I pulled out of the farmyard, I could still hear Tommy Branningan screaming.

## Lauren North's Story:

Des sat in the back of the car, eyes closed, silent.

I'd never seen him so angry, so out of control. I was convinced he was going to shoot the woman at the traveller's site.

That said, even with her still alive, we had major problems. As we drove from Haslingden to Blackburn, the nearest accident and emergency unit to the site, we saw three police cars, lights flashing, sirens wailing, all headed in the direction of the supermarket car park we'd just left.

The shit and the fan were conspiring against us.

There were other hurdles, too. Even if Kaya was at the Royal Blackburn, it would be almost impossible to see him, or even confirm his admission.

As far as the NHS were concerned, they'd had an unconscious and unidentified child, dropped on their doorstep. No doubt, we would have more cops to contend with there.

Parking on a small development of industrial units close to the hospital, we took stock.

"We have to get him out of there," said Des, removing his boot painfully.

"We need to get you in there," I said, looking worriedly at the wound to his foot that had reopened and was bleeding badly.

"Maybe that's the answer," offered Sellers.

"Go on, hen," said Des wincing.

Sellers shrugged. "Well, you're in need of some new stitches, that's for sure. I say, one of us takes you into casualty, and whilst you get sorted, the other has a snoop about."

I shook my head.

"Look, I believe Kaya is suffering from cerebral hypoxia, a condition that occurs when there is not enough oxygen getting to the brain. The woman at the site said that they couldn't wake him up. That tells me that he was breathing, but unresponsive."

"A coma," added Sellers.

I nodded.

"Exactly. Now, the team in ICU are going to put Kaya on a ventilator that delivers extra oxygen to the brain. Then they'll do all manner of tests. An angiogram, blood tests to check arterial blood gases and blood chemical levels, a CT scan, ECG, EEG, MRI and a thing called evoked potentials, which test to see if the brain recognises certain sensations such as vision and touch."

"You mean to see if the kid is brain dead," said Sellers, somewhat coldly.

Des was on her in a flash. Fists balled, eyes narrowed. "The kids no brain dead. He's going to be just fine," he spat.

I did my best to keep my voice level and keep the peace at the same time.

"We need to let the medical team do their job," I said. "The faster Kaya becomes responsive, the more likely he is to make a full recovery."

I looked at Des knowingly. "The fact is, the longer he's in a coma, the more likely he will be to remain vegetative."

Des pointed at me, his face etched with worry. "Come on, now... You have the expertise Lauren. You worked in HDU back in Leeds. I was there, I saw you. Maybe you could...?"

I wanted to heal his pain. Tell him that everything would be fine. But at that very moment, I couldn't. False hope was worthless. There was just too much at stake.

We listened as more sirens wailed in the distance.

I looked into the Scot's troubled face. Finally, he let his head fall.

"You're right, hen," he said.

I sat and thought over our very limited options, pulled out my phone, stepped out of the car and called the only person I knew could help... Cartwright.

He listened to what I had to say without asking a single question.

"I take it you are still on friendly terms with our pet Chief Inspector?"

"If you mean Larry," I said cautiously. "Yes."

"Good, I thought as much. Then you need to call him and get him to go around to Mrs Yakim's home in Manchester. Tell him to take the report of the missing child and call it in. Once that is done, call me again."

The line went dead. I looked at the screen on my phone as muffled voices from the car discussed our thorny problem. I considered that they had no idea how difficult this was becoming.

Larry answered on the first ring.

"I wondered if you'd call," he said quietly. "When you left without saying goodbye... well, what was a guy to think?"

"You figured my guilt had got the better of me?"

"Something like that."

"Look, Larry, I'm sorry to spring this on you, but I haven't had the best of days, and this isn't the time to talk about what two drunken adults did or didn't get up to.

I need your help, and this time there can't be any ethical crisis on your part. A child has been kidnapped. We believe we've located him, but he is seriously ill. His condition could prove fatal. I need you to go around to the mother's house, get her to make an official complaint."

"She hasn't called the cops?"

Larry sounded suspicious. I couldn't blame him, after all every time I spoke to him, I was always asking him to bend a rule or two. But since his last stuttering efforts had led to the unnecessary death of a civilian, I hoped that he'd realised that we were on the right side of the argument, even if we were occasionally on the wrong side of the law.

"No, not the cops… she called us, Larry. And before you ask, yes we've located the kidnappers."

"And they are where?"

"Not sure."

"You've lost them?"

"Not exactly."

"I don't like the sound of this, Lauren."

"You never do. But there's no time to waste here. I'll tell you everything in good time… but Larry?"

"Yes?"

"If you let me down on this one, you'll never hear from me again… that is a promise."

"Harsh," he said quietly.

I gave him Grace's address. "Ring me back the moment you've called it in."

I took a breath. "Oh, and one more thing… I had a nice time."

I stood outside the car and waited. I've never smoked in my life, but at that moment, I think I could have started.

As if reading my mind, Des stepped out into the night and began the process of filling his pipe.

"Who'd yer call, hen?" he asked, his eyes piercing me.

"Cartwright," I said watching his efforts.

"What did that crabby old bastard have to say?"

"Not a lot, just to involve Larry."

There must have been something in my voice, or in my face. Des lit his pipe, took a long drag and exhaled. "He's like a fuckin' bad penny, that boy."

I could feel my hackles rise. "We need him on this one, Des."

He examined me. "Pillow talk is a dangerous thing, Lauren."

"It's not like that."

"Really?"

I shook my head.

"Let's just concentrate on the job at hand, eh? Let me worry about my love life… or the lack of it."

Des examined the bowl of his ageing pipe. "So, now what?"

"Soon as Larry calls in the job, I call Cartwright."

"A waiting game, then?"

I nodded.

Des tapped out ash on his heel and winced.

"We need to get you fixed, too," I offered.

"There's time for that," he said, looking into my face again. I don't think I'd ever seen so much sorrow and turmoil in a man's eyes.

"I'm tired, hen," he said. "I'll tell yer this, just between the two of us here, once we sort out these boys across the water, if wee Kaya is in any fit state, I'm going to ask Grace to go up to Scotland with me. No strings attached of course. They can live in the cottage and I can get back to my place on the Loch. Keep an eye on them. Breath some clean air, walk the streets without a gun in my belt."

I turned. "What about Rick?"

Des watched me knowingly. "What about him?"

I looked down at my feet. "I know he cares about me, but… "

"But it's not enough?"

"I don't think he'll ever get over Cathy. There would always be a ghost in the house, even if I could persuade him to give up this crazy life."

Des refilled his bowl. "And you think this Larry guy is the answer?"

I shrugged. "I don't know."

My phone saved me from any further awkward questions from the Scot.

"I'm at the house," said Larry, all businesslike. "Grace wants to talk to you."

I'd had many hard conversations with worried parents, husbands, wives, sons and daughters. Before I'd met Rick and Des, I'd lived my life with people, who for whatever reason, lay in comas. Some woke up, some never did. We lost more than we saved, and those that survived often had serious ongoing problems.

As I related what we knew to Grace Yakim, I did my best to remain positive, yet I could hear her heart breaking over the phone.

I closed the call and took a deep breath.

"Grace is with Larry, they are both on their way to The Royal now."

Des continued to smoke and judge me with those sharp blue eyes.

"Better call the spook then," he said.

As it turned out, I had no need to. He'd sent a welcoming committee.

As I held my phone to my ear, I saw the headlights approaching. Moments later, a Vito minibus with blacked out windows drew up across from us.

Two men slid from the vehicle.

They were suited and booted, but unlike the reception that the Americans had afforded us outside the Thirsty Scholar, these two were anything but polite.

"Cogan and North?" snapped the first guy. A broad shouldered blond with a broken nose.

"Who's askin'?" said Des warily.

The blond ignored the question. He just lifted open the rear door of the Vito and began to remove two plastic buckets and a bag of what appeared to be clothing.

"Step over to me, Cogan," he said.

The second guy was leaning into our Audi. He spoke quickly with a hint of a Liverpool accent.

"Leave all your weapons and personal effects in the car. Do it now, quick as you like."

I saw Mitch and Sellers begin to move. Maybe it was their years in the army. That, 'don't question authority,' thing.

Des and I, however, stayed put.

"No one is going anywhere just yet," I said with as much confidence as I could muster.

"Aye," added Des. "I'm no leavin' until I've seen the boy."

The two guys shot each other a look.

The Scouser shrugged.

"Our orders are to collect you lot and destroy as much evidence as possible. We figured that as we are here to cover your sorry backsides, that you might be a tad more helpful."

There was pleading in Des' voice. "Come on lads… What about the boy?"

Blondie gestured towards the back door of the van. "Look, Cogan, you know the script. Contaminated clothes in your car, scrub your hands and forearms in the white bucket, then dip in the red. Slip on one of the suits. Do it now, pal, we ain't time to chat about it. If we get a tug between here and where we're going, don't utter a fuckin' word until you see a very expensive looking lawyer. Clear?"

I looked into Des' eyes. "What choice do we have?"

He shook his head resignedly and limped over to the van.

The Scouser, stepped over to me and searched me roughly. He took my phone and pocketed it.

"You got cash on you? Coins? Keys? Purse?"

I shook my head.

He nodded. "Go put on a suit, throw your clothes in the Audi."

Moments later we all sat in the van as Scouser boy torched my rental.

He jumped back into the driver's seat and we were away.

"Where are we going?" I asked.

"Legoland," said Blondie.

I turned to Des, quizzically.

"The SIS building, hen," he said. "MI6 headquarters, London.

I'd felt unusually nervous the whole trip. Each time a car overtook us, or we saw a marked police vehicle, I'd convinced myself that we were about to get a pull.

As I watched the M1 give way to Staples Corner, Edgware Road, Marble Arch and finally Vauxhall Bridge, I was full of foreboding.

Our van was driven into a nondescript underground car park that gave no indication that we were in the most hallowed of halls.

Our Liverpudlian friend killed the engine and unlocked the doors. He reminded me of Rick. Probably ten years his junior, but he had that same stern determined look about him, and I wondered if he'd come via a similar background. We all stepped out cautiously. Des was last, and I could see that he was really struggling with his pain, both physical and mental.

From somewhere off to my left, I heard a lift door open and moments later we were joined by three other men, one obviously a doctor, as he wore the green scrubs associated with his profession. He smiled kindly at Des and helped him to an electric cart. I think the Scot was too tired and sore to argue, but he gave me a lingering look over his shoulder as he went.

I swallowed bile and did my best to stay calm.

Their job seemingly completed, Blondie and Scouse sauntered off without saying a word, leaving our party of three with two middle aged suits.

One had a clipboard. He was in his mid-fifties, greying at the temples but lithe of limb. I considered he spent a good few hours a week on a treadmill or bike.

"Which of you is North?" he asked, all matter of fact.

"Present," I said, with no small dose of sarcasm.

My mockery did little to help my cause and it certainly didn't break any ice. Clipboard looked at me with steely grey eyes. His expression dead pan.

"Quite the comedian, are we Ms North?"

Not bothering to wait for an answer, he turned to Sellers. "And you are?"

Victoria smiled serenely. In fact, during the entire incident, I couldn't recall her being in the slightest bit fazed.

"Obviously, someone whose identity MI6 is unaware of," she purred. Then, pushing a wayward curl behind her ear, added. "And until I know with whom I'm speaking, I'd like to keep it that way."

She gave Clipboard a beaming smile.

I felt instantly better.

Clipboard turned his mouth down and his attentions to Mitch.

"Mr Collins, please go with my colleague here. He will take you to one of the upper floors. Your associates from the United States are waiting for you. This…" Clipboard struggled to find his words for a moment, then almost smiled, "… Calamitous cock up, you appear to have involved yourself in, was not part of your remit my old chum. Despite your pals over the water not quite knowing who the enemy have been for the last forty years, it appears they don't take kindly to you running about the English countryside shooting up the local Gypsies."

Clipboard waited for the American to move.

Mitch gave me a resigned look, then stepped over, took me in his arms and hugged me.

"Ma'am," he said. "It's been a pleasure."

I nodded and managed a smile. "You're a good bloke, Mitch."

"See you Stateside," he said, and walked.

Sellers shouted after him. "Later big guy."

Mitch didn't turn. He just raised his hand over his head and was gone.

We followed Clipboard to the lift I'd presumed he'd exited from. Much to my surprise, rather than travel upwards, the elevator dropped like a stone. Sellers and I were firmly on a downward path.

The lift doors opened with a swish and we found ourselves in a long arched-roofed corridor which appeared far older than the building we had entered.

"Ooh, where's M?" said Sellers.

"My life is full of jokers," said Clipboard. "None of them funny."

We turned right and passed several other suits walking in the opposite direction to us. All wore ID cards around their necks. None took any interest in us, or our guide for that matter.

He finally stopped by a solid looking green door and looked Sellers in the eye.

"As you prefer to remain anonymous, Ma'am… you'll be comfortable in here, until Ms North is briefed."

Clipboard rapped on the door and it was opened by a very serious looking woman in nurse's whites.

Sellers raised her eyebrows. "I've had all my shots, honest."

Clipboard gave her a thin smile and watched her step into the room.

I instantly felt very alone and vulnerable.

"Ms North," he said. "This way please."

We walked for another minute until the corridor, which was becoming more like a tunnel with every step, turned sharply left and a pair of iron gates barred our way.

"This is as far as I go," offered Clipboard, tapping the said item on the metal bars.

A door opened somewhere along the darkened corridor and I heard footsteps approaching.

"Good luck," he said, and turned on his heels.

A woman approached. Power dressed to the max. My age, tall and willowy, with the straightest blondest hair, I'd ever seen. The cut was so sharp and precise, it looked like you would slice your skin by touching it.

She swiped her ID along a slot and the gates clicked open.

"This way," she said, turning her back on me and displaying seamed stockings right out of the 1940s. This was obviously not dress down Thursday.

Another green door appeared to my left. This time it was ajar, and I was ushered inside by the smartest PA ever.

Cartwright sat behind a small desk in an unremarkable room. The blonde woman perched herself to his left, those silk covered legs crossed, palms delicately resting on her thigh.

If the surroundings had been different, I'd have expected high tea to be served any minute.

"This is Camilla," said Cartwright. "She works for me."

I managed a smile.

"Just give me the number of her hairdresser and I'll leave you both to it."

Camilla remained stoic.

Cartwright leaned forward, elbows on desk.

"Lauren," he began. "It's late, I've missed a very nice dinner and I'm tired."

"I know a great kebab shop just south of the river," I said.

The old spy gave me a look. "I'm sure both you and Mr Cogan would enjoy such a delicacy, but I have no desire to eat anything that spins around in a shop window for days on end."

Never one to beat about the proverbial, Cartwright turned to the matter in hand. There was anger somewhere in his voice, but he held it inside.

"Why in heavens name did you not let the boys in blue deal with this kidnapping? What were you and Cogan thinking of when you decided to assassinate half the fucking gypsy population of Lancashire?"

I cocked my head. "I think they call it summary justice. If I recall, something that you hold dear to your heart. After all, that's why you pay us so well, isn't it?"

He was struggling to keep a lid on his temper and it showed.

"You shoot the fuckers I tell you to shoot," he hissed. "You don't take matters into your own hands, willy nilly. When you work for yourselves, you play by the book."

I sniffed and changed the subject.

"Why am I here?"

"I need to protect my assets," said Cartwright. "Of which you are one, and a very valuable one at that. Desmond is being well cared for and will recuperate quickly. We are fortunate to have the very best medical care at our disposal here, and this is an extremely secure building."

"We're here for our protection?"

"For now."

"How's Kaya?"

"Awake."

I felt instant relief. "Thank the Lord."

Cartwright pointed. "Well what *I'm* not thankful for, is the gang fuck out in the backwoods of Blackburn."

I watched him physically attempt to calm himself. "Now," he said, with as much temperance as he could muster. "I've always considered the three of you to be good professionals, but this? This is a balls up to end all balls ups. Is Cogan out of control?"

"No. Just pissed off."

That didn't help Cartwright's mood. His voice shot up three notches.

"Pissed off? I've just watched the fucking CCTV of the incident in Haslingden, Ms North. He murdered two civilians in front of dozens of witnesses. The Chief Constable of Lancashire Constabulary is apoplectic."

"They were both armed."

"He shot one of them in the back as he was running away, for fuck's sake."

I shook my head. I was not in the mood to take shit.

"Fucking double standards, don't you think? I'm sure those two pillars of the travelling community currently in the morgue, worked tirelessly in their social sphere. Unfortunately for them, they kidnapped a kid at gunpoint and stuffed him in a suitcase until he suffocated. Not just any kid, but the son of a recently deceased close friend and ally of ours, JJ Yakim. The man who saved my life by giving his. The man who gave his life for this bloody department. So... fuck them, and if you don't like it... fuck you. They're dead, bang, bang, oh dear, very sorry."

I sat back and folded my arms, feeling ever so slightly like a petulant child, but happy I'd fought my corner.

"Finished?" said Cartwright, one eyebrow raised.

He lowered his voice, the epitome of instant practiced composure.

"Look, Lauren, I understand your allegiance to Mr Cogan and whilst we all wish young Kaya and his mother well and are not ungrateful for the contribution that Mr Yakim made to the Albanian operation, we have had to make some serious decisions of how the team will look going forward... at least temporarily."

He took a deep breath. "As of right now, Fuller will work with other operatives of my choosing."

"Bollocks."

"Just until everyone if feeling a little better."

"I'm fine."

"Well, yes, but..."

"But what?"

Cartwright looked at me with those rheumy eyes of his. The ones that told you that he's seen it all, done it all, and walked out of the other side.

"I need someone to work alongside Mr Fuller, starting tonight and..."

That got my attention.

"Rick? You've heard from him? How is he?"

"In one piece, thank you for asking. However, the job in Ireland is moving very quickly and he is in need of some assistance for all manner of reasons."

"I'm all ears. I'll go… tonight."

"Yes, I considered you may say that, but under the current circumstances, the answer is… no."

"Why not?"

"You've become a distraction, Lauren. A problem."

I was about to remonstrate but he held up a hand.

"Yes, you are an asset to us, but to Richard Fuller, right now, you are not. You are too close to him, and as your relationship with Detective Chief Inspector Simpson has… how shall we put it… moved on somewhat. I can't take the risk of having Richard distracted."

I was open mouthed.

"You've been having me followed."

"Only in your down time, dear."

"Well, there hasn't been much of that."

"Enough for you to form a sexual relationship with a senior detective who is willing to put his career on the line to get close to you."

I let my head fall and rubbed my face with my palms. I was in bits.

"Jesus Christ. Look, Cartwright, I love Rick… I…"

The old spy was cold as ice. "Yes, enough to sleep with another man."

I felt tears approaching but held them back… just.

"It was a mistake, you don't understand… "

"What? You fell over drunk, and Larry Simpson just happened to fall on top of you? Then what? Before you knew it, you were copulating like a pair of dogs on heat?"

I raised my head and felt myself flush with a mixture of anger and embarrassment.

"Don't be a clever prick, Cartwright. You sit there all holier than thou, with your stocking clad blonde PA for company and judge me. Fuck you. What's she here for… to replace the missus?"

Cartwright fixed me with his stare. "No Lauren, Camilla is here to replace you."

I stood and eyeballed the woman. Any hope of containing my emotions had flown right out of the window.

"You're sending *her* to Ireland? Dumping me? After all I've been through? Belfast? Are you forgetting that? O'Donnell's boys? Do you recall what those bastards did to me?"

The old spy sat back in his chair and played with a pen.

"You are a fine operative, Lauren. There is no doubting your ability or your dedication to your duties, but…"

"But I had a moment of madness, went out, got drunk and shagged the wrong guy… is that it? Is that fucking it?"

"It's not just your actions that night, Lauren. Whether Fuller discovers your infidelity or not, is none of our concern. The fact of the matter is, you are distracted by him, and he by you. There is far too much at stake here. The operation in Ireland is growing, evolving minute by minute. We already have operatives in several locations around the globe all working tirelessly and in great personal danger, all dependant on Fuller's ability to bring this mission to a successful conclusion. I'm sorry, but the decision has been made and it's final. You and Cogan will work with another team leader until this phase of the operation is complete."

I sat back down, my heart banging in my chest. All those times I'd hoped that Rick would give up on his seemingly insatiable desire for danger, and here I was, desperate to be alongside him.

I ran my tongue across my teeth, took air in through my nose and locked eyes with Cartwright.

"Can I have a minute… Sir?" I shot a look at Camilla, who had remained silent and impassive throughout. "Alone?"

Cartwright nodded at the woman. She stood, smoothed down her skirt and clip clopped from the room on impossibly high heels.

The instant the door closed, I leaned in. "Have you lost your marbles, Cartwright?"

"Not at all."

I pointed behind me, towards the door. "You are going to send," I fought for the right words. "*That*, out to Ireland to support Rick? He'll eat her for breakfast and have her running home to Selfridges before the day is out."

Cartwright gripped the bridge of his nose between thumb and forefinger. He closed his eyes briefly, then looked into mine.

"I'm not a fool, Ms North. Please don't treat me like one. Camilla is an experienced and professional agent and is perfectly capable of dealing with Mr Fuller's negativity towards the fairer sex."

I laughed down my nose.

"I hope she has a return ticket."

Cartwright pointed. "This is not a matter for discussion, Lauren. My mind is made up."

My head was a teaming jumble of information and emotion. I did my best to concentrate. I needed to buy time. Time to sort out this mess.

I cocked my head. "Look, Cartwright, Des will be laid up for a few weeks, out of the game. Next to him, I'm your best fit…"

"Not at all," said the old spy. "Mr Cogan will be fine and dandy by the morning."

Now I knew I was having a nightmare.

"It's been a while since I worked A&E, Cartwright, but even so, after the trauma Des has suffered, he'll be three to four weeks before he's even close to…."

He shook his head.

"Treatment of wounds and their management have moved on a tad since then, Lauren. Believe it or believe it not, Mr Cogan will be ninety percent fit this time tomorrow, by which time, your new team will be complete, and you will have your own tasks to perform."

He pushed his pen into his top pocket, a sure sign our conversation was coming to an end.

"And if it makes you feel any better, your mission is directly connected to Mr Fuller's operation. Now, I suggest you follow the chap that is waiting outside that door and get some rest. You will be briefed at 0800hrs."

I was close to information overload, but I just couldn't let Cartwright make such a massive error with Camilla.

"Look, what if I proposed another operative to work alongside Rick? Someone on our books, like JJ was? Someone I know who can deal with him? Someone who is as good, if not better than me?"

Cartwright shook his head. "It has to be a woman. You don't know the full story. Undercover work…"

"It is a woman," I said. "And she's here… right now and ready to go."

## Rick Fuller's Story:

I'd briefed Cartwright the moment I'd left the farm. I'd told him all I knew and that I needed support, in the form of Lauren North. Having a female operative on this job was going to be very useful. Covert ops need females, ask any terrorist.

He hadn't seemed phased that Fin had planned to steal the AK's. He didn't even seem to mind that his long-time undercover operative was dead.

However, he did seem preoccupied when I told him that our gun runners had a visit from a mystery man driving a 7 series Beamer, giving them the nod about Finbarr's intentions. All within a day of him meeting yours truly.

I'd told him I suspected that we had yet another informer in the camp, and as we were in bed with the Yanks on this deal, notorious historical supporters of the Irish cause, it didn't bode well. Cartwright said he would, 'look into the matter,' and that 'support would be forthcoming.'

That was spy speak for, 'I'll make the decisions.'

I'd wanted to ask him if he knew that the owner of the farm had been O'Donnell's man, but there was no time, and I reckoned that I probably knew the answer to that one, anyway.

I pulled the truck over at a small service station fifteen miles north of Cork and bought myself coffee and a sandwich. Driving the wagon had been a real chore. Each AK weighed in at 3.9 kgs which meant the payload of 800 boxed weapons came in at three and a half tons. Add to that, the hundred and twenty 1000 round boxes of ammunition that hadn't been mentioned in the deal, and the truck was well over its 7.5 ton maximum.

The old lorry had rolled about like a jelly and laboured under the payload, but it had got me over halfway to my destination, so I couldn't complain. Parking on the services was a sound idea as I was sandwiched between other drivers all bedding down for the night. It may not have been ideal, but it gave me some modicum of security as I waited for the next move.

As I'd devoured my ham and cheese roll, I realised I hadn't eaten for a while. The food made me instantly drowsy and although my wagon didn't boast a sleeper cab, I slipped down across the seats and fell asleep instantly.

Well, at least until my phone vibrated in my pocket.

When I saw who was calling, I knew there was trouble. You didn't speak to Cartwright twice in four hours unless things had gone to rat shit.

"Your fucking friends are a fucking liability," he ranted. "Cogan has only gone and executed two bloody gypsies in front of half of Lancashire."

Obviously, I'd known about the kidnapping. I'd also known Des Cogan for long enough, wounded or not, to realise that the boys who had taken the kid were on borrowed time if he caught up with them. So, it was my turn to be non-committal.

"Nothing that a man of your calibre can't handle, is it, Cartwright?" I said, stretching.

"Not the fucking point, Fuller. What happened to bloody common sense? A bit of restraint for goodness sake?"

It was unusual for the old spy to swear so much. It almost made me smile.

"How's the kid?" I asked. "I take it they've got him back?"

Cartwright seemed to calm slightly.

"They'd kept him in a suitcase," he said. Damned animals…Miraculously, he's awake and talking, but you know how these things are… early days. We have him under observation in Blackburn. The mother is in a safe house for the time being."

That made me feel better. JJ had given us everything. It was all we could do to protect his boy. But I detected trouble in the air.

"That's good news," I said. "But I sense an issue here, Cartwright. The reason for this update on my team is what exactly?"

"Lauren North will not be joining you."

That made me sit up.

"What?"

"Now don't go all girly on me, Fuller. Your little band of happy clappers are lucky not to be sitting in a cell as we speak. It took a great deal of political goodwill to afford them their liberty, I'll tell you."

I scratched my head. "Okay, fair one. But why bin Lauren? I told you, with your man Finbarr gone, I could do with another pair of hands. A couple can move about far easier than a single male, you know that. The drop is in a holiday town. We need to blend in. The Bosnians may already smell a rat. Who's to say our grass hasn't given the boys from the Balkans the heads up? None of this will be any good if I end up floating in the Irish sea and your AK's go missing."

"That won't happen Richard. Now, I realise that you need support, but Ms North is not in the right frame of mind to give it to you right now."

"Meaning?"

"Meaning, what we discussed over luncheon the other day. I think the two of you need... space."

"Ah, this cooling off period you mentioned?"

"Exactly."

I could feel my hackles rise. "Well, I don't want a cooling off. I want her here... now."

"Not a good idea."

"What are you trying to tell me here, Cartwright?"

"What I'm telling you is for your own good, Richard. Listen to a man who knows about these things."

"And what exactly do you know?"

There was a silence.

"Ms North is... confused right now."

"Confused, how?"

"This... this policeman..."

"Larry? The detective guy? No, you're barking up the wrong tree there. Lauren and me put that to bed before Albania. He had a thing for her, she knocked him back. That's the end of it."

Another silence. Longer this time.

"What if it isn't?" said Cartwright. "What if he's closer than ever?"

I felt my gut tighten. Everything I'd told the Irishman, just before I'd gut shot him, flashed through my head. Was I dead inside? Was I incapable of caring... was that all true?

I sniffed and ran my hand through my hair. How did I feel? What was in my heart?

"I need support," I said flatly. "And whoever you've got had better be on it."

"And you'll have it, Fuller," said the spy. "Drive south from where you are now, to a place called Riverstick. There's a GAA ground in the village. There will be a chopper dropping in there in just under thirty minutes. Your support is on board."

"What's his name," I asked.

"*She's* called Sellers," he said. "Victoria Sellers and she's as good as I've ever seen. I've fully briefed her, she's up to speed... Oh, and Fuller... be nice."

I sat, stared at my phone for a while and considered ringing Lauren. Considered asking her the question, asking for the truth. Jealousy is a vicious emotion. It won't leave you alone. It eats away at your insides. It's physical, sickening and spiteful. But I couldn't have it both ways. I couldn't tell myself that I was incapable of love one minute, then tear myself apart wondering what Lauren had been up to the next.

It seemed that I'd had my chance, and for whatever reason, I'd blown it.

Pushing all thoughts of love and remorse to the back of my mind, I drove to Riverstick, and just as Cartwright had said, within ten minutes I heard the rotors of a chopper above me.

The aircraft was in complete darkness, no lights or beacons for this landing, so I figured that the pilot would be using NV to navigate the bird down. Scary for the passengers, but better safe than sorry.

As the helicopter lifted off and disappeared into the inky blackness, I saw a figure walking towards the truck.

Victoria Sellers was maybe five ten and had all the attributes that a woman needed to attract any man to her. But she didn't walk like a woman. She strode. She marched.

Sellers was dressed in designer jeans and a beautifully cut leather jacket, both as expensive as they were serviceable. Her dark hair was tied back in a ponytail and she carried a very full looking Bergen on her back.

As she reached the truck, I dropped down from the cab and extended my hand. When she gripped it, I realised that she not only walked like a man but shook like one, too.

"Fuller," she said with an accent straight out of the 'how to sound like a posh twat' guide.

"Vicky," I offered.

"No," she said. "No, Fuller, not Vicky or Vic or any other abbreviation."

I had to stop myself from taking the piss. "So, what would you like me to...?"

"Victoria... or just Sellers... You can call me Ma'am or Captain if you like, but that is technically untrue these days." She shrugged off the Bergen. "Any of those will do, Fuller. But I suggest we fuck off from here and find somewhere else to hold this inane conversation."

I shot her a look and jumped back into the cab.

Sellers sat alongside me, her Bergen ensuring we were sufficiently separated.

I shook my head and started the engine. We were on our way, but I wasn't happy.

"I ask Cartwright for support, and he sends me a female Rupert."

Sellers glared at me. "Do you know why British army officers were nicknamed, 'Rupert', Fuller?"

"Not a clue... maybe because it's a posh name, and most officers are upper class, like you?"

"In one, Fuller. But I'm not upper class, darling. I'm way posher than that."

She turned in her seat. There was no doubting that she was beautiful. She had fine chiselled features, large expressive brown eyes and fabulous raven hair, but there was far more to this woman than her looks. The way she moved and conducted herself was unlike any female I'd met before. She pursed her lips.

"Operation Buzzard... Do you know what *that* is, Fuller?"

"Is this twenty questions?"

"I like to know if my subordinates are up to speed, so to speak. So, do you know, or not?"

I gritted my teeth.

"No, but I get the feeling you're going to tell me."

"Afghanistan, May 2002, Fuller. Buzzard's aim was to prevent the freedom of movement of Al-Qaeda and Taliban and destroy their base camps. My unit and 45 Commando deployed into Khost close to the Afghan-Pakistan border. We were accompanied by several US Special Forces guys and the usual CIA paramilitaries. My boys fought alongside 45, the Yanks and the spooks, clearing caves and bunkers at altitude. It was horrendous."

"Your boys?"

"The Intelligence Corps, Fuller. Manui Dat Cognitio Vires."

"Knowledge gives strength to the arm."

"Ah, you have a brain to go with the muscles... good. Anyway, the point I'm making is most men can't see past a pair of tits and a bit of lipstick, including you probably, so, let me point out a couple of things so we get off on the right foot. I had seven confirmed kills during Buzzard, four more in Basra. Unofficially, there are another half dozen Iraqis laying in unmarked graves in and around Erbil. If you are unsure where that is, it's about seventy clicks from Mosul and is the capital of the official Federal Region of Kurdistan."

"You fought with the Kurds?"

"I wasn't keen on civvy street."

"You were a mercenary?"

"Officially, I was a defensive driving instructor. I went there because my partner was there doing the same kind of work."

"Partner?"

"None of your business."

I turned up the heat in the cab.

"Okay, so you're an ex solider, you have an intel background, combat experience and you work for Cartwright. Lose the chip and we'll get on just fine."

She smiled, and her face lit up.

"Sorry, Fuller. The chip comes as part of the package and I don't work for Cartwright, I work for you. I'm on your books. Lauren fought tooth and nail to get me here."

"Now I am all ears."

"I think it best you pull over somewhere. There's more to this than meets the eye."

There always was.

## Des Cogan's Story:

I opened my eyes to find myself in a hospital bed again.

My first thought was that it was becoming too much of a habit. My second was that I felt really quite good.

The guy that had met me at the underground car park, the wee man in the green scrubs, stood by my bed.

"Time is it, Doc?" I asked.

"A little after two in the morning… Are you feeling better, Mr Cogan?" he asked in a strong Slavic accent.

"Actually, Doc, I feel tip top."

"Good, good. I always like it when my Guinea pigs survive."

I frowned at that. "I only had some burst stitches, Doc. Hardly life threatening."

"This is true, Mr Cogan. But the powers that be insisted that we have you," he seemed to struggle for the words. "… combat ready asap."

I looked down at my injured leg. It was encased in a metal box from which various coloured wires snaked downwards to another rather fancy looking contraption.

"What's going on?" I asked.

The Doc's face lit up. I'd seen the expression before when I'd mistakenly asked some fuckin' train spotter what his favourite steam engine was. I wish I'd kept my mouth shut then, too.

"Well," said the Doc, rubbing his hands. "This machine here increases the level of a chemokine, CXCL12, directly to the wound surface. In addition, bioavailability of the CXCL12 is synergistically increased within the wound, as the bacterial produced lactic acid causes a slight pH drop. That inhibits degradation, you see?"

"Oh aye, I see that, the now," I said.

He wasn't finished.

"Now, this unit ensures the chemokine, is endogenously upregulated in the injured tissue and by increasing the levels further, more immune cells are recruited. These specialised cells heal the wound and accelerate the whole process."

"I take it, this is a fairly new idea, Doc?" I asked.

"I've used it in mice and it's been very effective," he said and actually fucking smiled.

"So, what ye sayin' is, that I'll be up and about quicker?"

"You'll be up and about first thing, Mr Cogan. Good as new."

I fully expected Q to walk in and hand me an exploding fucking pen.

## Rick Fuller's Story:

I pulled the truck over into the nearest layby and killed the motor.

Sellers began undoing the top of her Bergen and laying kit out onto the seat.

"So, what's the big news?" I asked as she made ready a very nice looking Rohrbaugh R9 Stealth Elite SLP.

"One moment, Fuller," she said checking her handiwork.

The Rohrbaugh was a very classy weapon. If you could actually find one, R9's were trading on the black market for over three grand apiece. Thanks to its many aircraft grade aluminium components, the little weapon weighed in empty at less than a pound. Sellers' gun was finished in diamond black over stainless. I was impressed.

She gave the gun a final wipe.

"Okay… Cogan, North and Collins are being briefed first thing by their new team commander."

I felt my temper flare. "Their new what?"

She held up her hand. "Let me finish, Fuller… Right now, they're all tucked up in their shiny new bunks in the depths of Canary Wharf. Cogan has undergone some radical wound treatment therapy and will allegedly be as good as new by breakfast. North is pissed that she didn't get this gig. None of my business, but I understand that you two have some kind of thing going on that makes the spooks uneasy."

"Lauren and I could have easily worked things out," I offered.

Victoria tucked her R9 into her jeans, dropped a box of spare rounds into the top of her Bergen and re-fastened it.

"Not the time or place though, eh, Fuller?"

Fair one.

"Anyway," she said. "As for Mitch Collins, we figured he was going to be sent back across the pond after Cogan shot the two Gipsies. Politics and all that…"

She slipped her hand inside her jacket, removed a lipstick and began applying it and speaking at the same time.

"However, not so, darling. This new team commander is CIA… another Yank. A guy by the name of Theo Varèse, and he requested Collins stay on as he'd worked with him previously in Iraq. I didn't get the pleasure before being sent here, but I understand this Varèse's a big hitter. A proper war hero."

"Really?"

"Oh yeah. When I worked in the Kurdish territories, all the local boys ever talked about was Operation Viking Hammer. You ever heard of it?"

"Are you always full of these questions?"

She shrugged and popped the lipstick back from whence it came.

"Operation Viking Hammer eliminated Ansar al-Islam's presence in northern Iraq and allowed Kurdish units to join the fight, a massive objective for the Americans after the Turks refused them the use of their territories. Viking Hammer went down in the annals of Special Forces history. A battle fought on foot, under sustained fire from an enemy lodged in the mountains, and with minimal air support. Three U.S. Army Special Forces soldiers were awarded the Silver Star for their actions, and several members of the SAD paramilitary team received the Intelligence Star for extraordinary heroism in combat. Varèse was one of them."

"So, this Varèse is CIA Special Activities Division?"

"If you believe the hype, yes."

I let out a whistle. "Do you know this new team's role?"

"Well, Cartwright… he's an absolute sweetie, isn't he? He tells me that they are tasked with looking after our sorry backsides during the handover. If all goes according to plan, once the deal is done, we regroup and track the shipment into Europe. From there we follow it until we find Al-Mufti."

Sellers pulled off her jacket.

"And on that note, apparently Intelligence Services, Stateside, have been working flat out since MI6 gave them the nod about Yunfakh. They, like the Firm, believe Al-Mufti is indeed the end user of this shipment and the two Bosnians meeting us at the dock are just go-betweens. However, the plot thickens… The Yanks have been going through loads of old PIRA files and have discovered a connection between Al-Mufti and a Provo quartermaster by the name of McMullen."

"I know that name."

"Really, well, despite what Finbarr told you about the demise of the

PIRA, apparently McMullen was still required to sanction this deal. Seemingly, he is still a big player and was due his cut."

"I knew the deal was supposed to be a three way split, Fin said as much. But he never mentioned the name of the quartermaster." I was racking my brains. "McMullen you say?"

"Quite… However, the Yanks are also convinced it was McMullen that got old Fin slotted. They think he somehow got wind of our involvement. They don't know how, maybe his connections across the Atlantic. You see, after Good Friday, McMullen went to live in Chicago and continued to drum up support and donations for the cause. He has fucking dual nationality would you believe?"

I knew MI6 had already figured that the Bosnians were just middle men for Al-Mufti, so no surprises there.

But McMullen?

I began to leaf through the old pages in my memory banks. "Sean Patrick McMullen?"

Sellers shrugged. "Didn't get that far."

"I'd figured we'd killed him twenty years ago," I muttered almost to myself.

"Sorry?" said Sellers.

"Nothing," I said. "Probably nothing."

Sellers opened her Bergen again.

"I have pictures," she said.

I waited for her to pull a file from the sack. She leafed through until she found what she wanted and handed me three pictures. The first was of Abdallah Al-Mufti, the same shot I had seen back in the day before we'd set off to Tiji to destroy him. The second was again one I had seen before, it was of Sean Patrick McMullen, the man I'd believed to have died in that burning bungalow in Colgagh, County Monaghan, Boxing Day 1987.

Then Sellers passed me a third shot and it took my breath away.

\* \* \*

There was no doubt, it was the same guy. McMullen was older of course, his hair totally grey, swept back behind his ears. The shot had been cropped from some kind of holiday snap, and he was smiling. He revealed perfect

Hollywood teeth.

"You bastard," I said.

"What?" asked Sellers, eyeing the picture.

I was almost funny. I'd been compromised from the very beginning.

In my haste to find Finbarr, I'd taken the chance of causing a ruck in town, making my presence felt. Well for once it had come back to bite me in the arse.

The guy in the early bar in Cork. The Welcome Inn. The guy with the pearly smile and the Sinn Fien badges in his pocket, had been no other than Sean Patrick McMullen, head quartermaster of the Provisional IRA.

He'd clocked me. No danger. It had been my impatience that had let me down.

There was no mole, there was no grass hiding inside MI6 or the CIA. It had been my own sloppy practice that had given the game away.

And by now, the alarm bells would be ringing that the boys at the farm couldn't be reached and McMullen would have half the gangsters in Ireland looking for this truck, these AK's, his cut of the money and yours truly.

"We're in the shite," I said. "I need to call Cartwright. This new team needs an early start."

## Lauren North's Story:

The knock on my door was insistent, as was the voice that went with it.

Not that I'd slept much.

I'd persuaded Cartwright to send Sellers to Ireland, rather than the stocking clad, Camilla, then spent much of the night considering that I'd made the wrong decision.

Sellers was just Rick's type.

Shrugging off those thoughts, I rolled off my cot and opened the door.

"Briefing, ten minutes, said the suit standing in the corridor. "Please be ready when I return to collect you."

I checked my watch, it was 0350hrs. Cartwright had said an 0800hrs briefing… something bad had happened.

"No breakfast in bed, then?" I joked.

The guy managed a weak smile and walked away.

There was a small shower cubicle in my room. A hotel style set of mini toiletries were piled in a chrome basket screwed to the wall, so I quickly stepped under the hot jet of water and did my best to get my shit together.

Eight minutes later, I stood wearing the same set of clothes I'd arrived in, towelling my hair dry and fastening it back in a ponytail.

At precisely 0400hrs, the knock came, and I was ushered along more long narrow corridors. The suit finally stopped at yet another green paint-ed entrance.

"This is you, Ma'am," he said.

I smiled. "Thank you."

I opened the door to find Des already seated next to Mitch Collins. Both were stuffing their faces with delicious smelling bacon sandwiches.

Des looked as perky as I'd seen him for weeks. He gestured to the pile of rolls on a table against the wall.

"Fill yer boots there, hen," he said. "Ne brown sauce like, but the piece is fresh."

Mitch gave Des a look. "Piece?"

"Bread," I offered."

"Ah," nodded the big Yank. "That makes sense… not."

"You sound chirpy," I said to the Scot. "You've got your colour back, too."

Des stood and stamped his wounded foot on the floor. "I'm brand new, hen. I'm like the six million dollar man."

"What did they do to you?" I asked.

"Eh, fuck me hen. Dinnea ask that question, ye might not live long enough for the explanation like."

"Really?" I said.

"Everyone got something to eat?" said a deep American voice from behind me.

I turned to see a man in his early forties. He was of medium height with a boxer's physique, his shaved head and fine chiselled features accentuating his shiny black skin.

This guy moisturised.

He stepped over to the table full of sandwiches, lifted the top from one and then turned to the group.

"No vegetarians, I hope."

I shook my head. Des confirmed his meat eating status by grabbing a second sandwich.

"Good," he said. "Okay, for those of you that don't know me, my name is, Varèse. First name Theo, but everyone calls me Marvin."

"After the boxer there?" asked Des through a mouthful of bacon.

"Exactly," said Varèse. "I picked up the nickname as a grunt in the Corps and it never left me."

"Fair one," said Des. "Could have been a lot worse."

Marvin smiled to reveal unsurprisingly perfect teeth. "So it could, Mr Cogan. So it could."

Marvin pulled up a chair.

"First of all, let me apologise for the rude awakening at such an un-Godly hour, but the situation with Mr Fuller and Ms Sellers over in Ireland is extremely fluid right now, and we have a change of priorities."

"Meaning?" I asked.

"Meaning that we now know that Mr Fuller was compromised early into this operation, and that in turn now puts him and Ms Sellers in extreme danger."

I flopped down in a chair and waited.

Marvin clasped his hands together and rested his elbows on his knees.

"It would appear that Mr Fuller was recognised in a bar in Cork by a man by the name of Sean Patrick McMullen."

"I know that name," said Des. "But he's dead. We blew the hell out of his house back in the late eighties."

Marvin shook his head. "Apparently not. He is very much alive."

"Well, even so," said Des. "I cannea see how the boy would recognise Rick, we've never met him close up."

Varèse nodded.

"As I understand it, some ten years after the operation you mention there, Mr Fuller was the subject of an assassination attempt by the IRA, where his wife was sadly murdered."

"Aye, that's true," said Des.

"Well," said Marvin. "We know that the persons who gave Mr Fuller's attackers the details of his family home, also gave them his photograph. That was kept by the PIRA along with many other shots of police and military personnel. Our understanding is that this collection still exists, runs into the hundreds, and is still in the possession of McMullen himself."

Des blew out his cheeks. "Them fuckers have a lot to answer for," he said.

"They do," said Marvin. "But I'd appreciate it if you would refrain from profanity there Mr Cogan."

Des shot me a look, then turned to Marvin.

"Did you and Mitch go to the same bible classes as kids?"

Marvin's eyes grew dark.

"My religion is my strength, Sir. I've fought many battles alongside Mr Collins and stood in many a church with him, too. Now, Mitch and I may disagree on some things, and I'm sure we all will have our moments, but it is my job to get Mr Fuller and Ms Sellers from their present location, safely to the port of Kinsale, so they can negotiate this transaction. Once that is achieved, all six of us, under my leadership, will begin the long tail of those weapons, in the hope they lead us to Abdallah Al-Mufti."

"Halleluiah to that," said Des.

Marvin soldiered on.

"We feel," said Marvin, standing. "That as Mr O'Rourke was cruelly tortured, much of our intelligence could be compromised including the location of the drop and identities of the buyers. However, we don't believe that McMullen will do anything to jeopardise this deal by warning off the Bosnians. He needs this business to go ahead. His criminal gang are desperate for the cash and won't want to scare the buyers off by talk of MI6 or the CIA sniffing around the place. No, the bottom line here is, McMullen's men are now gangsters rather than soldiers. They need cash. They need those AK's back."

Mitch rubbed the top of his head with a giant hand.

"I reckon they won't risk any fireworks at the drop, Sir."

"I agree," I said. "They'll try and take them on the road. The IRA are masters of the ambush."

This posturing from the American was all well and good. However, no one had noticed the elephant in the room. How would Rick feel about being relieved of his command? I'd kept my mouth shut, but Des was a different matter.

"Now, let me get a few things straight in my head here, Mr Varèse. Have you ever been to Ireland?"

"I have not," he said. "The majority of my combat experience has been in Iraq, but…"

Des cut him short. "Have you ever met Richard Fuller?"

"I have never had that privilege, Sir."

Des nodded slowly. I could see that his dander was up.

"So, let me explain something to ye. One, Rick and my good self have spent years on the Emerald Isle. We've fought street battles in Belfast, tracked terrorists through South Armagh and dropped in HALO into Co Kerry. We know men like McMullen, we know what they are capable of. We know how they think and how the hierarchy of the Provisional IRA works. We know the weather and the ground. So, I'll ask ye this. What qualifies you to lead this team? Because right now. I don't see it."

Right on cue, in walked Cartwright. Considering he'd had less sleep than us all, he looked immaculate. Black Savile Row three piece, white shirt and striped tie.

Surprisingly, it was his clothing that he referred to.

"Recognise the tie, Cogan?" he asked sharply.

Des turned, had a look and shook his head.

"Royal Inniskilling Fusiliers," said Cartwright proudly. "I remember when I joined up, all the old boys would tell their tales of war and battle and I would jealously listen. You see, before my time, the 1st Battalion was engaged for many months hunting insurgents in the jungles of Malaya. In '52 the chaps were posted to the Suez Canal, and afterwards to Kenya, where they helped to suppress the Mau Mau uprising. It was a vicious, terrible conflict."

"Aye," said Des. "But you'd be too young to see those actions."

"On those occasions, yes, Cogan. But I ask you this. When later in my military career, I was sent to Ireland on a completely different matter, one of the utmost importance, I was given the choice of whom I would take with me. Now, do you think I chose the chap who had spent all his career fighting the Irish, or a man who had seen jungles, deserts, oceans and mountains?"

"That would be up to you, pal," said Des.

"Quite," offered Cartwright. "And unless someone has recently superseded my orders, I have chosen Mr Varèse to lead this mission both in Ireland and beyond. Do I make myself clear?"

That was us told.

## Rick Fuller's Story:

I pulled the truck around the corner, away from the main road and killed the lights.

"So, you deliberately caused a ruckus in this bar, to flush out O'Rourke?" asked Sellers as she emptied more of the contents of her Bergen around the cab.

"That's about the strength of it," I said, trying to make sense of all the various bits of kit.

"He was a bit on the eccentric side was our Finbarr, the Firm had lost him, and the clock was ticking, so it seemed like a good idea at the time... What's all this shit?"

Sellers tapped two tiny grey boxes perched on the dash. "Tracking devices, darling. I'm going to pop those two inside a couple of the crates in the back... So, this guy that clocked you, you didn't recognise him?"

"McMullen? No chance. I'd only ever seen the first picture you have there, and that was back in 1987. I'd figured the face in the bar was a Sinn Fien boy, it was written all over him, but I didn't have him down as a major player at all."

"So how do you think he identified you?"

I picked up what looked suspiciously like a limpet mine. "Probably my shite Belfast accent... Why the fuck have you brought these?"

"For the boat," offered Sellers, picking up one device. "Latest tech these. I'll tell you, there's some wacky shit knocking about in that basement at Canary Wharf. I felt like Miss Moneypenny."

"What do you mean, 'for the boat'?"

She cocked her head.

"Ah, well, you see Cartwright is insistent that we don't lose the AK's. So, these little babies are a bit of insurance. MILA's, smart limpet mines. They incorporate a detonation system controlled by a computer. They can be remotely detonated from anywhere in the world. In this case, from Cartwright's office. Basically, if things go tits up, and we lose our targets, the boat goes to the bottom with the booty."

"But we have the trackers."

"Belt and braces, Fuller."

"And who is going to attach these little babies to the hull? That's a diver's job."

"I am."

"You?"

"I got my bronze medallion in lifesaving at school."

I shook my head and checked my Rolex. "The team should be on the ground now. I'm going to try Lauren and organise an RV."

# Des Cogan's Story:

Its amazing what can be achieved if the will is in place, eh?

By 0450hrs we were at London City airport and boarding a private jet to Cork.

Armed with no more than fake documents, some personal radios, good waterproofs and a few hundred euros each, the plane lifted off exactly ten minutes later.

The flight took me back to the time when we had first sought out Mc-Mullen and his stash of explosives, intended to murder and maim RUC officers in Belfast.

At least this time, I didn't have to jump out of the fucking plane.

I had genuine concerns about Theodore 'Marvellous Marvin' Varèse. Even though Mitch had done his best to convince me the guy was the real deal, I felt he was there for the wrong reasons, to placate the Yanks, rather than for good operational sense. I also knew that he would have to lock horns with Rick to gain control of the team, no matter what Cartwright said.

And that could get messy.

I felt the same about Sellers, to be fair. No matter how good someone looks on paper, you're taking a massive chance on a mission like this. When you bring a new face along it can mean trouble, and I wondered why Lauren had been so keen for Victoria to take the place of the wee girl Cartwright had selected.

Some questions are best left un-asked though, eh?

Still, on the plus side, whatever the good Doctor did to me back in London, appeared to have worked, and other than a really weird feeling of tightness around the wound, my foot was almost brand new. So, feeling at least physically fit, and with the knowledge that the nucleus of our team would be working together, I settled down for the short hop to Ireland.

Thirty six minutes later we touched down, and using our shiny new driving licences, we hired two cars. A nondescript silver Ford and a larger VW SUV.

As usual, our plan was simple. Escort the wagon containing the AK's the ten or so miles from its current location to the port. Keep an eye on Rick and the wee lassie whilst the deal was conducted, then get ready to follow that boat wherever it decided to go.

I was in full agreement with Lauren. The players would try and hit the truck on the R600 between Riverstick and the harbour at Kinsale. The boys would lie in wait, use the land as their friend, and attack us from a position of strength.

McMullen's problem would be that he would have to rustle up men at short notice. Not easy in these times of alleged peace and tranquillity. I reckoned that whoever he found would be down the terrorist pecking order and not too switched on. After all, from what I'd been told, Rick had already slotted eight of his best men.

Whoever they found to take us on, would be in for a nasty surprise, too, and I was confident that with the overwhelming firepower at our disposal, we could pull this little job off and be on our way to France in no time.

After all, we had eight hundred AK47's to play with.

The Yanks had taken the Ford and Lauren sat next to me in the VW as I drove. She'd been quiet all journey. Pensive, withdrawn.

Whatever was or wasnea going on between her and Rick, I was confident that they wouldn't let their personal problems interfere with the job in hand.

She had a map spread across her knee and squinted at it using the interior light in our car.

"We just stay on this road," she said. "Once we pick up the truck, it's no more than a fifteen minute drive from Riverstick, to the port."

I detected a slight tremor in her voice.

"The lay of the land worries me," she said.

"It's fighting country," I explained. "Just like Scotland."

She nodded wistfully.

"Apart from one small village, Belgooly, it's pretty much open country all the way with deep ditches either side of the road. Ideal if you just want to lie in wait for a slow moving convoy."

"Or plant a nice wee IED, hen," I offered.

Lauren looked out of the window into the darkness. She looked genuinely concerned.

"The fuckers could be out there right now, nicely dug in, waiting."

Her phone buzzed, and she hurriedly answered. From the tone of her voice, I knew instantly that it was the big man himself.

"Okay," she said. "Yes, fine. I can see it here now. We'll be less than ten minutes. You okay? Yes, I'm good, thanks." She looked over at me. "He's fine too, strangely enough. Okay, okay."

And she closed the call.

"He's parked in a side road, here," she said tapping the map. As Lauren caught my eye, I thought I saw fear in her face.

"I don't like this, Des. I've got a bad feeling."

## Rick Fuller's Story:

Sellers clambered into the back of the truck and began to open some crates. She needed to secrete the tracking devices into two of them and, as we were both of a mind that this little job was about to turn nasty, we figured that some extra firepower wouldn't go amiss.

The Bosnians wouldn't miss the odd AK, eh?

I still had my BAP, MAC10 and the Irishman's Uzi, but when you needed real punching power, there was no replacement for a fully automatic 7.62 rifle.

"Well, well," said Sellers as she opened the first crate. "Did you actually have a look inside these boxes before you set off, Fuller?"

"No," I said. "Strangely enough, I was in a bit of a hurry. Don't tell me. Make my day. They're full of fuckin' teddy bears."

Sellers pulled a rifle from the crate, racked back the action and checked the spout before throwing it down to me.

"Jackpot," she said.

The guns had been described as AK47's. Now, the first AK's were initially a fixed stock weapon, but by the time the first production models were in service, Kalashnikov had already produced the AKS. The S standing for Skladnoy, meaning folding, in Russian. I opened the underslung stock on the weapon in my hand and had a closer look. At first glance that's what I thought we had, but…

"These are AKM's," shouted Sellers as she rooted deep into a crate pushing one of the tiny grey trackers into a corner and covering it with packaging.

"AKMS actually, Sellers. The M is for modernizírovann which means…"

"Modernised," said Sellers, dropping down from the rear of the truck and wiping her hands on her jeans. "The most ubiquitous variant of the entire AK series of firearms."

She inspected her own rifle and slipped in the magazine. "Strangely beautiful, don't you think, Fuller?"

I shook my head, "You know your AK's I'll give you that… And I think, you're a bit crazy."

"When you fight the Afghans, you get to know these babies pretty quickly. And yes, it's been said before, darling. I'm mad as a hatter."

My phone buzzed. It was a text from Lauren.

*Thirty seconds.*

As the two cars approached our position, I considered how much fun this was going to be. I mean, think about it. Here we had, a real life Captain, with proper battle experience in the form of posh totty of the year candidate, Victoria Sellers. Mr Theodore 'Marvellous Marvin' Varèse, genuine US war hero and Cartwright's choice to lead this mission… and then of course, you had me.

I didn't give a fuck what the old spy in Whitehall said. This was my team.

The moment the crew debunked, I made my presence felt and began barking orders.

"Sellers, issue each of these guys with an AK and two full mags, please. Mitch, good to see you. Grab Des and take out the rear window of the Ford… Oh, and do the two rear passenger windows in the VW slide all the way down?"

"No, Sir," he said.

"Okay, remove those too, then, pal."

Much to my satisfaction, everyone got straight onto it and Marvellous Marvin kept his mouth shut.

Nevertheless, my mood was about to change dramatically.

Lauren strode over. Beautiful, businesslike, purposeful. Her eyes never leaving mine, growing ever closer with each resolute step.

I'll tell you this and you can believe what you like. The very moment I looked in those eyes, I knew.

I just fucking knew.

"Hi, you okay?" she said, her lips suddenly trembling, eyes filling with tears. Guilt etched on her face like a written confession.

My whole body was screaming. I swallowed big lumps of jealousy. Chewed on them. I hated myself for feeling the way I did, and at that very moment, I hated Lauren North for what she'd done to me. But him? Lawrence? Oh, there was a special place in my heart for that bastard.

I could see she was about to cry.

"It ain't the place for this, sweetheart," I said, and gestured towards Sellers. "Get an AK and I'll brief everyone presently."

"I think you'll find that falls under my remit, soldier."

I turned towards the voice.

Theo Varèse was standing with his arm outstretched, broad smile, hand offered.

"You must be Richard Fuller," he said, in a deep Southern State accent.

I took his hand but gave him the hard stare.

"I am, and I'm fully aware of Cartwright's wishes and instructions, but right now, I don't have the time to play pissing contests with you, Varèse. I know why you're here. But I also know this team, I know this country and I know the enemy, so…"

"And, I'm very much aware of your experience," said Varèse, his grip faltering and smile fading. "But I'm in command here, Mr Fuller. Her Majesty's government have given the US security services their utmost assurances regarding the outcome of this operation. I'm here to ensure that they don't renege on their side of the bargain."

He finally let go of my hand. "Now, I've worked alongside Mitch here on more than one occasion…"

"In Iraq," I said. "You worked with Mitch in Iraq."

Varèse screwed up his face. "That may be so…"

"So, what I'm saying here… *Marvin*. Is that if we were about to take on Saddam's finest, I'd leave you and Mitch here to it… but we're not… therefore to coin one of your American phrases. That means, you ain't the man."

## Des Cogan's Story:

I could see this little meeting of minds going tits up. Rick and Marvin were stood toe to toe. Rick was a good four inches taller than the American and a bigger guy all round. But Varèse had a fighter's build. He looked and moved like a boxer, and that normally meant, he'd punch like one, too.

"Have you forgotten how to follow orders, Fuller?" said Varèse, voice raised a notch and taking a step back to give himself room to move. "I thought you were a soldier?"

I saw Rick roll his neck… not a good sign. "Trooper, Varèse. I was a Trooper and note the past tense. I don't take orders from anyone anymore."

"Well, you're going to take them from me, Fuller, or stand down from this operation. None negotiable."

"You think so? And how are you going to enforce that little fairy-tale, Marvin?"

It was a split second from going off. The most disciplined of men are prone to playing my dick is bigger than yours once in a while. Just not at such a crucial point in the mission.

Sellers strode over from the back of the truck and pushed herself between both men. She shoved Rick square in the chest.

"Back off, Fuller!"

Rick looked shocked, but before he could say a word, she'd turned and given our American friend the same treatment.

"Step away Varèse! Now! Do as I say."

She stood between the two men with a furious look on her face, hands on hips.

"Right," she spat. "Technically, I outrank all of you by some way, but unlike you pair of sweethearts, I'm able to use my brain for the greater good. More importantly, *I've* left my fucking skirt and heels at home."

Varèse opened his mouth to speak.

Sellers held up a finger and wagged it in his face.

"No, Marvin. Listen up. I know all about your antics and medals during Viking Hammer and I know that being a member of SAD makes you an extraordinary fighting man. However, I too, have fought in those mountains and seen more action there than in any place on the planet. But this..." she waved a hand towards the darkened countryside, "This, is a whole different ballgame, Marvin. This is urban warfare, of which you have no experience. Fuller and Cogan have spent half their adult lives fighting over here. So, this is how this little contest is going to pan out."

She turned to Rick. "Fuller, you will take charge from here until the sale is made. Varèse, the moment we leave these shores, the team is yours. Now... can we get on for fuck's sake?"

There was a long silence as both men eyed each other suspiciously. Finally, each gave a short, almost imperceptible nod and the deal was struck.

Sellers strode past me and resumed filling mags with 7.62. I left my car stripping duties for a moment and followed, tore open a box of rounds, and began to give her a hand.

"That was impressive, Ma'am," I said.

"Men are like overgrown children, Cogan. Sometimes they have to share their toys and like it." She looked up from her task and gave me a smile. For the first time I noticed just how handsome a woman she was.

"Well, ye sorted it, that's fer sure," I said.

Her smile broadened. "Fuller's face was a picture, wasn't it?"

## Lauren North's Story:

He knew. Of course, he fucking knew. It must have been written all over my face. That, and whatever Cartwright had actually said to him behind my back, had given me away.

I watched him organising the crew. A man totally focused on his task. Not once did he look over towards me. Not once did he give me a second glance.

I collected my AK, slid in the magazine, stuffed the spare in my jacket pocket and made the weapon ready. Sellers was hammering lids back on crates in the rear of the truck.

"You okay?" she asked. "You look out of sorts."

I managed a smile, but it was short lived. "Have you got a man in your life, Sellers?"

She crawled out from between the boxes of weapons and sat on the tail of the ageing wagon. "Strange question at this point in the proceedings?"

"Oh, you know, just asking."

She followed my gaze and saw just who I was watching.

"Ah," she said. "The oldest story in the world."

"Meaning?"

"Meaning, how many women are sitting at home right now, wondering, what if? What if I'd made different choices? What if I'd left? What if I'd taken Mr Handsome up on his offer?"

I turned my head and caught Sellers eye. "What if I've already taken Mr Handsome up on his offer, and now, I realise I've fucked up?"

"He knows?"

I nodded.

"And you were together at the time?"

"Not exactly, but we were getting there."

Sellers slid off the tail of the truck and zipped up her jacket.

"Not exactly… now that is an interesting phrase, darling. I followed a 'not exactly,' all the way to Kurdistan. We were like a pair of dogs in the pound with a wire mesh fence separating us. All the time that fence was there, we were desperate to be together. Yet the moment the fence was removed, we couldn't wait to build another one."

"He was Army?"

"Had been. He was working out in Basra in what was politically labelled, an advisory capacity. Basra was a mess. There was no clear idea about what we were trying to achieve and certainly no resources being put aside to do it. The Americans came in all heavy handed and the Brits began to take casualties as a result. We both thought that we had seen enough fighting to last us a lifetime and decided that a return to Blighty and civvy street was the answer. Not so. The moment we left Iraq, something changed. You must understand that, Lauren? Come on, you've gone from being a nine to five kind of girl, to this. Could you really go back?"

I shrugged. "I don't know. I feel so confused."

Sellers' eyes glazed slightly. "Simon, that was his name, he persuaded me that we would be happier back in the Middle East, doing what we did best. He found a private security firm that would employ us both in the Kurdish region of Iraq. Good money, lots of excitement, lots of danger."

"So, the fence was back up again, no time for normality?"

"See, you already know the score, Lauren. Men like Simon, men like Fuller and Cogan, they will never change, never grow up."

"You split then?"

"He was killed by an IED seventeen months ago. I was sitting next to him in the Land Rover and didn't even get a scratch. Figure that out, eh?"

"Oh my, I'm so sorry."

She shrugged and picked up her own rifle. "Best make sure this crew don't fall foul of the same trick."

My eyes widened. "What do you mean?"

"Meaning," said Sellers. "That this is ideal country for it. Come on, the IRA virtually invented roadside bombs."

"I suppose, but they wouldn't want to damage their goods, would they?"

Sellers nodded but her thoughts were elsewhere.

"Maybe, but who's taking the lead car?" she said, eyes unfocused.

The penny dropped, and I instantly knew what she was telling me.

I heard Rick raise his voice.

"On me guys, please."

We circled him.

"Okay," he said. "Lauren, you take the VW. You'll have the point"

That answered that one.

"Mitch and Marvin, you ride in the back with her. I'll drive the truck. Sellers, Des, you take the Ford and follow on… you'll be tail end Charlie. If we get a contact, we do our best to keep moving. Let's not have any hesitation here."

He held up the most recent picture of Sean Patrick McMullen.

"If we get the opportunity to take this boy out, we slot him there and then. And we don't take prisoners, are we one hundred percent on that?"

Nods all around.

"If we encounter any kind of roadblock, Lauren, you move out of my way and let the truck do the ramming. Once we arrive in Kinsale, we'll park up close to the old fort where there is natural cover. Don't forget we have another," he checked his watch. "Eighteen hours before the sale is supposed to take place and we will be vulnerable up until then. Should things go to shit, and we get split up. We'll RV back at the GAA ground where Sellers was dropped. Any questions?"

There were none.

I slipped myself into the driver's seat of the VW and propped my AK, muzzle down in the passenger footwell. Marvin and Mitch squeezed themselves in the back. The boys had torn out the parcel shelf and seat back, as well as the rear passenger windows. This gave the guys the widest arc of fire possible. Though it would be a chilly and uncomfortable ten miles or so to the port.

I started the engine and turned up the heater.

Rick strode over and handed Marvin a walkie talkie through the missing rear window.

"Eyes peeled, guys," he said and walked away without turning his head.

## Rick Fuller's Story:

I tested our comms and climbed into the wagon.

Sellers was standing by the passenger door. "Throw me down my Bergen, Fuller," she said.

I grabbed the heavy bag and pushed it out of the passenger window. Sellers caught it with both hands, opened the top and rooted inside.

Moments later, she pulled out a set of body armour, pushed two ceramic plates into slots front and back, climbed the step to the cab and pushed the set back through the open window.

"There you go, Fuller," she said. "Bit exposed up here, eh? Better safe than sorry."

I handed the kit back to her.

"Give it to Lauren, please. She has point."

Sellers shrugged. "Your call, boss" she said, holding out the Bergen.

I grabbed the sack and lay it across the double passenger seat. It was still very heavy.

"I thought you'd dropped those mines in the back with the AK's?"

She gave me a fleeting but beautiful smile. "I did, but a girl still needs to be prepared, Fuller."

With everyone in place, we set off along the R600 for Kinsale. The sun was just about to rise, and the sky was a clear deep violet. Had we been here in different circumstances, it would have been idyllic.

There was virtually no traffic on the road, although twice we encountered tractors with large buckets or other vicious looking attachments on their way to work the surrounding fields. Each time, the sight of them set my nerves on edge. The IRA have used farm machinery and diggers on several occasions to attack the police and military and I'd learned to trust nothing and no one.

We entered Belgooly just as dawn broke and trundled by the Church of the Sacred Heart. Shortly after that, we passed a small service station and picked up a dark coloured saloon car that pulled off the forecourt and slipped in behind us.

Des was straight on our comms.

"Blue Vauxhall Astra, two aboard, both male, Caucasian, late thirties. The woolly hats are a bit much for this time of year, don't ye think, pal."

"Balaclavas?" I asked.

"Aye, possible," said the Scot.

We were all skittish and a little wired. We knew McMullen wouldn't allow us to steal his money, but it was a guessing game as to how he would try to stop us.

Moments later, the Astra overtook. I closed the gap between the nose of the truck and Lauren's VW to make sure he didn't separate us. The boy just put his foot down and sped off into the distance and we all breathed a collective sigh of relief.

The final part of our journey saw the road run parallel with the river Stick. The sun was almost fully up and our little convoy cast shadows on the glistening water to our right.

With just two kilometres to run, I began to feel better. That was until the river turned east and split, and we hit the first of two bridges that we had to negotiate to take us into the port of Kinsale. This was the Ringnanean crossing.

Just before the bridge proper, is a left exit road, the L3215. On our map, the narrow lane was shown as a dead end.

But it wasn't.

Once upon a time, this small, tight road was the only river crossing. It formed a half-loop, re-joining the main drag at the other side of what is now the Ringnanean bridge. It had been blocked off for many years using concrete slabs, but the moment I saw a large JCB nestled in the jaws of the far exit, the hairs stood up on the back of my neck.

"Heads up," I said into my comms. "Check out the earth mover ahead."

It was only as our old wagon drew level with the side road, that I caught a glimpse of a similar seven and a half tonner to ours, parked just metres from the main road. When I clocked the blue Astra partly hidden behind it, I knew we were in deep trouble.

The R600 bridge is a low flat construction, fifty to sixty metres in length. As one of McMullen's boys pulled the digger across the road in front, blocking our path forwards, it was a simple matter for the boys parked in the side road to slip the truck in behind, and we were ambushed.

To make matters worse, the bridge was no more that ten feet above the river bed and the raised, tree lined banks on the right hand side of the road, gave any shooter cover, and a clear view of any traffic on the bridge.

We were sitting ducks.

## Lauren North's Story:

As the big yellow digger rolled across the road in front of our VW, Rick began barking his orders to the team. I saw armed men scuttling behind the machine, starting to take up positions in front of us.

Moments later, Rick's instructions were drowned out by the sound of Mitch and his AK. He leaned out of the window behind me and began laying down rounds towards the huge JCB. The terrific noise from the Kalashnikov punching at my eardrums.

I saw the glass in the cab of the machine crack and spider, and a man jump down from it, holding a rifle. As his feet touched the ground, there were two more sharp cracks from behind me. The guy's knees gave way and he fell to the floor.

I swung our car to the right and slowed to allow Rick to pass me as we'd agreed.

"He's too big to ram," shouted Rick into the radio. "Just drop behind me into cover."

Before I could think, my whole world exploded.

There were at least two men tucked in behind the massive wheels of the earth mover and they opened up on our car with their weapons set to fully automatic.

The VW's windscreen was instantly shattered and for a moment I was blind.

Varèse saw my issue, rolled himself to face forward and smashed at the screen with his AK. He immediately opened up from inside the car. Each round felt like someone was poking my eardrums with a pencil.

"They've got us blocked in," shouted Mitch over the bedlam.

"Fuller's right," bawled Varèse. "We need cover. Drop back. Drop back."

As I turned the wheel, we instantly took fire from unseen shooters somewhere on the riverbank to our right. Rounds clattered into our car's panels, the big calibre bullets slicing through the metal and tearing at the interior. I ducked instinctively, and in the heat of the moment, let my foot slip from the clutch.

I stalled the fucking car.

Mitch was back out of his window, firing in short bursts towards the tree line. Varèse clambered between the front seats and with the muzzle of his rifle resting on the dash, let go the AK on fully automatic towards the JCB.

I was now totally deaf from the gunfire. The barrage was incessant. Lumps of plastic trim flew around the inside of the car. Some rounds were so close, I could actually feel them against my face. We needed to move, we needed cover. I dipped the clutch and fired up the VW.

Then I was hit.

## Des Cogan's Story:

All journey, I'd been lying down with my belly flat to the floor pan of the wee Ford, risking an occasional peak out of the hole where the back window had once been.

The moment I heard Rick on the comms, I knew the shit had hit the fan.

I lifted my head and saw a wagon pulling out of a narrow side road behind us. As in ground to a halt, blocking the road, that same blue Astra that had passed us earlier came into view.

No sooner had I clocked the car than we began taking fire from somewhere off to our right, my left. Maybe from the river bank or the trees beyond. I couldnea see those boys, so I listened to my old instructor's voice in my head and concentrated on the Astra.

*Shoot at what you can hit, son.*

The Vauxhall had accelerated towards us, then slewed to a halt. The boys knew they had us in their wee trap, the road blocked both ahead and behind, so they debunked, firing as they went. This time the two players had pulled down their masks.

I lifted up my AK into the aim. "They willnea help ye, pal," I muttered.

I was doing my best to keep the Astra boys busy, but the shooters in the trees were tearing our little Ford to pieces, and it was only a matter of time before one or both of us was hit.

Sellers seemed to read my mind and nipped the little car up the inside of our truck, giving us some cover from the riverbank.

For a brief moment, we could get our heads up and take stock.

I scrambled straight out through the missing back window and, using the rear wheel of our truck as cover, began to give the two masked men behind more of their own medicine.

Finally, one of the players showed me a little too much balaclava and I caught him around the ear or throat. A fountain of claret sprayed into the air as he fell backwards, but he was instantly replaced by the driver of the wagon who ensured that I began to take heavy fire again.

Sellers crawled out of the driver's door and under our truck. She began taking aimed single shots towards the riverbank. Maybe she could see what I couldnea?

It was then that I heard those dreaded words from Mitch Collins.

"Man down… Man down."

## Rick Fuller's Story:

I'd begun to take fire the instant the JCB trundled across the road. I'd seen Mitch pop his head out of the offside of the VW and slot the boy that had driven the digger. Then, Lauren moved over as we'd agreed, but it was obvious to me that I had neither the weight or the power to knock the earth mover out of the way without writing off the truck and killing myself in the process.

That said, my main concern was that I'd been taking so much 7.62, that all I could do was hold the wheel steady whilst lying across the seats, driving blind and hoping for the best.

I'd told Lauren to slip the V Dub in behind me to give her and the Yanks some modicum of cover, but I couldn't see if they had made it or not.

I hit the air brake and the old wagon juddered to a stop. Dozens of rounds fizzed and spat around the cab as I crawled across the floor towards the passenger door, dragging my AK as I went.

I was covered in razor sharp shards of glass and plastic. All I could do was hope that a round didn't find its way through the engine bay and into my guts.

As I reached for the handle and gave the door a shove to open it, the window was instantly shattered, and the door skin was punctured by multiple rounds, tearing the metal open like tissue paper.

The noise was horrendous.

I dropped to the tarmac and saw that Sellers had pulled the Ford up my nearside. She and Des were out. Des firing back towards the Astra, whilst our newest recruit was under the truck and giving the boys in the trees the good news.

I'd just turned my attention to the players tucked in behind the JCB, when I heard Mitch's voice on the comms.

It was my worst nightmare. Lauren was hit.

I dipped my head and looked under the truck to see the V Dub stranded in the middle of the opposite carriageway some ten metres away. It looked like Lauren had been shot as she'd been in the process of pulling the car into cover. I could see her slumped over the wheel of the VW.

Her hair covered her face. She didn't move.

Varèse had jumped out of the motor and was backing up Des' efforts, laying down fire to the rear of our position. It appeared that even more of McMullen's men had taken up positions there to reinforce the boys in the Astra.

We were now taking heavy fire on three sides, and anyone who has ever been in a gun battle will tell you, if you are outflanked, you're in the shit.

We had two choices. Do one into the countryside behind us, or fight on.

I never was one for giving up, and I certainly wasn't leaving Lauren behind, or the AK's for that matter.

On hearing Mitch's transmission, Sellers had crawled further underneath our truck, and I saw her begin to make her way towards the VW. She was terribly exposed to fire from either side, but she showed great expertise and bravery as she rolled left and right, firing out towards the treeline between movements.

Either she'd been hitting the targets out there, or the boys on the riverbank were low on ammunition, because the onslaught from that position had slowed and it gave Varèse, Des and me precious seconds to take a closer look at the boys at either end of the bridge.

Whatever had gone on before, I had to admit Theo Varèse was a tremendous shot with the AK. He took out two players inside a minute, using short bursts and saving precious ammunition.

Mitch displayed lion-like bravery.

Reaching inside the VW, the American dragged Lauren across the passenger seat. He pulled her limp body out into the cordite filled air, as high velocity rounds sent sparks flying off the road surface all around him. I risked a short glance in his direction as he struggled with Lauren's apparently lifeless body. With herculean effort, he lay her on the glass covered ground.

Varèse and Sellers did their best to cover him as he worked on her.

I desperately wanted to go to help, but the cacophony of gunfire from both flanks was unrelenting and my job was to help keep the fuckers quiet and let the Yank do his job.

As I emptied my first magazine, my comms burst into life. "Fuller, come in. Fuller, can you hear me?" It was Sellers.

"Go ahead," I shouted over the unrelenting noise.

I dipped my head under the body of the truck, so I could see her position. She caught my eye and pointed to the cab.

"Bergen," she screamed as another burst of 7.62 was hurled in her direction. "Get the fucking Bergen."

Easier said than done.

The moment I made any movement back towards the cab door, I was met with a hail of gunfire.

Mitch had managed to drag Lauren underneath the truck and was checking her airway. I looked into his eyes. He gave me the slightest nod and a thumbs up and I felt a tremendous weight lift from me. At least she was alive.

My jealousy, my covetousness was washed away with that single movement. For that split second, life was good again.

I rolled forwards, landed on my feet for a change and pushed myself upwards towards the open door of the wagon. I instantly took fire and as I crawled across the floor of the cab, I felt a tremendous shock to my right boot.

The force of the impact tore at my ankle ligaments. It was as if someone or something had tried to rip off my foot.

Screaming in pain, I looked down to find a round had clipped the heel of my Timberland. It felt like Godzilla had hit my ankle with a seven pound lump hammer.

Taking in massive gulps of air, ignoring the agony and stretching my body, I found the Bergen that had fallen to the cab floor. Once I'd got a firm grip of it, I wiggled my way back out into the fight.

By the time I hit the tarmac again, Mitch had left Lauren lying in the recovery position, under the truck and had begun returning fire towards the JCB.

That took the heat off me for a few seconds as I rummaged in Sellers' Bergen. The second I put my hand inside, I realised what she had been screaming at me to recover.

One thing I had quickly learned about our very blue-blooded young recruit, was what she meant by being prepared.

I almost smiled as I pulled four M67's from the bag. The US made explosive fragmentation grenade has a spherical steel body that contains 6.5 oz of composition B explosive and weighs 14 oz in total.

Because of its size and shape, the Yanks call it, the baseball.

I bawled at Des, who gave me a sharp look over his shoulder.

"Let's finish this," I said, tossing him one of my new-found toys.

Des caught the spherical device and nodded. "Good job, pal. I'm almost out of ammo here."

I then rolled two more devices under our truck towards Sellers and the Americans.

Varèse didn't wait for my call, he simply grabbed the M67, pulled the pin, let the spoon slip from his fingers, did a mental two second count and threw his grenade towards the Astra and our enemies.

Not exactly in the rule book but fuck me it was effective.

The gunfire from behind was silenced in a split second and replaced by screams.

I tossed my grenade the twenty or so yards towards the JCB, and saw two figures decide that discretion was the better part of valour and make a run for it.

They were in the shit either way.

The grenade exploded, taking one man down with it, and Mitch picked off the second with his AK.

Varèse pulled the pin on his second grenade and with a throw any college quarterback would have been proud off, tossed it into the treeline. It exploded, sending branches crashing to the ground.

I held up a hand and bawled at my team to hold their fire.

Gingerly, I stood on my rapidly swelling ankle and took stock.

Other than the screams coming from behind the now ruined Astra, there was silence. If there were any boys left in the trees, they were dead, or they'd done one.

Des scrambled under the truck, desperate to tend to Lauren.

"She's taken a round to the chest, Mr Cogan," shouted Mitch. "Looks like it bounced upwards off the plate. Ms North is a very lucky lady."

Des cradled her head and she opened her eyes.

"This is lucky?" she asked.

"Aye," said the Scot. "I reckon it is."

"Where's Rick?" she said quietly. "Is he okay?"

"I'm here," I said, kneeling so she could see me.

She turned her head. There were tears forming in her eyes. She grimaced in pain.

"I'm so sorry," she said.

## Des Cogan's Story:

The R600 is not a busy road, but it needed to be opened and the carnage dragged away from the prying eyes of any early commuters to Cork.

Mitch and I walked the scene and put two wounded players out of their misery. The American held onto a modern day picture of McMullen and checked it against each corpse. Sadly, our quartermaster wasn't amongst our victims.

We rolled seven dead bodies into the hedgerows. Not having the time or inclination to start searching the riverbank or treeline, there could well have been another two or three out there.

Not a bad morning's work, eh?

We moved the JCB back into the far entrance and drove the battered VW, Ford and Astra around the wee looping road out of sight. Rick reversed the player's wagon up to the rear of our lorry as it was leaking oil and fuel and we transferred the AK's and ancillary kit to our new commandeered truck.

Twenty minutes after the last shots were fired, we were back on the road to Kinsale.

Thankfully, the second of the two bridges didn't hold any further surprises and, just as the town was waking up to a new, very pleasantly warm sunny day, we trundled into the port.

Rick parked the truck on an open square of land adjacent to the ancient fort. Everyone was tired, none more so than the big man himself, who hadn't slept more than a couple of hours for close on two days.

Lauren was very sore, and her head banged, but although she probably didn't feel it, she'd been very fortunate. I'd been hit square in the back during our battle against Stephan Goldsmith's men in Albania. That cracked a few ribs and knocked me cold.

However, Lauren's armour was modern day and had done a better job than our makeshift stuff. I sat examining her in the back of the truck, and she appeared not to have any broken bones, but she was disorientated and dizzy. Bullets do crazy things and the one that Lauren had taken had hit the ceramic plate of her armour and ricocheted upwards, grazing her temple and exiting through the roof of the VW. That graze would have felt like being hit with a sledgehammer. I managed to rustle up some meds for her and within seconds of removing the needle from her arm, she was asleep.

Rick wouldn't let me even look at his leg.

The round that struck him, had taken the heel straight off his boot, pushing the ankle joint in an unnatural direction and tearing the ligaments, often more painful than a clean break.

He'd hobbled around the truck chuntering away to himself until the shops opened, then went to buy himself some more boots.

He returned an hour later with six bags of footwear and clothes.

At first, I thought it was his OCD kicking in, until I realised that we were all dressed for urban combat rather than for strolling around a pretty fishing village in the height of the season.

The two Americans were our best form of decoy, as they fitted right in with the tourists. Rick handed Marvin and Mitch a bag apiece and sent them off to the quayside to hire a boat.

Well, we were going to need one.

I eventually persuaded Rick to jump in the back of the truck and get some shuteye. Within thirty seconds of him settling down between the crates of weapons, he was snoring.

That left Sellers and my good self to put the world to rights.

I'd left her watching Rick, Lauren and the truck whilst I found us hot sandwiches and coffee. When I returned, she had changed into the clothes that Rick had bought for her.

She sat on a low wall to the right of our wagon with her hair down and her face to the sun. There was no doubt, the girl was stunning.

"Here ye go," I said. Handing her a roll and coffee.

She smiled and took them gratefully. "Thanks, Cogan," she said, tearing open the bag and taking a large bite.

We ate in silence for a minute or two, before I broke it.

"Ye like yer formality there, don't ye, Victoria?"

She swallowed, took a drink of her coffee and nodded.

"I come from a family of academy, ceremony and solemnity, Cogan. Stiff upper lip doesn't even scratch the surface."

"I come from a family of righteous indignation."

She grinned at that. "Nothing wrong with a bit of good old Godly resentment, Cogan... I take it you are a Catholic?"

"Aye, I said. Realising I was talking to an officer with my mouth full. "I have to say though, I'm very much in the lapsed category these days."

Sellers cocked her head and looked at me quizzically. She took straight talking to another level.

"Is that why you spared the woman? You know, the one back in England, the traveller?"

I had a think on that one.

"She was saying the Lord's prayer, wasn't she?" pressed Sellers.

"Aye, but it wasn't for that."

"Then why?"

It was my turn to smile. "You ask a lot of questions for a posh bird."

"It's how one learns, Cogan."

"Aye it is. So, with that in mind. What on earth are you doing here with us?"

She looked across the ruined fort battlements and out into the basin.

"Simon Garcia," she said.

That knocked the wind out of my sails. "Si? Big lump of a fella? Sandy hair? Beard? Loved blowing stuff up?"

She didn't turn back to me, just nodded and studied the water.

"That's the chap. He worked with you guys for a while, didn't he? He was always talking about Fuller and Cogan and the good old days here in Ireland."

"I wouldnea exactly call them that, hen. So, you and him were...?"

Now she turned.

"An item? Yes, I suppose you could call us that. He was a lot like you two. Couldn't leave the job alone. When he left 22, he came to work in Iraq for one of those big American security companies. Not much different than a private army really. By the end of 2005, I'd finished my last tour and we decided to come home."

"Can't see Si as a home bird."

"He wasn't... I wasn't. So, he found another firm who were working alongside the Kurds and we went straight back to Iraq."

I shook my head and found my pipe. "Well, what a small world, eh hen? And how is the big man?"

She gave me a look that told me everything.

"When?" I asked.

"Almost a year and a half ago. Roadside bomb, just outside Mosul. We'd been there a matter of weeks."

I nodded.

"Shame that, good lad."

"He was... so when I found RDL Security's website and noticed the names Cogan and Fuller on there, I figured you might be worth a try."

I shook my head ruefully.

"Well, ye certainly have done that, hen. I can say, ye played a blinder out there on the road. Yer as good as any man I've seen."

"Thanks, Cogan."

"Des," I offered.

"If you don't mind," she said. "I'll leave it at Cogan."

## Lauren North's Story:

I woke to find Rick lying beside me, his arm draped around my waist. For a moment, I considered that we should just stay in Kinsale, slip out of the back of the truck, find one of those quaint bed and breakfast places we'd passed on the way in and try to mend our broken lives.

It wasn't to be, of course.

He opened his eyes and gave me a long look.

"How are you feeling?" he asked.

"Probably as good as you."

He sat up, stretched and checked his Rolex.

"Let's go find Des," he said.

We dropped down from the back of the wagon into bright sunshine. Des and Victoria were not hard to locate, they were sitting on part of one of the old battlements. They'd both changed their clothes and looked, to all intents and purposes, like a pair of holidaymakers.

Rick limped over.

"Any sign of the Yanks?" he asked.

Des shook his head. "Not so far."

"Maybe they've gone fishing," offered Sellers.

Rick gave her a look, rummaged in his pocket and pulled out a battered old Nokia.

"What's that?" asked Des.

"Finbarr's old phone," he said. "It has the numbers of our alleged buyers in it, Hamza and Imran."

He fired up the old brick.

"Don't know about you, but I reckon it's about time we made our presence felt."

He dialled the number and whoever was at the other end answered immediately.

"No, it's Devlin," said Rick in what I could only presume was his best attempt at a Belfast accent.

"O'Rourke is dead, murdered."

There was a silence, then he said. "They're all here... and the ammo. Where's the handover?"

Rick scribbled a name on a paper. "Okay, midnight as agreed."

He closed the call.

"Well?" asked Des.

"Ardkilly Ridge," said Rick.

"Sounds like a place for a last stand."

It was Varèse. He stood alongside Mitch and wiped his bald head with a tissue.

"You got a boat yet?" asked Sellers.

"Sure have, Ma'am," offered Mitch. "She's a real beauty too. All modern conveniences."

"You can sail?" asked Des warily.

"Of course," smiled Marvin. "I have my own boat down in the Glades."

"Aye," said Des. "That's all well and good, but this trip is going to be a wee bit different than a river cruise. This is the Celtic Sea we're talking about here, son."

Marvin waved a dismissive hand. "Aww, don't stress, man. These things virtually sail themselves."

Rick walked back to the truck, found a map, then returned to the group.

"Okay, here's the exchange point. Where's our boat right now, Varèse?"

Marvin took a quick glance at the map. "Here, the marina."

"Good," nodded Rick. "You pick her up, sail her and drop anchor... here, Lower Cove. From there you should be able to spot any decent sized craft entering the sound at Ardkilly. More importantly, you'll see them coming out again. Once the deal is completed, we will RV with you, here... at Sandy Cove beach. You and Mitch go pick up the boat. Stay in touch and try not to get fucking lost."

Varèse gave Rick a hard stare "Why do you guys always choose to use that dysphemism?"

"A what?" said Des.

"Dysphemism, repeated Varèse. "An expression with connotations that are offensive either about the subject matter or to the listener."

"Load o' shite," said Des.

Rick allowed himself a grin. "Sellers..."

"Aye aye, sir," she said, throwing up a mock salute.

"Are you still determined to fit these mines?"

"That's what Cartwright said, Fuller. Who am I to argue?"

"Okay. So, the rest of us will drive up to the spot now, check out the lay of the land and where Sellers can get in and out of the water, undetected."

Des turned to me and lowered his voice. "Mines? What the fuck is going on here, hen?"

"I don't know," I said. "But I don't like the sound of it."

## Rick Fuller's Story:

We all stood at the front of the truck. I held the keys in my hand and squinted in the bright sunshine.

"It's going to be a long night," I said. "We okay for food? Water?"

"We could do with a few bits," said Lauren.

I nodded. "There's a service station come mini market on the main drag, we need diesel, anyway. I'll stop there."

Des and Sellers clambered in the back of the truck, leaving Lauren and me to sit rather awkwardly in the front.

As I pulled the wagon out of the car park, I could sense her eyes on me.

"Don't say anything," I said. "Not now. Wait until this is over."

"There's that fence again," she said.

"What?"

"It doesn't matter, Rick. Just drive."

I pulled into the garage.

Des stepped straight to the pump and began to fuel the truck, whilst the girls went into the mini market for supplies.

"I'm bursting," I said to the Scot. "You seen the bog?"

He gestured towards a hand written sign on the wall by the pay booth. I nodded and wandered around the back of the services.

I'd done what my body needed me to do and began to wash my hands at the sink. Again, I found myself examining my face in the mirror, only this time, the mirror wasn't glass at all. It was made of polished metal which distorted my features.

Even so, I looked tired.

*What fence was she on about?*

I splashed cold water on my face and reached for a paper towel. As I opened my eyes again, I heard the door of the toilet open.

I had company.

It was none other than Sean Patrick McMullen and he didn't look happy.

He was very pale and unsteady.

In his right hand he held a SIG Sauer P226. He clutched his stomach with his left, and I could see blood seeping through his fingers. His pure white hair brushed back over his forehead was streaked with claret.

"Richard Edward Fuller," he said quietly, stepping carefully behind me. "I have waited so long for this."

"I hope you're not disappointed," I said.

"Take the Browning from your belt and drop it in the waste basket there, sonny."

I eyeballed him through the mirror. He waved the SIG to make his point. I did as I was told.

"You have caused me a great deal of problems, Mr Fuller," said McMullen, wincing in pain, yet keeping the SIG firmly pointed at my back.

"It's what I do best," I said. "I like to be a thorn in the side to the average terrorist."

He smiled. Those fucking shiny teeth that always annoyed the life out of me smeared with his own blood. He was in a bad way, which didn't bode well for yours truly. The boy had nothing to lose.

"The moment I saw you in the bar," he coughed. "I knew it was you. You haven't changed much in twenty years." He staggered slightly but straightened and held the gun firm. "Her Majesty's SAS Trooper, dishonourably discharged, and now what? Thief, gun runner. How the mighty have fallen, Fuller."

"You seem to know a lot about me."

He snorted, and blood trickled from his nose. He didn't even appear to notice.

"People tend to tell the truth after the second kneecap," he said.

So, Fin had kept to our back story, despite his agony. Brave boy... deserved a medal.

"We all have to make a living," I said. "And I do enjoy ripping you Paddies off... Just like old times."

"Aye," said McMullen. "I hear you relish doing the dirty work for Manchester's drug dealers and pimps these days. So, in a way, what I'm about to do, well, it's almost a public service."

I had to smile at that.

"Yeah, you always were a pillar of the community, McMullen. You'd kneecap your own mother if you thought she'd rob you of a euro."

"But it's you who's robbing me, isn't it, Fuller? I have to say, I'd had you down as a company man. More in the MI6 category, doing Whitehall's bidding. But you fell off the perch, didn't you? After Cathy, I mean. After Paddy and Tommy paid you a visit. That's how I recognised you. Paddy O'Donnell had your picture you see?"

"I gathered."

"He was given it by… "

"I know the story, McMullen. I made it my life's work"

"Yes, of course you did… And now you have your vengeance. Tommy Brannigan died slowly, you know?"

"Every cloud," I said.

His breathing was shallow and even through the grubby mirror, I could see his pupils were dilated. The bullet wound to his gut must have caused some serious damage. His body would be pumping epinephrine, into his bloodstream to try and fix the problem. His pulse banging in his head, his muscle strength waning, blood pressure dropping. He was dying.

McMullen gulped air.

"Y'know, I didn't have you down as a gun runner, Fuller. Getting in bed with scum like O'Rourke. Just goes to show, ye can't trust anyone these days."

He stumbled slightly but recovered his composure.

"I'd hoped that Tommy's sons would see to you, but sadly they failed me. Then, there was always the possibility of taking you out on the road, but, as you well know, it wasn't to be."

"Sorry to disappoint you… And it looks like you caught one of your own rounds. That's brightened my day."

"I'll live long enough," he said baring those teeth again. "Long enough to see you dead…"

I heard the safety click, and then the crack of a pistol hurt my ears, but nothing else.

I turned to see Sellers standing in the doorway, arm outstretched and that beautiful R9 smoking in her hand.

McMullen had slid down the wall, a line of his own blood etching his progress along the plaster.

"We can't leave you alone for a minute, can we, darling?" she said.

I gave her a look. "Help me shove him in the cubicle, Sellers… He's a dead weight."

*  *  *

Ardkilly Ridge is actually a narrow road that runs alongside the banks of the river Bandon at a place called Sandy Cove. The thin stretch of water is shallow at low tide and is popular with small pleasure boats.

We got the truck as close to the water's edge as possible and Lauren got a brew on whilst I sat alongside Des on the pebbled shoreline, looking down the inlet towards the open sea.

"Quiet spot this," I said.

Des smoked his dreadful pipe as we watched Sellers wade into the river.

"It is, bet it makes for fine fishing, though."

"Never could get my head around that."

"Peace, mate," said Des. "Peace and quiet."

He changed the subject. "Hey, remember Si Garcia, pal?"

I nodded. "Course I do. He was part of our patrol when we went after McMullen first time around. We should have gone back to his house and slotted that fucker back then."

Des tapped his pipe on the heel of his boot and refilled it. "Probably right, pal... anyway," he made a show of nodding towards Sellers. "They were an item. Met in Basra. Si was working for some Yank security firm."

"Jesus, small world, eh?"

"He was killed last year. Roadside bomb."

I shook my head. "Oh dear."

Des lit his pipe again and took a long drag. "Apparently, he talked about us a lot, and when she saw our names on the RDL website, well, that's why she applied."

"She's good. No doubt about that."

"Aye, but she's fucked up, too. Lauren says that she was in the same Snatch Land Rover as Si when the bomb went off. Sat right next to him. She never had a scratch."

"When it's your time, eh?" I said.

Sellers walked over. "Fucking brass monkeys," she shouted. "But I reckon I can get in and out without a problem."

"Good," I said. "Des was just telling me about Si Garcia."

She looked at the Scot and then to me. "Some people have a big mouth," she said, and walked off.

\* \* \*

With the tracking devices safely in place and the mines stowed in the long grass a safe distance from our position, all we had to do was wait.

Night fell, and with no ambient light to spoil their show, the stars came out in abundance. Yet again, I was left feeling that had things been different, I would have loved to spend more time on this beautiful island.

At 2320hrs, my comms crackled into life. It was Varèse. A vessel big enough to transport our cargo was making its way up towards our position.

Ten minutes later we saw the navigation lights on the boat in the distance.

I turned on the headlights of the wagon to guide them in. Des and Lauren sorted their weapons out and took up their positions.

Game on.

Just before midnight, the boat dropped anchor and killed its engines. Once again, the night was silent apart from the lapping water.

I stepped forward. Lauren and Des flanking me. All of us armed, ready, tense.

Two men appeared on deck. Both were tall, slender and sported full beards. They wore dark coveralls and gloves. Both carried rifles.

"Devlin?" one shouted.

"Aye, that's me," I said, doing my best with the accent. "Will you be Hamza?"

"I am… but we need to check the cargo," he said. "To be sure it's all there."

"And I need to see the colour of your money."

A third and fourth man appeared on deck. Both carried M16's. I heard Des rack his AK. Violence filled the air. Hamza held up a hand towards his men.

"We all need to feel secure, Mr Devlin," he shouted. "With O'Rourke gone, we feel nervous. He vouched for you, but we are most anxious."

Hamza lay down his weapon on the deck and showed his empty hands.

"Can I come ashore and take a look at the merchandise?" he shouted.

"You may," I said, removing my Browning from my belt and handing it to Des.

The boy stepped forward and pushed a gangplank onto the pebbles. In my peripheral vision, I could just make out the dark shape of Sellers as she waded silently into the water, fifty metres away.

Hamza strode confidently down the plank and held out a hand.

I took it.

"What happened to O'Rourke?" he asked.

"There was an argument about the price," I said. "The old guard got greedy."

"Money is a terrible curse, Mr Devlin."

"Only when you don't have any," I said.

I opened the rear doors of the truck and Hamza climbed up onto the tail. He prised open the first crate and pulled a rifle from it.

"Nice," he said. "Very nice indeed. You are a man of your word, Mr Devlin."

"I am," I said.

Hamza jumped down from the truck and shouted to his men. "Imran, Ivan, Josip. Come now, move the goods aboard."

It was my turn to halt the proceedings.

"Steady there, my friend. Let's you and I go to your boat, there. You can show me the money. Then you can load the goods, and we'll all relax a wee bit."

Hamza thought for a moment, then smiled.

"This makes me happy," he said and beckoned me aboard.

We climbed the plank and Hamza stepped below deck. I followed, finding myself standing in a small cabin that had a square table fastened to the centre of the polished wood floor. Hamza disappeared into a second room for a moment and returned with a briefcase. He dropped it in front of me.

"Three hundred and twenty thousand euro," he said dramatically.

I pulled some random bundles from the case, checked that they were as they should be and closed it again.

"All there," I said. "Let's crack on, eh?"

"Of course," said Hamza.

We made our way onto the deck again and watched as Hamza's boys got on with it. They worked methodically, opening each crate in turn, then re-securing the lid before carrying it onto the boat. Twenty minutes later, the crates were aboard, and I made to leave with the cash.

As I picked up the case, Hamza stood in my way. "Please, Mr Devlin. The tide is in our favour for at least an hour. Will you have a small drink of tea with me to celebrate our business venture?"

I instantly smelled a very large rat. "I'm a coffee drinker myself, son," I said.

"Yes, yes, of course you are, how impolite of me. Coffee then."

He turned and shouted behind him. "Imran! Coffee for our friend."

It was a play for time, we all knew it was. Off to my left I could see Des moving himself into cover. Lauren was in the kneel, tucked into the trucks front wheel arch. AK in the aim. I couldn't see Sellers, but I knew she was there. If this went off, there would be no winners.

Out of the corner of my eye, I saw the boy, Imran, appear from below. He carried a circular metal tray, balancing it, one handed. Behind him was a big brute of a man. Shaved head, black t-shirt, shoulder holster.

"Ha," offered Hamza. "The very best Columbian."

Black t-shirt stood behind Imran, hands clasped in front of him, eyeing me closely.

It was then I saw it. There, on his hand, sat between thumb and forefinger, picked out in the moonlight. That simple tattoo of the sail in the wind. This guy was indeed Yunfakh.

Imran held the tray under my nose. Sitting there were two small cups of coffee. Next to those were the two tiny grey transmitters Sellers had concealed in the crates.

Hamza's smile receded, his dark eyes turning black as the night.

"You try to betray me, Mr Devlin," he whispered. "Although, that is not your true name, I'm sure. This, of course is not my issue. We will concern ourselves with such trivialities at a later date. But for now," he picked up the transmitters and tossed them onto the shore. "For now, you will be our guest."

T-shirt gave me a gentle reminder with the pistol and I held up my hands to show all watching the proceedings that I had a gun in my back.

Hamza turned to the crew on the shoreline. "One shot," he shouted. "Just one shot in our direction and we will kill your friend and feed him to the fish… make no mistake."

T-shirt grabbed my elbow.

"This way," he said in a heavy Eastern accent. "Abdallah sends his regards, Mr Fuller."

I've mentioned to you before, when Lauren was captured and when we've talked about the lads in Iraq, I'd never been taken. I have never been frightened of dying. But to be held captive…

"Shoot the fuckers," I shouted. "Come on, Des, slot the bastards."

But no shots came, and I was led below.

## Lauren North's Story:

"Where do we go from here?" I asked as the three of us sped towards the RV.

"We follow them," said Des, manoeuvring the wagon around the narrow lane. "We follow them and get Rick back. Then we slot the fuckers."

"How can we follow them without the trackers?" asked Sellers. "We can't even see them. They turned off all their navigation lights the moment they sailed. It's pitch black out there. They could be ten yards away and we wouldn't see or hear them. They have to be using NV."

"Then we have to find a way around it," barked Des. "We get NV kit dropped in. Get air support. Use radar. Fight fire with fire."

Moments later we pulled up at the boat the Americans had rented. Des briefed Varèse who looked extremely serious. Mitch looked on.

Marvin turned to Sellers. "Did you fix the devices?"

She nodded.

"Whoa there, Cowboy," shouted Des. "Dinnea even be thinkin' about that as yer solution, pal."

Varèse pulled out a mobile. "My orders are very specific, Mr Cogan. Those weapons are not to reach their intended destination under any circumstances. That was the deal, track them or blow them. And as we can no longer track them…"

Des was in Varèse's face. "Cartwright will never sanction that. Not with Rick Fuller on board."

The American began to open his phone.

"Cartwright isn't required to approve the action, Cogan. I have the authority of the US government. I'm sorry, but orders are orders."

### End.

Look out for Book six in the Rick Fuller Thriller Series as the story continues in, THE FIGHTER.

Printed in Great Britain
by Amazon

41422561R00132